THE MANY NAMES OF MAGDALENA CRUZ

Colleen McCarty

The Many Names of Magdalena Cruz
Copyright © 2017 by Colleen McCarty

All rights reserved. No part of this publication may be reproduced, distributed, or transmitted in any form or by any means, including photocopying, recording, or other electronic or mechanical methods, without the prior written permission of the publisher, except in the case of brief quotations embodied in critical reviews and certain other noncommercial uses permitted by copyright law.

The characters and events in this book are fictitious. Any similarity to real persons, living or dead, is coincidental and not intended by the author.

Design Vault Press, LLC
www.designvaultpress.com

First Edition: September 2017

ISBN: 0976897415
ISBN-13: 978-0976897415

For my husband.

"North Americans don't understand... that our country is not just Cuba; our country is also humanity."

-Fidel Castro

PART I

CRIMINAL INFORMANT #1160

ONE

1992 1993 1994 1995 1996 1997 1998 1999 2000 **2001** 2002

May 1st, 2001 – New York City, New York

"Budget cuts and all, Burke. You know how it is. I'll gladly give you a reference." His hollow eyes—the kind of eyes only a newsman can understand—were apologetic as he went back to sorting papers on his desk.

Burke couldn't let his disappointment show. He went to his desk to begin updating his résumé. As soon as he sat down, the phone rang.

"Burke, here," he answered, trying to hide the quavering in his throat.

"Hey, Burke." Her smoky, casual voice was unmistakable. It always sounded as if she gargled gravel every morning. "It's Liz."

"Oh, I know who it is. Unfortunately, now isn't a great time. I'm in the city for the next few days so I can call you and we can get together…"

"This isn't about rekindling old flames. That ship sailed

when I didn't hear from you for six months. It's what I get for cornering the one man at the party with more airline miles than me."

"Well… I… you know," he stumbled, never really intending to say anything or make any excuses for himself. Burke was just buying time until she got to the point.

"I've got an assignment for you." Liz—Elizabeth Waller, Editor-in-Chief of Five Media Group—was not the kind of person who called individual reporters to offer them assignments. Whatever she had, it had to be big. This was some validation that she'd heard what Burke was saying in her ear that night. She'd heard it and it stuck with her—he was a great reporter, and he wasn't afraid to take risks.

"Which magazine is this for? Wander Magazine, Vacation Magazine, Five-Star Traveler…?" Burke rattled off her publications, saying them as distinctly as one says the names of their children. His experience reminded him: it never hurts to tell someone how important they are.

"Vacation," she broke in. "It's rather urgent. We need you to leave tomorrow."

Burke had never worked for her before. Vacation Magazine was the most widely read of all her publications and had the biggest budget. Burke was just a lowly NPR correspondent—what kind of story would she come to him with?

"That could be arranged." He tried not to expose the desperation in his voice. Getting Elizabeth Waller on the phone was akin to ringing up Medusa—she was mythical, fierce and if you looked her in the eye and lived to tell about it, you were a legend in your own right. "What's the story?"

"Cuba." She let the word sink in like a marinade on an aged steak. Words caught in Burke's throat. He'd meant to ask, "What's the angle?" but seconds ticked by until he realized he hadn't been able to eke out a single word.

"I have information that suggests now is the prime time to send someone to do a piece on the state of tourism," she continued. "The consulate is processing visas; the Canadians can't stop raving about it—even the British want a piece of those white Cuban beaches. My contact at the State Department says the administration is looking for a PR boost. They want to be the ones to lift the travel embargo, but they can't do it without credible intel that the country can support an influx of tourists. We need to make sure it's..." She paused for effect. "Safe. For Americans. Do you get it, Burke?"

When she said his name, he tasted scotch and felt satin sheets. "Test the viability of a third-world communist country's tourism infrastructure. Got it."

She ignored his quip and continued. "If there's money behind it for American businesses, we can push through all the noise that the Cuban ex-pats are going to make. 'Still communist,' 'human rights violations,' 'political quagmire.'"

Burke could hear the air quotes she was making pseudo-facetiously.

"None of that can hold water if we make a legitimate case that there's money to be made for American companies. Castro's old and weak. Since his watchful eye has more or less closed, Cubans have become rather industrious. But we can't run the risk of opening the flood gates and then having the government turn on us again—they could seize assets, detain tourists, refuse extradition..." She seemed to be considering her own words.

"Sounds pretty serious for a piece on white sands and pork sandwiches," he said. He knew she was a woman who liked brazen men—if only because she met so few who were more brazen than her.

"Plane leaves at seven a.m.; are you in or are you out,

Burke?" He could hear the hint of a smile in her voice.

"In," he said, without hesitation.

"Good. I'll be in touch." The receiver met the cradle on the other end of the line, but Burke still sat holding the phone, shocked. He took out a pen and began groping about his desk for the post-it notes that were never far away. *Send roses to Elizabeth Wat—*

An envelope was carelessly dropped on his desk. "You Richard Burke?"

"It would appear," Burke replied, looking up at a very insistent courier and gesturing to the nameplate plastered to the side of his desk.

"Sign here," he said, jutting a clipboard and pen into Burke's field of vision. He reluctantly did as requested. The courier slunk off back down to the elevator and Burke—never one to resist opening a package right away—tore open the envelope. Inside he found a Cuban Visa, a press pass, a letter from Elizabeth herself detailing his assignment for her, and a typed page of instructions.

```
BURKE -
ARRIVE AT TETERBORO AIRPORT AT 6:30 A.M.
111 INDUSTRIAL DRIVE, TETERBORO, NJ
07608

A PLANE WILL FLY YOU INTO HAVANA.
AWAIT FURTHER INSTRUCTIONS TONIGHT.

P.S. BE CAREFUL WHEN BUYING CIGARS, THIS
YEAR'S TOBACCO CROP IS COVERED IN
APHIDS.

TAKE CARE,
-E. WALLER
```

She knew Burke would take the job. She had baited him, all along knowing that he would say yes. It must've been love. He was possessed by the thrill of holding a Cuban visa in his hands. Peering around to see if anyone was watching, he carefully brought the visa to his nose and inhaled. He didn't know what he was expecting—sugar cane and tobacco, he supposed; instead it smelled like an office supply store. The visa, like Burke, had never been to Cuba. It was just a simple piece of paper printed with ordinary ink, but it smelled like the truth—and it proved that Burke was one step closer to uncovering just that.

But something was nagging at him. The timing of everything was so in sync, so... planned. Did Liz tell Lou—nay, *force* Lou—not to renew his contract? Burke knew she'd been miffed when he hadn't called her back months before, but could she really have been upset enough to ruin his career? He'd been deep in a story and had come back home to New York for just a few days before returning to Seoul. She'd cornered him at an office cocktail party and grilled him on seemingly unimportant details about his relations with the North Koreans. He buckled under the weight of being listened to by someone whose first language was English, intoxicated by returning to the familiar—and by the Glenlivet scotch she kept absentmindedly refilling.

They stumbled back to her penthouse—the kind of place that made you blush at your own appearance, for lack of knowing how to behave around expensive things. Elizabeth was ten years Burke's senior, but her body moved like someone twenty years younger. They had a great time together, but the next morning he was on a flight back to the other side of the world, and she was back to overseeing everything that reporters like him said about it. He never thought to call, and his hotel phone's light blinked long into his trip, until he pushed *erase all messages* without listening to a single one.

Burke pondered all this as he packed up his desk and said his farewells. The frequently rotating staff in the New York office barely knew his face. His editor, Cindy, who received phone calls from him at all hours of the day and night—and yet never sounded like she'd been asleep—along with a few longtime news pals, marched out of the break room with a funeral procession of cupcakes. He smiled wearily and took a big bite of one, deliberately getting icing on his nose. They laughed sadly, and Burke tried not to belie his excitement about the new assignment. Four years as a reporter for National Public Radio, and his leaving felt like a rushed homework assignment—busywork he had to get through before the real story could begin.

As he walked out, Lou waved another dreary goodbye, and the others mostly murmured their parting words while shuffling through stories and line editing segments for the evening lineup. A newsman would never wonder why postal workers always seemed to lose it and start picking people off from the top of the bell tower. News and mail had that one thing in common: they never stopped. There was always more coming. The job was never complete.

Before his foot was out the door, Burke's head was already swimming with possibilities. These people made his stories comprehensible, sorted through the confetti he called field notes, checked his facts—and just like that, they were merely another stop on his bus route. Such was the life of a wanderer, he supposed. Laying roots that would make a goodbye feel substantial was just not worth it for him. A small sacrifice for a life of seeking truth—of getting swept away in a room full of strangers who by night's end would be the closest friends he'd ever known. These were the kinds of friends he preferred: unexpected, seasoned, weathered; people who have lived. People who could pack a lifetime of friendship into one night in a small corner bar in Prague. The dead-eyed newsroom had nothing on people like that.

And what was there to be sad about? There was a whole island of people waiting for him.

He got back to his apartment after a quick dinner of hot dogs from the cart on the corner. He was in a rush to pack and felt anxious that he hadn't had time to properly wrap his mind around what was happening. His familiar, brown leather duffle bag sat open on the bed. That worn bag had seen even the most unloved corners of the globe. Next to it, his dopp kit, which housed only aftershave, a straight razor, a bar of Irish Spring, his toothbrush, and toothpaste. He threw in the stick of deodorant and a small sample of his favorite cologne. He'd learned from experience that bringing an expensive glass bottle would be excessive and costly when it inevitably broke on either the bumpy plane, or in the jostling car rides to and from locations on underdeveloped, sometimes non-existent roads.

He examined his travel essentials—four cotton button ups in various colors, three pairs of cargo khaki pants, a utility vest, and one grey suit—which had just been returned to him freshly laundered by his door-to-door laundry service. He had sent them last week, the day he touched down in New York following a three-month assignment in Islamabad. He hadn't felt the need to remove the thin plastic sheeting surrounding each piece. As he fumbled with the cheap hangers and tags, his buzzer rang.

Setting the clothes on the bed, still robed in plastic, Burke strode to his front hall and called down on the intercom, "Who's there?" He wasn't much for visitors, at least not here. He stayed at this apartment so infrequently that most of his friends knew not to drop by. If he was in town, he'd call. There were a few girls he knew who were so far removed from shame that they might do a walk by, checking to see if he was home, but he hadn't heard from any of them in many moons.

"Special delivery," a gruff voice called back. "Need a signature."

TWO

1992 1993 1994 1995 1996 1997 1998 1999 2000 **2001** 2002

May 1st, 2001 – New York City, New York

Burke opened the door when prompted by a stiff knock. He was met with a thick head of black hair combed neatly into a pompadour. The man was about six inches shorter than Burke; his black coif jumped out at the reporter as soon as he opened the door. He pushed past Burke, juggling a few files thick with paper and a steaming pizza box. He wore a trench coat and sunglasses, because apparently being subtle was beyond him. As he sat the pizza down on the kitchen counter, throwing open the box and nearly inhaling the first slice ravenously, Burke began to divine that this was not a delivery man. At least, it wasn't his primary profession.

"You going to get in on this?" the stranger asked, gesturing to the pizza.

Burke sat gawking at him.

"Oh, I'm sorry, I thought you were expecting me," he said between bites. The stretched cheese still hung from his mouth.

Burke touched his forehead, searching for even a

modicum of recognition. "Who are you?" he finally said, after nothing came to him.

"Dean Wright. Special Operations Officer Dean Wright. CIA."

"What are you doing here? I'm just a reporter. I don't have anything the CIA would be interested in," he said, feeling a fuzzy, frantic anxiety begin to rise in his chest.

"Not yet you don't," Wright said, reaching for the paper towel roll and tearing one off. He dabbed his mouth and crumpled it into a ball in his fist. He was still chewing the last bit of crust as he said, "and you're no longer *just* a reporter. You're my newest field asset." Those last two words—*field asset*—rolled around in Burke's mind as he went through the motions of making this complete stranger more comfortable.

"What exactly does that mean?" he asked, leading the agent into the living room where Burke sat on the stiff couch and his visitor sat opposite him in a cheap, knockoff tufted arm chair. The agent grimaced as he attempted to get comfortable in the chair but could not. Burke came home so infrequently, this might have been the first time anyone had actually sat in that chair.

Agent Wright sat his plate down on the coffee table, and it was the first time since he'd arrived that he wasn't eating. He looked into the reporter's eyes seriously and said, "Welcome to the CIA, Burke. You're my newest agent. I'm sending you to Cuba undercover. You are playing yourself: a reporter. The job is for Vacation Magazine. You're to tell the Cubans that the president is thinking about lifting the travel embargo, and that you are one of many reporters we are sending to 'get an honest feel for the place.' You must uphold this cover at all costs. If you are compromised, you'll have to signal me immediately or else I might not be able to get you out."

"What was that? You might not be able to get me out? Are

you fucking kidding me?"

"This from the guy who sat on the demilitarized zone between North and South Korea, refusing to leave, refusing bathroom breaks lest you miss the first shot? It never came, by the way. You must've known that—you must've known there was no real danger, because I can see it right now that you're a pussy. Goddammit." He tore a cell phone from his pocket and began dialing.

"Wait—" Burke started to say, but the agent was already talking to someone.

"Liz? Yeah, it's Dean. You brought me a dud." Burke could hear the female voice on the other side of the conversation, but couldn't make out what she was saying. He felt like a dolt as the pieces started to come together. Elizabeth Waller had set him up.

"Start getting ready to move down the list."

Pause.

"I thought this was the one, too," he said, remorsefully. He put the phone down and started for the door.

"Wait, just wait a goddamn minute! You're the reason my contract didn't get renewed. You cost me my job. You barge into my house, you embarrass me in front of Elizabeth fucking Waller, and now you're just going to leave? Oh no, I'm going to Cuba and you're going to pay me a shit ton of money to do it. Once I accomplish whatever it is—the mission, whatever the mission is."

"And that's how you work a newbie, Burke." The agent smiled and tossed Burke the phone, where he could see that he'd only dialed 411 for information. The voice Burke had heard was a robotic response.

Wright leaned back in the chair and opened one of the tan files he'd brought in. Burke could see from the contents of the file that it had to be compiled by a government agency. The file was so disheveled and full of different kinds of media—newspaper clippings, photographs, film negatives, printed pages—there was absolutely no organization to the system. The way he tore through the material made the insides of Burke's ears itch. He squirmed in his seat.

"Let's get through as much as we can get through tonight," the agent said. "Wheels are up at seven a.m., so this is my only chance to brief you." His fingers flew over the file so roughly that Burke feared there might be nothing left of it by the time it was his turn to hold it.

"One thing first," Burke said, getting up. He cleared the table and put the single remaining pizza slice in the fridge, then headed back to his room to pull his notebook and pen out of his suitcase. He also grabbed post-its and a few of his own empty files and brought them to where Agent Wright sat. "This needs to be reorganized, which I'll do as you talk. I can't work with this." He gestured to the two files. One was held together by a green flimsy rubber band, the other file's contents were strewn about on the floor and the table.

As Burke scanned through the papers he came across a paperclipped stack that read *Criminal Informants*. This list had names, each paired with a city and a number ascending past three thousand. Many of the names were in red with parentheses around them. This, he knew, meant they were dead.

"Okay," Dean said in an exaggerated tone that indicated he thought Burke was some kind of OCD nut case. "I'll spare you the details on the last sixty or so years of Cuban-American relations, except to say that not many people really know the actual state of things. Information gets major spin on both sides. Castro has always been a master at controlling what goes in and out—especially information. He's a paranoid motherfucker. Back in '59 when he marched on Havana, taking complete power, he 'extinguished' every American asset on the island, even those he had no proof against. Some nationals, others ex-pats. He did it in secret. Since then he's kept a tight grip on the intelligence there. If you're caught participating in 'counter-revolutionary' activity—since he's the ultimate revolutionary, you see—you disappear, then reappear a number of years later missing teeth, toes, sometimes worse. After that, you're on a surveillance list. The last few years we haven't heard much coming out of Cuba. Blogs and a few political Cuban-Americans say it's improved, that Castro has softened. Some say he may even be dead—a phantom regime running things with look-a-likes. It's the prime time to stage a coup. We can install someone who will be a win-win for everyone."

"Wait a minute," Burke broke in, sifting through photos and organizing them chronologically. "Are you asking me to help the U.S. install a puppet government in Cuba? They have the most successful communist system in the world. They have a near perfect healthcare system. Their literacy rate makes Alabama look like a third world country. You're asking me to go in and commercialize utopia? You do know who I am, right? I work for National *Public* Radio. Or at least, I did... until today."

"I have your file right here. Active supporter of Amnesty International, you dabbled in the Communist Party at Amherst, and you voted for Ralph Nader in '96. You're the perfect communist minion to go looking for utopia in Castro's Venus flytrap."

"What makes you think I'll do it? Why wouldn't I just disappear into the blaring trumpets and mojitos, and finally write that tell-all about what it's really like in Cuba?"

"Because you're you. And you've seen enough of the world to know when something's not right. If the healthcare, the education—the 'utopian' systems—are so perfect, why are there twenty thousand Cubans actively applying for U.S. visas every year, and two thousand Cubans washing up in Key West? Why were Elian Gonzalez's relatives terrified for that boy to go back to his father on the island?

"I can tell you that we've had a rough go of finding out the truth. Usually the truth is more complicated than it seems. With Cuba, the truth is a choppy black sea—the undercurrent is strong, there's glass and sharp coral along the bottom, and the closer you get to the surface, the more desperate you get for air—the harder you get pulled back under." His face was drained, and he looked up at Burke as if remembering that he was still there. His eyes belied that he was younger than he looked. Searching for this so-called truth had leeched the years from him. "I'm drowning in it, Burke." His voice rasped, but it was clear as a bell.

Burke was shocked by the transparency of the moment. The agent had no reason to trust him, to show him his vulnerabilities; and yet here he was, this stranger, this agent, near tears in Burke's armchair. The reporter wondered if this was another ruse, but he couldn't help himself. He felt an instant soft spot for the man. He'd obviously lost people. Burke could tell by the slump of his shoulders, the rush to move him in, and the guilt he carried tenderly; a newborn child, requiring him, possessing him, needling him all the time.

Wright continued after a hushed moment. "In the eighties and nineties we had active assets on the island. Natives. We paid them handsomely for information on the regime, on revolutionary activity. Every time we'd get a tip, it would come up bunk. When I took over as National Intelligence Officer for Cuba, I realized that I'd gotten the job because we'd uncovered that every single one of those assets was actually working for Castro. He was feeding them information and watching us chase our tails like a bunch of fucking amateurs. He probably doubled what we were paying them; that, or seized their money as soon as they got it.

"We're the premiere intelligence operation in the world, yet we have no idea what's happening on an island ninety miles away." His face was turning red now.

"Well, actually, it sounds like Cuba is the premiere intelligence operation in the world..." Burke couldn't help himself, but immediately regretted the gaffe. The agent looked pointedly at him, then burst into laughter.

"We've got a lot to cover, Burke. You're the first external asset going into Cuba in ten years. Even though they say they're communist, the almighty dollar always seems to loosen a few lips. We've leaked a bit of information into Cuba that the president is considering lifting the travel embargo. Things have been very strained recently with the Gonzalez thing, so it's meant to be an olive branch—a gesture of goodwill. Goodwill wrapped in money.

"In reality, we can't lift the embargo. Not with Castro still in power, that is. They will be suspicious of you from the moment you arrive. You might be followed, even actively shadowed by Cuban police. But at the same time, they'll want to impress you. You'll feel in constant flux between terrified and pampered."

"Wait a second, you're just going to keep talking? I might turn on you. I might go to Castro myself and become a double agent. Why me? Why are you so sure I'm the one for this? By the way, I haven't said yes yet." Burke was incredulous even though they both knew he was ecstatic about the prospect and could hardly wait for the plane to take off.

"Well, you have said yes—you said yes on the phone to Liz, who told you in code that she was CIA. And..."

"What?" he broke in too loudly. "Elizabeth Waller is CIA?"

"Covered in Aphids. CIA. It's the code you'll use with

anyone on the island, and we use it here to determine if the person we're talking to is someone we can trust. Anyone involved in Cuban missions knows it. You ask how the tobacco crop is coming in, they answer 'covered in aphids.' So, since you consented to the job to one of our agents, you have agreed to do it."

"But I didn't know the code," Burke retorted, a little whinier than intended.

"That's the thing about spies. We're sneaky." Wright smirked and took a moment to gauge Burke's reaction.

The reporter touched his hand to his temple in disbelief and yet, surprising even himself, he was ready to continue. He wanted to devour all the information—his reporter's brain had taken over. Any regard for his own safety, the objective of the mission, or the sanity of any of this would have to be put on the back burner. Right now, he needed to become a sponge and soak up everything within his grasp.

"The second question you had—why you? I'm trusting Liz on this one. She says you're incorruptible. Aside from the fact that you've searched 'Cuba' or related terms on the internet every day since you got internet access in 1998, she tested you. She's vouching for you."

"Tested me?" Burke could feel the heat beginning to rise in his neck. He couldn't tell yet if it was from anger or embarrassment.

"She said she asked you some sensitive questions about North Korea, even offered you an exclusive on it. She knows you've been; hell, the New York Times knows. 'Richard Burke is First American Journalist to Cross the Demilitarized Zone, Welcomed by Kim Jong-il.' Whatever it was she asked you, you answered right. She said you're a vault."

"I couldn't expose my sources. Saying anything about North Korea—anything at all—would mean people dying. No scoop is worth that."

"'A journalist with a soul and a conscience.' That's how Liz described you. That remains to be seen, doesn't it?" He chuckled smugly, and Burke stood to turn away. His head was swimming. Did Liz sleep with him as an assignment? Was she trying to get a read on him? Trying to get him to talk? But there was something more. Something in her breath, something in the kisses that lingered too long.

"She likes you Burke. She wants to see you succeed." He stood too, following the reporter as he paced the room.

Burke looked at him cagily.

"We all do," Wright said, more seriously.

"What's really at stake here, Agent? We've got terrorism in the Middle East, ethnic cleansing in the Sudan, a crack epidemic in New York City—why are you going after Cuba? And why now? Doesn't the CIA have bigger fish to fry?" He had so many questions running through his head, but he needed to focus on Wright. He needed to watch his reactions to these questions to see if the agent was just gaming him.

"This might shock you, Burke, but I am not a very high ranking agent in the CIA. In fact, the opposite is true. There are much more qualified agents working Istanbul, Iran, Kenya, Egypt. There are more qualified agents than me working Peru, for fuck's sake. Cuba is the bottom of the barrel. It's been considered a lost cause for twenty years.

"Sure, there's a threat there, but it's not imminent. Until Elian washed up, most people had forgotten it existed. That being said, I am an agent of the Central Intelligence Agency. I have been assigned to Cuba—it is my duty to keep Americans safe and keep the republic intact. I believe the best way to do that is to eliminate communism and create a cooperative government. This is my job, and I'm going to do it. Are we done with question and answer time? Like I said, there's a lot of stuff to cover if you're going into Cuba in twelve hours, prepared to aid a nation's unrest."

"Okay," Burke finally relented. Wright was a tough read. Burke felt this was the first time since walking into his apartment that the agent was telling the truth: this was his job, and he'd chosen Burke to help him do it.

Burke looked down at the pictures on the floor. He began to pick them up one by one, reading the notes scribbled on the back. He was quiet, waiting for Dean to start in on his briefing.

The agent stood up and headed to the kitchen where he'd set down a plastic bag next to the pizza box. He reached inside and pulled out a beer that had been sitting there since he'd arrived. He wiped the beads of sweat on the bottle into his shirt-sleeve, and in one fluid motion, swiftly twisted his forearm over the cap, listening to the small metal clang as it hit the counter.

He might be a low-level agent, but he was a high-level drinker. No casual drinker—or casual gym member for that matter—could twist off a beer cap with the grip of his forearm. Dean took a long pull from his beer and headed back to the living room, reclaiming his seat in the armchair.

"Okay, now." Dean picked up the pile of papers Burke had discarded and began to go over the details of the last ten years in Cuba. "We don't know much about what's going on—like I said, Castro's regime has cast the whole island into a maze of smoke and mirrors. What I hope to accomplish with you is to get a few trustworthy counter-revolutionaries under my belt—people hell-bent on taking Castro down. We can help them, give them resources, but they need to be on our side completely."

"How can you tell that about someone, Dean? How can you know someone won't betray you?" It was something the reporter had always wondered about spies.

"That's the first lesson of your very fast employee orientation. In Cuba, when someone has disobeyed the regime or tried to escape, they are put on a list. They will be relegated to the positions in society that no one else wants. Orderlies, waiters, laundresses, you get the point; the lower rungs of society. It's a lifelong punishment, and you're kept on surveillance perpetually until you die.

"This group of people is the most likely to be dissatisfied with the status quo and to be engaging in counter-revolutionary activity. They are master secret keepers and they never give up hope that someday a coup could be realized. They are descendants of Che. It's in their DNA to topple the system, constantly seeking a better one. Revolution is a drug to them.

"These are the people we need to find and connect with. You need to dig in, get one of these people alone and give them one of these." He handed a stack of small white cards to Burke. On them were the words:

```
Every night, a star burns bright

En la Sierra Maestra, motherland of the
revolution

Find the beacon of hope, and be saved
from all injustice
```

"What are these?" he asked.
"Directions to a safe house, the one stronghold we've been able to establish. It's manned twenty-four hours a day by an agent. There's support there for anyone who's been compromised. We can airlift them out, whatever they need."
"Has anyone ever made it?" Burke inquired, cautiously.
The agent looked at him seriously. He leaned forward and

placed his elbows on his knees. An intense, buttoned-up air came over him, and Burke could see that the pizza-eating, fumbling lout was gone. In its place, a soldier remained; the kind of soldier who ran meetings and operations and watched people die in front of him.

Burke was suddenly possessed by a need to ingratiate and please. It reminded him of his mother when she had guests over to dinner. He always got this feeling in the presence of soldiers—a profession he had strongly considered before settling on Amherst. "Never mind, please continue. I'll hold my questions until the end." Burke bowed his head without a note of sarcasm.

"If you can get them this card and tell them it's a last resort, then we'll be able to get them out safely. But we need information from them. Lists of names, the people they work with. Where do they find resources like weapons? How do they send messages? How do they recruit people?

"So that's the first step, Burke. Seek out the disenfranchised, the downtrodden. Hang out with them. Show them yourself, have experiences with them. Do not let them see you as someone different than them—you are the same. You're not some rich American coming to help pillage their island of its resources. You're a poor writer, a revolutionary in your own way; a lonely traveler. This is crucial in earning trust."

Burke nodded curtly, motioning for him to continue. The reporter began really looking at the pictures scattered around him while Dean talked.

"Something we always teach new recruits is the value of reciprocity, and the importance of graduation. First: the value of reciprocity. Do something for someone because you want to. Do it because it's your idea, because it's the right thing to do. Then, they will feel an unconscious need to repay you. Note, this doesn't work with everyone. Some people are heartless bastards who will rip you off and never look back. But for your average, run-of-the-mill person, a little kindness goes a long way.

"Second: graduation. You've got to start small, and then graduate to the big request. Of course, if I approached you and asked you to make me a bomb, you would say, 'Fuck no,' and 'Get the hell out!' But what if I asked you about an old flame? Or how you pass messages? Sure, that's easy. The next ask is a little bigger. And so on. Graduation. Depending on the informant, you can have Castro's head delivered within a week, if you've graduated properly. Asking the human mind to make large leaps is impossible. But incremental jumps are the secret. That's how the Nazis took over Germany—incremental jumps.

"Of course, there are advanced trainings for these tactics, but we're short on time."

Burke could feel his heart rate begin to elevate and more questions rose in his throat. He held them back.

"Look, Burke, I'm not excited about this, either. I don't want to send a civilian asset into this situation, but the Cubans check their visa applicants down to the letter. If you weren't a real journalist, they'd know it. You were the top of the list, but your file reads like a one-man show. You might as well have 'Does Not Play Well With Others' stamped on your forehead. That's going to be your biggest headache—people. You'll have to trust people and they'll have to trust you. Start getting right with that now, tonight, because you won't have time by nightfall tomorrow.

"Now, when you approach a potential asset, what are you going to do?" He stopped talking for the first time and looked at his new asset.

Burke set down the pictures he was gazing over and thought for a moment. He closed his eyes and pushed his sleeves up to his elbows. He furrowed his brows, trying to calculate the exact angle the wind would hit him on an overcast day, looking down the Malecón. The taste of fresh coconut milk. The feeling of being gazed upon by people who didn't want him to know he was being looked at.

"I'm going to look for a person who's hard on their luck. An older person who looks weathered, looks like they've been to hell and back. A man, probably. He'll be washing dishes or cleaning toilets. I'll watch him for a few days, long enough for my Cuban police escorts to believe that I am a Cuban-at-heart, simply born in the wrong country; this should be taken care of by a little palm-greasing. I'll buy an extra cigar or an extra sandwich and offer it to him. I'll begin a conversation on the state of his home, where he grew up—does he still love it? I'll tell him I'm a writer. From Che to Fidel to Jose Martí, they were all writers at heart. Cubans love reading like white women love Moscato."

Dean—the man or the agent; hard to say which—chuckled at this.

"He will tell me of his dreams, and eventually of his transgressions. They will lie in the crook of a frown or a faraway look, those dreams that went awry; the mistakes that left him there, at the end of a dead-end street.

"I'll invite him to dine with me. The Cuban escorts' ears will prick at this—an American journalist dining with an outlaw. What would he want with this outsider? And more importantly, what might this outsider say that could damn the regime? But they won't worry enough to intervene and risk me seeing their island harshly.

"This is why I can't let him out of my sight—our dinner will have to immediately follow. On the open terrace at the hotel, I'll choose a table close to the edge of the balcony. Other tourists will stare at the rugged man and me—an odd and curious couple. I'm sure my escorts will want to sit within earshot. A mariachi band will be helpful here, both in getting the information I need and handing him the card. Near the end of the song—*Alma Llanera*, I think, or *Celito Lindo*, both being about five minutes—I'll see that he slips away unseen via the side entrance off the veranda, before my friend peeks around the musicians to realize that I am sipping wine alone."

Dean's smile was captivated by the story and Burke could tell that he realized he had underestimated the reporter.

"I was at the top of the list for a reason, Agent," Burke said confidently. "Investigative journalism is not unlike being a spy."

"Yes, but you haven't really been able to flex those muscles as a foreign correspondent, from what I understand." For the first time, he looked genuinely intrigued about Burke's experience of the world.

"I was working on a terrific lead in Seoul about six months ago," Burke said. "A man who had worked as the private chef for Kim Jong-il for twenty years. He'd seen everything. He became a great friend, actually. I had files of interviews about what it's like in North Korea—a similar situation to Cuba, I think you would agree."

"What happened there?" Wright rubbed the stubble on his chin, which made a sound like sandpaper, and took a ferocious sip.

Burke felt that familiar darkness enter his chest. A therapist might call it guilt, but he knew it better as fault. "He disappeared. He'd been out of the North for four years; he felt safe enough to talk. Qi was the best sushi chef in the world. He was seventy-three when I met him, and he could drink sake bombs with a bar full of frat boys until dawn. And now he's gone, and it's my fault and it's for nothing." Now it was Burke's turn to search the bottom of his beer bottle.

Dean got up and grabbed two more bottles from the six

pack, putting the rest in the fridge. "You need these more than I do," he said. "And when you're the one who disappears, I'll need them again, so I'll come back to claim them." He looked at his asset, deadpan, and began to laugh harder than Burke had seen anyone laugh since grade school. His laugh sounded like a blimp as it popped; a great expulsion of air with little sound, squinted eyes, his hands grasping his stomach.

Burke tried to resist but soon fell in with the guy. He laughed so hard that he dropped to the floor, the side of his face sticking to the Polaroids and paperclips in the files around him.

THREE

1992 1993 1994 1995 1996 1997 1998 1999 2000 **2001** 2002

May 2nd, 2001 – Havana, Cuba

Inside the small biplane, Burke gripped the armrest as the landing gear jumped and rumbled awake. He tried to resist mentally critiquing the pilot's every move, but couldn't help it. The landing gear should've been put down fifteen minutes ago, and now they were touching down just as the wheels locked into place. It had been a few years since Burke renewed his pilot's license, but any rookie knew the landing gear shouldn't be an afterthought.

He should've told Dean he'd fly the plane down after they dropped him in DC, but he thought it best if he didn't attract attention. As they skidded down the runway, excitement and adrenaline coursed through him. *Cuba.* He could finally mark it off the list of countries he'd always wanted to go to. The secrecy... it was like he could sense it just beyond the tree line. He tried to remember what Dean said. "Don't stand out. Don't attract attention. You're just a reporter. You travel all the time, it's just another dot on the map to you," he'd coached.

The pilot was out of his seat now and the co-pilot was pushing open the small staircase that would lead Burke out onto the tarmac.

"Isn't it a bit suspicious that I'm arriving on a private plane?" He'd asked Dean.

"You work for a news conglomerate. They fly reporters all over the world in their charter planes. Just act like you're supposed to be there and no one will question you. You have the travel visa. That's all they'll need."

Dean had made it seem easy. Just walk into an isolated, communist country and gather information about the burgeoning revolution against a dictator who's been in power since 1959.

Sure. Piece of cake.

Burke breathed deeply and grabbed his attaché case. Stepping out into the Cuban sun felt like being bathed for the first time. It was an unfamiliar yet not unwelcome feeling. It felt like this country could see all of him and she didn't turn away at the unappealing parts. He breathed in the tropical air, puffing out his chest and smiling for the first time in what felt like years.

"Mr. Burke," the captain said. "Mr. Burke, there's the main door to the terminal." He pointed to the small door framed by black glass. "You'll find customs in there and everything you need. There's a driver waiting to take you to the Hotel Royaliza."

"Thanks for everything," Burke replied absentmindedly. Whatever pleasantries were keeping him from this strange island, he wanted them out of the way fast.

Hi heart pounded as the customs agent looked over his passport. "Visa?" She flipped through the blue papers of his passport, seeming to admire the many stamps from so many countries. Her face formed a scrutinizing frown, accompanied by a nod. Burke fumbled with the papers in his inner jacket pocket, finally producing the rectangular card that read:

```
REPUBLICA DE CUBA
VISA - TARJETA DEL TOURISTA
```

Burke also began unfolding the letter from his editor at Vacation Magazine which detailed the work he was doing as a journalist, and his press pass. He hoped the sweat on his temples was not visible to her, and immediately decided to wave it away as part of the tropical heat if she asked. Though it felt like his hands were shaking, he was relieved when he looked down and saw that they weren't. Thank Christ, she waved him through and he breathed a sigh of relief. The breath came in smelling of pineapples and fresh seawater.

He walked through the airport, following the signs that should lead him to the street. He was propelled by sheer curiosity and an ardor for a country he had longed to see since he was a boy. He almost felt like flinging off all his CIA connections and just disappearing here. How bad could the life of a Cubano be? The scenery was beautiful, rents were dirt cheap, pre-war American cars flooded the streets. And the women...

Don't think about the women yet, Burke. You can't just ditch the CIA. They have plenty of practice finding people and wringing information out of them.

"There's no such thing as a dream," he could hear his father saying. "There's what you do day in and day out to make your life what you want it to be, and there's bullshit. Nothing in the interim."

"Señor Burke!" A thin, unusually tall Cuban was running toward him. He was holding a sign that read *Ricardo Burke*.

"Yes. That's me," Burke said stiffly. He marched to greet

him with his hand outstretched. He shook the man's hand and gripped his forearm confidently when they met. He locked eyes with the Cuban. A message seemed to pass between them before any words were spoken.

We're on the same team.

"It is very nice to meet you, sir. It is an honor. I listen to your segments on NPR..." he trailed off. "I mean I have heard of you, a famous reporter, no? Welcome to Cuba!" He attempted to cover his near-gaffe with enthusiasm. Cubans couldn't listen to American radio unless they owned an illegal Ham radio. "I am Paolo, your driver and guide." Paolo bowed, as if he was about to begin a dance.

Burke kept walking, electric with potential. Paolo fell into step with him and Burke wondered how much he knew. *Am I to confide in him? What if he's playing both sides?* Burke frantically searched his memory for some snippet of advice from Dean.

It had been a long night and it was hard to remember everything the agent had said. Though it was foggy, something began to come back to him—a code; a way of knowing who was a CIA asset without exposing himself.

"How's the tobacco crop coming in this year?" Burke asked, casting his eyes downward.

"Covered in aphids," Paolo said, unremarkably. "I don't know what they'll do if they can't get rid of them."

Covered in aphids. CIA.

He's one of us.

Us—a classification he had only been able to assign to himself for the last twelve hours. He breathed out in relief, and felt a little better knowing that Dean—perhaps he should call him Agent Wright—hadn't sent him into Cuba completely blind. Burke also felt better knowing that this was all real; knowing that Paolo was involved meant he wasn't being hung out to dry, the journalist's equivalent of getting stuck writing obituaries.

He walked Burke to a black Lincoln sedan. In the back seat, he had placed a coffee and a stack of newspapers—the New York Times, the Guardian and the People's Daily were the ones Burke could see. Sliding into the car, he smelled not just any coffee, but a small cup of espresso, still steaming. The man had done his homework.

Of course he had. He was CIA. Homework was all he did.

"I'd like to take you back to New York with me, Paolo. It seems you know me better than my own news desk." Well, his former news desk.

"I'm kind of locked in here, sir, or I would take you up on that." His accent, which had been faint to begin with, had now completely disappeared. He didn't sound earnest, but Burke attributed this to his concentration on pulling out of Jose Martí International. Paolo was quiet, so Burke sat back in the seat and sipped the espresso. Even though it was hot enough to burn his tongue, he could still taste that it was the best coffee he'd ever had. It was round and nutty and felt alive in his mouth. He took a moment to savor it and realized it had been almost two days since he last slept.

FOUR

1992 1993 1994 1995 1996 1997 1998 1999 2000 **2001** 2002

May 2nd, 2001 – Havana, Cuba

Paolo had said something. He'd left the airport and continued on the Avenida Rancho Boyeros into Havana. They were driving through the Plaza de Armas.

"Burke, you alright?" he was saying.

Burke could see his eyes in the rearview mirror. "I think I just need some air."

As Paolo rolled down the window, a hand came in. "Señor! You want drive my Cadillac? Fifty dollars only!" The owner of the hand was wearing a thin beige shirt, under which he was sweating profusely. This was the first real Cuban Burke had met; he couldn't just say no.

"Paolo, let's do it. Let's switch cars. Let's walk around the square for a bit." He pulled the handle and began opening the car door, even though they were still moving. The cars there were legendary—pre-war American cars filled the streets from before the trade embargo, patched with love and spare parts. They gleamed in the sunlight in jellybean tones—cerulean blue, cherry red, and mint green.

"Orders are to take you straight to The Royaliza. We can't

just—" Paolo stopped abruptly because the man was taking hold of Burke's hands. His fingers felt rough with dirt and calluses, but his eyes were kind.

"Come on, man. It's great car. Purrs like kitten." Burke was completely swept up. They continued holding hands as he led the reporter across the square. Burke looked back to see Paolo cursing behind the wheel as he looked for a nearby parking space. Burke thought the 'dumb tourist' cover was more believable than the 'men in a black car.'

They passed two ancient men playing chess at a stone table and a girl sketching the statue of Che Guevara a few feet beyond. On the other side of the manicured square, Burke saw a gleaming red Cadillac.

"It's not...?"

"Si, si," he assured Burke. "Es mí car. Se llama Marilyn Monroe."

It must've been a 1956 or '57 Cadillac El Dorado. It was in pristine condition. The camel tan leather seats looked as if they were straight off the showroom floor—smoothed and oiled like a treasured baseball glove.

"Is this what you do? You rent this car to tourists?"

"Si, I make good the money. She is a beauty," he said, the last bit ringing with the clarity of Humphrey Bogart, and the charm of Bing Crosby. Burke saw from the man's gray teeth and dirty fingernails that their definitions of 'good money' were not the same. Still, he had to admit the man was right—she was a beauty. They stood admiring the cherry apple dream—such a stark picture against the Spanish tiled roofs and brick roads reminiscent of the turn of the century. It was easy to forget that it was 2001. Here he had no email address, no cell phone, no World Wide Web.

"Christ, Burke!" Paolo breathlessly appeared from across the square. He said something to the man with Burke, who, he realized absentmindedly, was still holding his hand. It didn't even feel strange and Burke made no move to take it away.

They began to argue in Spanish that flew by too quickly. It made Burke wish he had done more than listen to the five hundred most frequently spoken Spanish words on the plane. Of course, he partly spoke it—and Japanese, Korean, French, Tagalog, and Farsi—but he found more than twenty-four hours necessary to do a full language refresher. In his sleep-deprived state, he picked up, 'preying on poor tourists,' 'trying to make a living,' 'mind your own business,' at which point he decided to step in.

"Paolo," he whispered calmly. "Paolo—wouldn't it be beneficial to change up transportation? And just to clarify, I am a *journalist*." He waved the tag on a lanyard around his neck. "It's my job to have an experience in this country. I need to get a feel for what it's like to be a tourist here. And for me, part of that is driving this gorgeous car down the coast to the Royaliza." Paolo looked at Burke as if he was making too much sense to work for the government. "Pay the man, let's go."

"Fifty pesos for a ride around the square," the man said. "How long you going to be gone?"

"I can drive the car back to you tomorrow," Paolo said, now fully on board with the new plan. His eyes darted around the square suspiciously.

"Okay, for overnight it be one hundred fifty pesos." The owner tried to cover his excitement.

"Sure, whatever," said Paolo, whose eyes couldn't seem to leave the car. He pulled money from his pocket and half-heartedly counted it out to the man. "Meet you back here tomorrow, sí?"

"Sí, si." The owner practically threw the keys at Paolo and galloped toward the cantina on the south side of the square.

"We'd better get going," Paolo said as he headed back to

the Lincoln. "Let's get your stuff moved over without too much fanfare." Again, his eyes were searching the square. He lingered on the chess players. The girl who was sketching was gone now; Burke could see her hurriedly shoving her sketchpad into her bag as she briskly walked across the street and down the sidewalk, her hair trailing behind her like a black, waving sheet.

"Something funny going on here, Starsky?" Burke prodded. "Has there been a disturbance in the force?"

"Get in the damn car," he said. "And you can't just mix pop culture references like that. Starsky and Hutch being put in the same sentence with Star Wars is a crime punishable by death."

"You got it, Hutch." Burke reached in the Lincoln and pulled out his attaché case and leather duffel. The starch in his button up shirt was beginning to make his skin itch. He looked around to see that everyone was wearing flowing linen shirts, floral prints, straw hats. Paolo and he were all business. They stuck out like turkeys in a cockfight.

"I thought I was Starsky!" Paolo said, taking Burke's luggage from him.

"Fine, take this stuff. I'll be right over." Burke headed for a shop with a men's hat rack outside the door.

"I don't think you get how this works, Hutch!" Paolo called after him. "You're supposed to stay with me..." His voice trailed off behind him as Burke heard the bells of the shop door jingle. The smell of cedar filled his nose and he heard the hum of a sewing machine. Behind the wooden counter he saw a man sitting on a stool, feeding beige fabric through the teeth of the machine.

"Hola," Burke said as he ran his hand down the row of jackets and shirts that line the walls of the store. The man did not respond, deeply entrenched in his work. He wore a dark green hat with a patterned band. It was pushed back far onto the crown of his head so that he could see what he was doing. Burke noticed a strip of gray hair peeking out from under the hat, and a tremor in his arm. He looked up to reach for a button and jumped at the sight of the reporter.

"Esta bien, esta bien." *It's all right*, Burke told him. His face looked frightened and he moved his mouth as if chewing something. Burke placed a few shirts and pants on the counter.

Not engaging, for fear of frightening the vendor more, he stepped out to pluck a hat from the rack. The man did not meet his eyes, but simply punched numbers into the antique cash register. He showed Burke the total, the tremble in his arm now more pronounced. Burke placed the pesos on the counter and gathered up the clothes, placing the light straw hat on his head. He pushed it back with the tip of his forefinger so that it mirrored the vendor's. He smiled his sincerest, most thankful smile. The old man's eyebrows pleaded, *Not now. Not here.*

Does he know who I am? Why I've come here? Does he have something to tell me?

Burke grabbed the brim of his hat and dipped his chin in gratitude. The ancient cash register spat out a receipt and the vendor handed it to him, placing it in his palm and then grasping his hand with both hands in a friendly handshake. Burke could feel him placing something else into his hands.

He waved as Burke headed for the door, feeling somehow as if he was seeing his grandfather for the last time. Paolo had loaded the Cadillac and pulled up outside the shop. Burked casually walked to the car and stepped in, wielding his new shirts and pants—still on their hangers—into the car. He laid them across the back seat, but caught Paolo's frustrated expression and turned to face forward.

"Jesus, Hutch." With that, his foot floored it on the gas pedal and they were whizzing through downtown Havana. The antique engine sounded like stampeding bulls beneath the hood. Pedestrians from all around waved at them, calling, "¡Arriba!"

"¡Arre!"

"¡Magnifico!"

Burke's smile beamed as he waved at each person going by.

"I'm going to stop calling you Hutch and start calling you Lucy," Paolo called over the whooshing wind.

They were leaving the city center now, and the streets were starting to look more like most of the places Burke had been; brightly-colored buildings with bars over the windows and plaster cracking off at the corners. Some of the buildings had Greek and Roman columns along the facades. Laundry hung across the alleys. Dust from the cobblestone streets was caked on everything, giving the city a kind of haze reminiscent of a sepia-toned photo.

"Call me what you will, I am never leaving," Burke said, his cheeks hurting from the permanent grin plastered on his face. "But I will indulge you. Why Lucy?"

"You remember 'I Love Lucy?' There's an episode where she and Ethel have to go to work in a chocolate factory. They're on an assembly line and the chocolates start coming down too fast for them to keep up. Lucy starts shoving them in her mouth, her bra, everywhere to try and keep up. That's you right now. You're stuffing yourself. Just take things as they come, man. Do your job. You're here for a reason. Don't forget that. And one more thing—this car, your buying Cuban clothes, your hobnobbing with street people—this is not keeping a low profile! I was instructed to keep you in my sight—"

"Lucille Ball was my first crush, so yes, I think it's fair to say I am familiar with the reference. And to your next point, I don't need a babysitter. I am quite capable of maneuvering in a foreign country without a handler. I understand why you're here, and I'm glad that you are." Burke glanced at the gun just barely visible in a holster outside Paolo's ribcage, beneath his jacket. "But think of me more as a colleague than a ward."

"Not an option. My orders are to keep you safe. You're untrained, completely green. Do you even know what was happening back there? Who you were buying your frilly panties from?"

The city seemed to dribble away in front of them, laying before their eyes a vast, curving road surrounded by a lush landscape. To the left, the ocean spanned out beyond the tree line. "I try not to discriminate against the people I buy panties from."

"Well that's good. Did he happen to say anything to you?"

"No, but it looked like he wanted to." Suddenly Burke remembered the note the vendor had placed in his palm. He looked down to see his hand still gripping it with surprising force. With the way Paolo was over-reacting, Burke wasn't sure he could trust him with the contents of what it said. "He didn't say a single word the entire time I was in there."

"Well no, he wouldn't, considering his tongue was cut out in '92 because he fashioned a car like this," patting his hand lovingly on the dashboard, "into a boat. He sewed the sails himself. He was caught by the Coast Guard and sent to a camp. A camp for 'outlaws.' Now he sells his handmade clothes to tourists in a government owned shop."

"The government owns that suit shop?"

"The Cuban government owns anything and everything worth owning in Cuba. That means if—like our friend who rents this car—you do business person-to-person mostly in cash, you don't have to worry too much. If you've got a good business, they're going to come calling. It also means they have ears everywhere. There are cameras in that shop, which means they now know your face—and that dumbass hat."

"I don't need to justify my fashion choices to you." Burke pulled the brim of the hat down so that it fit snugly around his forehead. The El Dorado being a convertible, there were no visors or visor mirrors. On a hunch, he opened the glove compartment to find a plastic hand mirror. He held it up to admire his new headgear, and to make certain that Paolo wasn't right. "A young Hemingway!" he said, half joking, half wishing he had left the hat back on the rack where he found it.

"So much for anonymity." Paolo's eyes traveled to the rearview mirror. Burke held the hand mirror so that he could see the road behind him without being seen. A black sedan—new and shiny—cruised up behind them. The two men in the car were undoubtedly members of the National Revolutionary Police Force, or PNR to friends. "Your escorts are here."

"Good thing we were expecting them, then," Burke said, replacing the mirror.

"I was hoping to get a foothold at the Royaliza before they showed up. Two of my guys are there wiring your room and checking for bugs. They'll be checking in with you tomorrow while I return the car and put my ear to the ground. Your arrival will have stirred up curiosity."

Cautiously, Burke unfolded the note the old man gave him. "Guardate la espalda," was scrawled in shaky jags.

Watch your back.

PART II

MADGE

FIVE

1992　1993　1994　1995　1996　1997　1998　1999　2000　**2001**　2002

May 3rd, 2001 – Veradero, Cuba

He's sitting at a patio table in a ridiculous white hat. We get them all the time, these wannabe Hemingway writers. He keeps looking at me with a carnivorous stare. I don't know that, though, because I don't see him. I'm not even looking his direction. I'll just keep ignoring him. Just ignore him, and he'll go away. They always do.

These American men, so used to getting everything they want like the world is their marketplace. I'm sure he thinks I'm just going to come up and offer myself to him, "Excuse me, mister, I am looking for the sex?" Yeah, that's not going to happen. Eyes forward, Magdalena, focus on not spilling the juice.

Goddamn Catalina, this is all her fault. I wouldn't be covering in the service area if she hadn't drank so much last night and called in. Silly girl. She's going to get called into a correctional meeting if she's not careful. I long to be down in the basement sorting linens and going through the methodical tasks of the laundry.

It's supposed to be a punishment, being a laundress, but I find it oddly satisfying. I recite poems to myself, I sing the songs that my mother used to sing to me, but most of all I think of nothing, nothing but the cotton weaving through my fingers, and the lightness of the breeze coming in through the cracked windows. One of my teachers in university used to quote the Buddha: "What you think, you become," he would say. If that's true, then if I focus on the breeze in my hair and the sun on my face, maybe I will just turn into air and blow away.

For two years, I've done laundry under the surveillance of the state. Every hour of every day I focus on the cotton in my fingers because to think of anything else is an exercise in futility. To think about the past is to feel black pain that pecks at my consciousness and reminds me what people will do to each other in the face of hunger and lack of control. To think about the future is equally insufferable even in the fact that there is one. Why hadn't they just killed me? Because now they have me under their power—I'm constantly looking behind me, looking for cameras, wondering who I can trust.

He's looking again, this time at my tray on which I carry a pitcher of grapefruit juice. My eyes fall to see that his glass is empty. Shit. I search the patio for another server to help him, but I'm alone out here. I draw in a breath and change trajectory, heading for his table.

His eyes sparkle at my approach. Did he have to be American? I could deal with a Canadian or even a prudish Englishman. The English, who've learned the errors of their ways, have consented to spreading money around the world in rounds of pints and zinc oxide. They're mildly tolerable.

I arrive at the table, his face having grown into an unabashed grin. Closer now, I can see on the table he has newspapers splayed out—the *Granma*, the *New York Times*, and a few that look to be in Chinese. My heart softens a touch. I realize that maybe not all Americans should be so harshly judged.

I feel the weight of the pitcher in my hand and extend my arm to fill his glass, but my eyes are fixed on the papers.

"I'd like to order breakfast," he says, noticing my fascination, but not commenting on it. His grin has been reduced to a smirk that could be called shameless. I feel a flush come up from my torso.

"What would you like?" I respond calmly.

"Chilaquiles, coffee and a side of mango, please." His eyes travel over me and I feel like a map; my latitudes and longitudes vibrating with a sense of significance. His gaze falls to rest on my forearms, Uruguay and Paraguay. I watch him take in the topography of scars there for the first time.

"I'll have it out in a moment," I say, turning to go.

"Wait," he says, a little too eagerly. I turn my head back but force my body away, pushing it like a boulder up a hill towards the kitchen. "What's your name?"

"Magdalena," I say, catching the eye of a man in a suit standing idly by, a few feet away from this man's table. He shakes his head at me almost imperceptibly and I turn my head back towards the kitchen, moving away from them as quickly as possible.

Nearly there, I discreetly pull a chair from the dining room into the dish pit and sit down. I'm taking the risk because I feel if I don't regain my place on earth, begin to feel the gravitational pull again, then I will simply float away like a balloon at a child's birthday party.

"Shoo!" Mona comes from behind me, arms full of clean plates to be restocked. "You don't want him to see you sitting!" She carefully shifts the plates to one chubby arm and uses the other hand to shoo me like a cat from the chair. She's talking about Anton, our Jefe—boss—for today. I roll my eyes at her, yet stand up and return the chair to its place just outside the kitchen.

"You sick?" she says to me. I catch myself leaning against the doorframe, absentmindedly watching her nest each plate on top of the next.

"Nah," I say, waving away the accusation. "Oh, shit! I almost forgot to put in his order!"

"You need to go back to the laundry where you belong. You're going to get us all fired!" She says it playfully. I'm already halfway to the food window, so I can't see if her expression carries a hint of truth.

The cook—Diego, I think?—is cracking six eggs onto the flat-top. They hiss and sizzle as he adds cilantro, chili powder, salt and pepper. My mouth starts to water and I wonder how long it's been since I had scrambled eggs—how long has it been for Diego? Does he sneak a few bites for himself when El Jefe isn't looking?

"Oye, Diego, Chilaquiles y mango al lado. Arriba!"

"Ay, chica, get back to the laundry before you give me a heart attack." He pulls out the remaining six eggs from the egg carton and expertly cracks them one at a time with one hand while the other hooks the end of the spatula into the carton, and casts it into the trash.

"The couple at table fifteen have empty glasses and plates, thirty-six is ready to order, and the linens are piling up, Lavandera," his voice comes around the corner before I can see him.

"Anton, I'm covering for Catalina—"

"El Jefe to you. And I know. That doesn't excuse you from your regular duties." A Cuban Military graduate, he's been placed in this job to test his skills. He'll be moved into a more powerful position with more subordinates if he proves his value here.

"I can't do both jobs at once–"

"Yes and the hotel can't bring dirty towels and sheets to the guests. You'll have to figure out how to make it work until Catalina is back to health."

I bite my tongue. I want to tell him that Catalina is just hung-over, but I know this will cost her this job and will call my job into question too. He takes a step closer to me. "May I take a break after breakfast to bring the linens down and start things?" I say, looking at the floor.

"You'll have to find someone to cover the floor for you," he snorts, looking down on me with his hands clasped behind his back. "And I expect you back at ten 'til eleven to get ready for lunch service." He does a rehearsed military kind of turn and walks stiffly out of the kitchen.

I turn back to the food window to find Diego staring at me expectantly with a toothpick between his teeth. The chilaquiles stand steaming under the heat lamp. The spicy smell sticks in my nose and I briefly fantasize about tossing them down as I walk down the dirt road back to the farmhouse, leaving this place behind forever.

But I know that's not possible.

I pick up the big plate in one hand, and the little side plate topped with delicate mango slices in the other. I realize that after being told to do two jobs in one day I should be infuriated, but as I get closer to the American's table all the trouble of this world sinks away and I keep floating higher above it.

SIX

1992 1993 1994 1995 1996 1997 1998 1999 2000 **2001** 2002

May 3rd, 2001 – Varadero, Cuba

"Madge!" Mr. Burke calls to me across the patio, as if he's seeing a friend who was presumed lost at sea. Madge? He is looking into my eyes as he calls this new, bastardized version of my name. I ponder whether to correct him or to let it stand. Are we going to be the kind of people who call each other nicknames? Who is Madge, and would she stand for Anton's treatment of her, or would she dump chilaquiles on his head and disappear into the Sierra Maestra mountains?

The serious man is still standing near his table, but there's enough distance for the American to enjoy his breakfast and maybe some light conversation with the waitress. This time it's my smirk that must seem shameless. Anton's denouncement of me has temporarily made me rash. I know they'll do nothing to me within earshot of the American.

I set his food down gingerly on the table. "And I didn't hear your name?"

"Burke. Richard Burke." The man says even his own name

with such unbridled pleasure. What it must be like to be him. "Will you be here at lunch?"

I flick my eyes to the serious man who hasn't taken his eyes off us.

"Si, yes." My cheeks burn at the thought of having to continue my morning with the knowledge that I'll see him again in a few hours. "But don't you want to sample some of our local cuisine? The hotel's menu is limited."

"There's plenty of time for that," he says, cocking an eyebrow and nodding his head ever so slightly in the direction of the looming man. His eyes gain a heaviness, little wrinkles springing up around them like blades of cheatgrass through the pavement. "So I wait for you like a lonely house," he whispers.

"Neruda," I whisper back, attempting not to show my surprise and genuine giddiness—a nearly foreign feeling. This handsome man I just met has quoted my favorite poet.

The serious man begins to approach Burke. I resist the urge to grab Burke's hand and run with him until no more eyes can follow us.

He turns. "Send for the driver. I'd like to tour the area this morning." He addresses the man decisively. I can see the outline of a gun in a holster below the man's gray suit jacket. I wonder if the Russian serial number has been filed off, like the ones in the State Security Camp.

The serious man looks at Burke, surprised and confused. "I... I am not working for you, Señor Burke."

I stand by defiantly, though no one has expressly told me to go. I can hear a buzz behind me and I assume Anton is coming this way to remind me of all the work that needs to be done.

"Well, why the hell are you looming around then? I thought you were an escort provided by the hotel. Private security or something. What are you doing here?" Burke is standing now, placing his napkin on the table. I can see the hint of a smile on his lips.

"I'm here to make sure you don't taint the Cuban people with your...American sensibilities."

Burke tosses a mischievous glance at me before resuming his collected manner. "And you do this with every tourist? I'll just make a note here." He reaches into the soft linen breast pocket of his shirt to retrieve a small leather-bound notepad.

"No, sir." The man jumps in at the sight of the notepad. "I've been assigned to you. For regular tourists, it's different. Every journalist has an escort from the Revolutionary Party."

"And what of free press, my friend? What of truth?" An inflection comes into his voice that makes him sound like one of history's great orators. He raises a hand and intensely waits in the pause for a thought-out answer.

I can see a glimmer in Burke's eye, and now the other diners have set down their forks and knives to observe the American tourist and his handler sent by the Cuban government. The serious man takes the bait, of course, as I knew he would. No Cuban can resist an ideological debate.

"Renaldo," he says astutely, thrusting his hand at Burke and moving promptly to sit at the table across from him.

Burke takes his hand and shakes it fervently.

"Mr. Burke, sir, I'm not going to change your story. I just need to be here to watch, to observe. I believe in truth."

Burke sits back down and engages Renaldo. "But, Renaldo," he persists, "how can I get the whole truth with you looming about, frightening people away from me? I can't get a sense of the country if people are afraid to talk to me."

Renaldo sits back, contemplative for a moment.

"Sssssstttt!" I hear the inevitable correction from Anton, who is creeping around the archway between the patio and the dining room. Looking his way, I can see his frantic arms waving me back in his direction. I suddenly realize that I've been idly standing by, openly eavesdropping on Burke's conversation. Although he has been sneaking me glances, no one has spoken to me in a few minutes. I'm sure if I could see myself, a loopy stare would inhabit my normally unapproachable face.

I can feel the red burn of embarrassment and turn to walk away. I'm just a waitress, who am I to him? I'm just the first Cuban girl he got to use the Neruda line on. And I fell for it hook, line and sinker.

Burke. Richard Burke. An American journalist obsessed with truth and Pablo Neruda. I have a sense that I've traveled to the Bermuda Triangle; a place that calls to you, somewhere you didn't know you wanted to go until it sucks you in never to be seen again, and this is the center. Richard Burke is the Bermuda Triangle, and I am a hopeless bi-plane destined to disappear.

It's not the first time in my life I've been faced with the possibility of falling in love, but it's the first time I've watched it happen with a mild indifference. Do I really love him so quickly? Or am I just desperate to feel anything other than the desperation I've felt these last few years? With Juan Julio, I railed against it—tried to keep myself from loving him. I knew that once I fell for him, I would never be free again. Luckily, I was wrong—but it's taken eight years to feel this way again. Burke feels like slipping into a hot bath; Juan Julio felt like slipping into a volcano.

SEVEN

1992 1993 1994 1995 1996 1997 1998 1999 2000 **2001** 2002

May 3rd, 2001 – Veradero, Cuba

I brush past Anton, who only stares in disbelief at the scene transpiring behind me. I force myself to keep going towards the service elevators, gathering linens and napkins as I go. There may not be a Richard Burke come lunchtime. He may be on the deportation list, or worse—put into a Cuban prison for dissent. It wasn't love I felt, it was pleasure at the sight of someone disobeying the status quo—someone who could actually get away with it. But the farther I get from his gravitational pull, the more I see that no one can get away with it for long.

The Castros will never let it fly. If he stands up and shows the world what Cuba is really like for us... well, they would never let that happen. They would lose everything. *Well, then why did they let him come here in the first place?* a voice in my mind wants to know.

They control the visas; they know who comes in and out. They control everything. If someone with a big enough reputation and media outlet behind them wanted to come do a story on Cuba, the Castros would simply refuse. Fidel would say, "The Cuban people have no need of the world to understand us—we need only to understand ourselves." He's always been the master of many faces.

Maybe this Burke isn't as big as he seems. He puts on airs to seem like a celebrity, but maybe he's just a small-time journalist—tourist, did he say? Maybe he's just a travel writer. We get those all the time—and yes, a standard escort is provided. The government will say it's for the journalist's protection, but we know better.

My mind is racing. When I get home I need to send a message. This time I'll need to take extra precautions because if Burke is sniffing around me, they'll be watching even closer than usual. I try to feel my hands wringing and wrapping the soft cotton, I try to feel the breeze on my face, but all I feel is exhilaration. I can't distract myself from the feeling that something is starting to happen.

A normal day in the hotel laundry room brings about fifty loads full circle. I try to get five loads through each of the five washer/dryers before lunch, and the other half after lunch.

Today, because of Anton's proclamation that I must cover two jobs, I am just getting the third load in when it's time to go back upstairs to get ready for the lunch shift. Not one to leave things to chance—or the responsibility of others—Anton exits the doors of the service elevator at exactly 10:45 to scuttle me back upstairs.

"Don't think I forgot about you down here, Lavandera." He calls me what I am, Laundress, as an insult. This only shows how little he knows about me, and still I harbor no desire to let him know what insults might actually sting. I don't consider my vocation a reflection of my worth or abilities—it is simply where I've been placed. I could have easily been a waitress, though thank God I'm not.

"I didn't think I could be so lucky," I tell him, as I remove the loads from the dryer into the large white rolling laundry tub. "There's no way I can get these towels into the guest rooms before check-in if I have to go back up to wait tables," I hold my head high as I tell him.

"Then you aren't working fast enough," he says, drawing closer and moving his hand to his belt buckle. He moves in behind me as I grab the last towel from the basin of the dryer. When I turn around I can smell the medicated scent of his standard-issue after-shave and see the glint of his hair gel. Being a military man, he's first on the list to receive such luxuries. His hair stands upright at attention in a swooped coif. A manicured mustache lays above his upper lip like a lazy dog. In his eyes is trained indifference.

"Do I need to show you how to work faster?" He begins to slip his belt from the loop. As he steps closer to me, I throw my eyes to the clock that hangs above the frosted-glass windows.

"It's almost eleven," I say, slipping past him and quickly darting towards the open elevator doors. "Don't want to waste any more time than I have to," I say brashly, glancing at the pathetic lump he struggles to readjust. I see a hint of hurt flash across his face before the smug expression he wears when he knows he will find me later, when there are no open doors and no quick-witted excuses.

I breathe a sigh of relief as the elevator doors close. Anton has cornered me before, but I just focused on the hard, cold metal of the washing machine against my back until it was over—which wasn't long. I never felt any reason to fight back, because what he was taking didn't feel like mine. He was trying to take something that was taken long ago, something I'm not sure was ever mine to give.

Now, after meeting Burke, the thought of having sex with Anton makes me physically ill. The thought of his loafing mustache twisting and straining as his lips tighten and release is enough to push me off balance. I put my hand on the side of the elevator to steady myself, and shake my head as if to erase the memory. I remember again that Burke might be waiting for me. I realize that I, too, want to wait for him. I wonder what would have happened if Catalina hadn't called in sick today—would he want her to serve him his lunch?

I look down to straighten my light blue laundry uniform shirt, and smooth my white pants. There isn't much to improve here—if he likes the way I look in this then he will like me in anything, I suppose.

Out of the elevator I bolt for the kitchen and turn into the nook just inside the door. The water feels cool on my hands and the soap feels needed. I scrub both hands and under my fingernails, as if I can wash Anton off completely. I don't want Burke picking up his scent. Even though he didn't touch me, I still feel as if I need a long soak in an icy sea. Being this close to the equator, a sole cube of ice is hard to find, so I will have to settle for the cool tap water and the antiseptic smelling soap.

Hands dried, I do a quick scan of the dining room. I see an elderly Danish couple settling in, a table of five middle-aged Canadian men who look like they haven't seen the sun since the last equinox, and a young honeymoon couple who could be Irish. Other than these guests, the room is empty.

I walk to the open-air archway and peer out onto the terrace. A quivering begins at the base of my throat when I don't see him at the table where I left him.

EIGHT

1992 1993 1994 1995 1996 1997 1998 1999 2000 **2001** 2002

May 3rd, 2001 – Veradero, Cuba

"Psst," I hear from my left. "Madge." A smile perches on my lips. I turn my head to see him sitting in the shadow of the hotel at a small two-person table. He is alone.

"What happened to your escort?" I ask, unable to quell my curiosity.

"We talked. He decided to dine elsewhere. He'll be coming back this evening to check in. He seemed to agree that his presence was not conducive to good journalism."

The cadence of his speech is intoxicating. I've always found words to be the most effectual aphrodisiac. I can't hide the surprise on my face that he was able to shake his state-provided escort so easily.

"I take it from your expression that you're surprised. The fifty pesos I slipped in his hand were also helpful in guiding him to make the right choice." He smiles and lifts a coffee cup to his lips. Thoughtlessly, I pull out a chair and sit down across from him, stowing my server's tray under my arm.

"I've never seen anyone get rid of an escort before, even for a bribe. They're beyond reproach—Castro's Eyes, they call themselves. What did you say to him? What did you talk about?"

"He was an educated man—hell, all of Cuba is educated, you know that. It didn't take much for him to see my side. I used a few old tricks, but I think deep down, he felt what he was doing was wrong and he wanted to do right." He takes another sip of the fragrant espresso and looks up as Anton—fuming—approaches the table. "Hello, we'd like to order lunch please."

The humiliation is almost too much for me to bear. I look at the table and bring my hand to my face in a belabored attempt to remain unseen. I know it's too late, though.

"Sir, my associate Magdalena would be happy to take your order when she can compose herself. I apologize very much for her rudeness and presumption in sitting down with you." Anton is so angry he's lightly stamping his foot, like a child who's not getting his way. Still, his tone remains falsely genial.

"No, you misunderstand. I'm going to have lunch with your associate, Magdalena. Could we see some menus please?"

This is one of the few times in my life I can remember actually having a choice in what happens to me. I want to relish it for a moment. In my past, even when defying the state, I knew that I only had one choice. I had to do what was right. Since being discharged from the prison camp, I've had one choice: to stay alive. I have done whatever I had to do to keep going forward without making waves. Here, in the face of Burke and Anton, I can choose. I can choose to sit with this American, enjoy his company, laugh at his jokes, glimpse into another world and then have to answer for it later. Or I can choose to stand up and continue my work, do as I said I would do, and leave Burke behind, maybe forever. What will the next waitress do? Will she remain seated, or stand and obey orders?

"No," I stand up, finally. "I can't. I'm sorry. I'm working now." I know if I continue my interlude with Burke the fallout from Anton will be much more than unpleasant. Burke will be on a plane away from here and I will have a hand pressed across my mouth for the rest of my natural born life. It doesn't matter if talking to him feels like gasoline in the water: strange, unnatural, and yet unexpectedly beautiful.

Burke's eyes fall to my light blue laundry uniform, my borrowed apron, and for a split second I feel that he knows how hard this life is for me. His face turns to Anton and his green eyes become crisp with distaste. "A menu, please?" He says again, dismissing Anton to the lowest possible station.

I take out my small notepad and pen as Anton hesitantly leaves to retrieve a lunch menu.

"Where can I meet you? What time do you get done tonight?"

"Sir, you're a stranger. I don't even know you. Why do you want to meet me?" I'm saying the things a girl should say to a strange man, the things all Cuban mothers teach their daughters in the face of a country of men whose only way of getting anywhere is by forcing through. But my tone is welcoming and sweet, as my body wants to open up to him like a day lily. I instinctually lean my chin toward him, feeling the breeze on my neck and collarbone. I try to push the corners of my mouth down, but the unwanted smile escapes me.

"By night, love, tie your heart to mine, and the two together will in their sleep defeat the darkness." Neruda again. As he says the word darkness, his eyes flick to Anton, and then seem to take in the world around us, too. Does this man know me? Has he seen inside my mind? How could he know that the weathered and broken down old farm house at the base of the peninsula is littered with books? This is the place I call mine—even though I happened upon it abandoned one day, and fully expect the owner to return and reclaim it. Can he know that I devour books like oxygen; sucking them in and then expelling them again when I've gleaned what I need from them? Of all my books, the Nerudas are the most sun-soaked and dog-eared of them all. I would never tell my sisters in Cienfuegos that I stay up late with a flashlight, and the precious 9-volt battery of which we are only allowed one per year, and read the sonnets over and over until my eyes are tired and my soul is full.

To my two sisters, I'm the hard one, the unfeeling one, the weathered and beaten down one. I am the cynic who doesn't believe in love anymore. But here is a man who seems to be Pablo Neruda incarnate. Has he truly come to liberate me from this hell I've been living in? He seems to think so.

Anton thrusts the menu in Burke's face with such force that I'm surprised he doesn't make skin-to-skin contact.

"Thank you, kind sir. Madge—Magdalena will take my order now, as you requested." They engage in some kind of male staring contest that I'm sure could be resolved sooner if they simply tackled each other.

Anton sniffs and stalks away.

I am suddenly livid at both of them. "You can't just saunter in here and put my job in jeopardy because… well, I don't know why you're acting this way, but it has to stop. I will be dealing with him long after you've gone." I try to sound as forceful as I can in a whisper. I look behind my shoulder to see Anton disappearing through the archway.

"I… I'm sorry. I wasn't trying to make trouble for you. In all honesty, I just wanted to have lunch and chat with you. Because you seem… like someone I want to get to know." He suddenly seems deflated and unsure of himself. He flicks his eyes from one side of the patio to the next and I wonder if he wishes the escort was back with him now, to guide him out of this situation. He brings a glass of water to his mouth and starts again, "I don't just quote Neruda to anyone, you know. I think you're beautiful and I can see in your eyes that there's more to you than a laundress—waitress—whatever you are."

"What a pompous thing to say. Of course there's more to me than being a laundress—that's true of all laundresses. We're not in America; we don't all get to 'follow our dreams.' Did you come here looking for someone to save? Someone who would swoon for your free markets and salivate over your Hollywood romances? Those girls are waiting for you down in town at the cantina. They wait for sailors and soldiers and think if they hike their skirts a little higher, a different future awaits them. It's the same future for them as it is for me: constantly trapped in a state of confusion, wondering what the truth is, who's telling it, and when this nightmare will end. Only there's one difference between them and me—I know that the truth only matters to the liars in the end."

This diatribe contains more words than I've spoken to any one person in years. I realize that my pointer finger is in Burke's face, my other fingers clasped so tight into my palm I can feel the nails digging in. His eyes have been locked with mine. He's been listening intently, without a trace of his previous mockery and mirth.

"There's something I want you, and the girls in the cantina, to know." He leans closer to me, his face suddenly seeming intoxicated at our closeness. "That future you described—confused, lost, not knowing who to trust?"

I feel myself nod.

"It doesn't matter where you go, those feelings don't go away. Cuba, America, Chile, North Korea, Sweden—that's the human condition. It only becomes easier to bear when you have someone to make the map with you."

"Make the map?" I feel as though I'm on autopilot and something else is propelling me further into the conversation.

"When I was deep in the bush in Uganda, my producer and I happened upon a village. We were thirsty and exhausted from days of walking in circles. It was a miracle we found any other humans at all. We told them we were lost and needed water, food and a place to rest. They helped us, we stayed there for weeks subsisting on cassava and coconuts. Every time we would go to the Won Yat—the medicine man—he would tell us, 'make a map.' It was all we could translate. We didn't understand.

"After a few weeks we realized that we wouldn't get back to the city unless we did something, because none of the villagers would take us anywhere. They thought it bad luck to go too far from their village. We went out into the jungle and looked for high ground. We walked to the tallest tree on the tallest hill. We could see for miles. I took out my notebook and drew the tree in the center of the page. We began to draw the map. First, we would go ten feet out and I would draw the trees and shrubs in a circle around the tree. We would continue out in circles. If we found a path, we would follow it, but never getting out of sight of the tree. I filled up pages and pages of a little notebook. Eventually we found our way back to the road we'd come in on, but I couldn't have done it without him—nor he without me. We needed each other, and that tree to anchor us."

When he stops speaking, it's like I've woken up from a dream. I realize again where I am and my face flushes red: I feel like I'm naked in public. I point my finger to the menu still propped in his weathered hands. I look down to notice that the skin around his nails is cracked and peeling. His hands are big and capable looking—the kind of hands not characteristic of a journalist. They look as if they'd be more at home on one of the fishing boats in the harbor.

"Oh, yes. I'll have the pork sandwich." He looks at me a little longer, to see if anything he's said is sinking in. I give a light nod and turn away from the table, afraid to waste any more time.

The rest of the lunch I stay away from him. One of the other male servers drops off his food to him and I occupy myself by standing near the food window and running food across the dining room quickly and efficiently and with as few words as possible. I glance at him a few times, and although he doesn't look antsy for me to return, his eyes are on me. He's coolly taking in his surroundings, and it's as though I'm just another shrub in the landscape of this land that's completely foreign to him.

I have a sick feeling in my gut. I know that, all emotions aside, this man is the closest thing to a way out that I have had or will ever have. I immediately hate myself for thinking it. I wonder if I would take it, given the chance.

He remains calm—he resembles a humming engine continuing down the road. The engine doesn't know there's an impending collision that will obliterate it, leaving pieces scattered up and down the roadside.

NINE

1992 1993 1994 1995 1996 1997 1998 1999 2000 **2001** 2002

May 3rd, 2001 – Veradero, Cuba

After my encounter with Burke, I clear the lunch dishes and head back down to finish the laundry. The heat and humidity have made the wet linens in the washer smell mildewy, so I begin to wash them again. Turning the cranks on the washers is a satisfying feeling; they make a sharp, fast clicking sound as they spin beneath my hands. When all five of them are running, I go to the dryers and begin folding the towels. I start to make up the cart that will follow me from room to room.

I keep hearing the sound of the elevator dinging, the sound of someone coming down. But each time it dings, the elevator doors open to reveal an empty box. I think what I feel is fear—the dull hum of terror that Anton will come looking for penance. Burke made him look stupid and I will be the one who has to pay.

I pass off the clean sheets to the housekeepers, who have agreed to help shoulder my load today. Now all I have to worry about is distributing the clean towels and collecting the soiled ones. I may actually get to leave the hotel before dusk, although I was anticipating working late into the night.

I pull the cart with me as I stop at each room. As each room is completed, I check it off the list. The more check marks fill my page, the more I start to hope Anton's forgotten about what happened earlier. Or maybe he is preoccupied with a bigger problem today.

I knock on room 627 and no answer comes. I enter by sliding my all-access key and pushing open the door. The room looks as any other—the hallway leads to the open bedroom that houses a single bed. On the suitcase rack stands an unzipped, weathered brown leather duffel. An almost too-basic lineup of toiletries lies in an orderly pattern around the sink. A newspaper fills the trashcan, and I gaze over the Chinese symbols I noticed earlier on Burke's table.

"Magdalena," a voice says from the bed. I hear the comforter rustle. A strange, liquid, honey feeling spreads across my chest and I realized where I am. This is Burke's room. My feet step quickly to the end of the hallway and I come around the corner like a boxcar down a hill.

I don't know what I expected to see there. I want Burke to be lying there with his reading glasses on, shirtless, but still in his trousers. I want the television to be on, but muted, as he rereads *Love in the Time of Cholera*. I want him to be waiting there for me.

Instead Anton stands by the bed with Diego, another bellhop and a fruit delivery man across from him. They all stare at me with a mixture of apology and excitement in their eyes. Anton's face is cold and intent.

"You seem surprised. Are we not who you were expecting?" I begin to back away and feel the luggage rack dig into the back of my calf. I try to move to the hallway but the bellhop effortlessly moves to block my way. I'm trapped. I open my mouth to scream, but I'm not sure if any sound comes out.

Anton moves to the closet and removes one of Burke's shirts from a hanger. It's a simple white collared button up. "Nice," he says. He walks to me, and stands close, his hot breath in my face. He puts the sleeve under my nose. It smells like fresh cut apples and shaving lather. "Smell that? That's your man. The man you thought you were coming in here to fuck. The man who embarrassed me and made you feel like you had the power to walk away." He grabs my arm and leads me to the bed.

I know what's going to happen here, and a part of my brain is sending signals to thrash, kick, bloody their noses, grab the letter opener... but that part of my brain is dead now. After the last time in the camp I realized that things go much quicker when you don't fight. And it takes something from them—they want you to fight, they want to chase you. In this case, not giving them what they want is a way to take back a bit of yourself.

He takes Burke's shirt from the hanger and wraps it around my face so that it covers my eyes but still hangs down in front of my nose. The smell fills my nostrils and I knit my eyebrows hard to fight back the tears.

"Every time you smell that, you'll think of what's about to happen." Anton says, the hot breath on my ear now. "You belong to this island like a dog, Lavandera. You're a criminal, and we're going to show you how we treat criminals. And somewhere deep inside of you, you're going to like it. Because you know you're nothing more than a dog begging for a leash."

As he says it, he roughly ties my wrists with something thin. A necktie? In another life, maybe Burke would have worn that tie to meet me for dinner. I feel the luxurious comforter beneath my skin as they remove my clothes. They are being strangely gentle.

"You're doing a service for Julius, here, so the first one's going to be sweet. It's his first time."

More clothes are coming off me and I hear movement and murmuring around the room. I actively think about Burke; where is he? Will he come back to his room and find us? Will he save me, just as I told him not to?

"I can't promise the rest of us will be as gentle with you," he says. I hear a muffled laugh and a clasping of hands. "Don't worry." I can almost see the patronizing tilt of Anton's head. "Your man won't be back for hours. We sent him with a driver friend of mine to tour the Peninsula. To get a real pulse on his story. Nice guy, that Burke..."

Anton keeps talking, but I stop listening. I hear him rifling through the room, touching Burke's things. The smell in my nose grows so strong that I pray for a hurricane to come wash everything away; the hotel, the men, the blood, the semen, the shirt, the whole island, even Burke. It's his fault I went into that room so late. His fault I had to wait tables and see his newspapers and ask him questions and see that there's another world out there. Him and Catalina. Fucking Catalina.

Anton goes last and takes longest. It's his way of having the last word. He knows it's dry, aching, burning by now. I have little left in me to care what's happening. He can do whatever he's always wanted to do, and he can do it in private since he forces the others out after their turns. Yes, they took turns like children on a merry-go-round.

The other three were so quick I wouldn't have known it was three different men if I hadn't smelled them and heard their different grunts. The first one, the bell hop, he couldn't have been more than fifteen. I remembered his doughy face from the check-in desk. He hesitated a little—as if he might've known what he was doing was wrong.

"Give it to her, or I'm going to give it to you," Anton said gruffly. The boy complied. I lay as still as possible for fear they would remember I was a person instead of a lifeless piece of driftwood floating in a murky sea of sheets.

I could sense them all there, watching each other, not knowing if it was okay to talk or to masturbate in front of other men. Anton was shameless about it, I could hear his whiney moans, the rustling of his stiff pants and the tinkling of his belt buckle as it jostled with his movements. He got it all out before his turn, sometimes on my face or my chest. It would take hours—hours, or minutes?—for him to come inside me and when he did there was almost nothing left but a dry sweaty heave.

"I would just leave you here for Burke when he returns, but we don't want *that* ending up in Vacation Magazine, do we?" He hisses at me as he unties my wrists. "Clean yourself up, and finish the towels." He zips his pants, tucks in his shirt and lets out the kind of satisfied sigh that makes me think he's just eaten a very filling meal. I sit up to gather myself and look expectantly at him.

"You think I'm going to leave you in here alone? Stupid punta. Wipe yourself down, replace the towels and get out. I'll make sure to put all of Burke's things back in order." As he says it he's rifling through a stack of papers on the desk.

I was hoping he would leave me at least one moment alone in Burke's room. I wanted to straighten it, to make sure he could never know I was here. I wanted to squirt shampoo up my nose and cleanse the scent from my brain.

Instead, I pull my clothes into position on my body as I find them in their scattered places about the room. It feels as if I am dressing a mannequin for a window display. When I hear the door click behind me, Anton is still sifting through Burke's possessions, as if he can find a way to consume him just by touching the things he's touched.

TEN

1992 1993 1994 1995 1996 1997 1998 1999 2000 **2001** 2002

May 3rd, 2001 – Veradero, Cuba

I walk out the basement door that leads to the back loading dock of the hotel. I asked the bell hop on duty, a young weekender I ran into by fortune on my way out of the bathroom, to check me out at the service desk so that I don't have to see anyone—especially Anton—before I leave.

I can see the sun melting into the ocean. This may actually be one of the best views of the sunset to be had on the entire peninsula. It strikes me that such beauty and such horror can coexist in this world.

I peer around, taking in as much information as I can in the half-light. I see a few parked delivery trucks, but the dock is quiet. Most of the other employees have gone home, except those who tend to the hotel at night.

I can see the ocean just beyond the fence of the hotel. It laps along, so peacefully. Below the delivery dock, beyond the fence, are a few rocks that lead down to the water. This side of the hotel does not have a beach, but if I was to swim out far enough, I would see tourists frolicking on the sand just down the shoreline.

I notice a place where the fencing has come apart. A clever staff member has bent it back into place, but looking closely a place big enough for a person to fit through is plainly visible. I am not in my mind so much, or even my body. I can see myself climbing through the hole, delicately placing one foot on each large boulder leading down to the sea. But in every other way, I'm already in it. I can already feel the salt accumulating on my skin, cleansing me and also stinging unbearably in my wounds. My clothes remain splayed on one of the rocks where I can see them.

The coolness of the water and the sound of the waves soothe me. I try to let it happen. The ocean bathes me. She holds me here for I don't know how long. Maybe she will carry me away. If I just started swimming, how far would I get?

It's almost dark when I climb out and put my clothes back on. The sting has subsided and I feel ready to walk home and fall into bed. But there is one place I want to stop first.

My first priority is to stop by Catalina's apartment and give her a nice, firm, open handed slap. The kind my mother used to give me when I would talk back or steal candy from her secret stash. Catalina is young, stupid, and doesn't yet understand how her actions affect others.

I amble onto the road home, trying not to feel the twinges of pain between each step. I walk out the gates of the hotel property, which measures three kilometers to the farmhouse. I usually walk it alone, but this time I'm flinching at every car going by. I feel the gravel beneath my feet, the night air on my neck. I am here, outside, away from the day. I'm trying to embrace this, to move on, to forget. This isn't the first time a group of men has taken me over, planted a flag and laid claim to my dignity, my peace of mind, and my autonomy. Those things were stolen from me long ago. But I feel for the first time that my scars have been laid bare. For the first time, I feel ashamed. How to explain this to him? That is, if I ever see him again. How could I explain that his very scent will cause vomit to rise in my throat?

I realize how very strange it is that I'm thinking about Burke at all. He's someone I didn't know existed twelve hours ago. This has all been his fault—his cocky insistence to have lunch with me, to force Anton away from the table, to denounce him.

I know, too, that if it hadn't been Burke, it would've been someone else. Another man would've made Anton feel small—it might have been today, it might be next week, but his reaction will always be the same. He will scramble desperately to regain his power.

It could've been Catalina—and not me—to fall prey to him. I'm suddenly glad she wasn't there today. She's not strong enough to withstand what those men did to me. She's just a waitress—it's the job she chose. She isn't being punished, this is just her life.

Me? I'm a prisoner. A criminal. I've been assigned to Veradero. I've been assigned to the laundry. And I will pay for my crimes in unimaginably cruel ways for the rest of my life. In a way, they believed they were serving the state. They're reminding me of where I belong—of what I am.

And still, beyond all my feelings of self-pity, I know beyond anything else that I have to find Burke. I have to tell him what life is like for me here—even if it kills me. Maybe I can get out. Maybe he is my last and only chance to get out of Cuba forever.

A pair of headlights saunters up the road towards me, jumping at each light bump in the road. The lights temporarily blind me and I notice it's because they're slowing to a stop. I feel the hot, twisting burn between my legs and remember to look at the ground and keep walking. I cannot withstand another encounter, even a pleasant one, today. I want to bury my face in my books and my blankets and forget the world.

"Madge!" A hand shoots from the car window into the night and I jump back. "How lucky it is to see you here, we're just on our way back to the hotel. This is Paolo, my driver. Do you need a ride home?"

I feel the raindrops before I notice the clouds that are now shrouding the moon. I keep my eyes trained on the ground, remembering what Anton said about his driver friend. I know that Paolo will tell Anton anything that happens here. I can feel both of them looking at me expectantly and I raise my eyes for just a moment to look at Burke. I can't resist letting myself have this one last glance at him. His eyes sparkle in the dim, amber light.

"Are you alright? Has something happened?" Burke moves to get out of the car and I hear him say something to Paolo. My legs quiver beneath me and my hands and arms feel like lead weights at my sides. I have an unbelievable need to lie down, and before I can think about it, I'm on the ground. Everything is shaking now. My breaths are loud and I think that if I was able to feel anything but panic, I would be ashamed of the jagged sounds escaping me.

I wake up to the sound of men arguing. I feel the tremor return to my limbs as I look around to get a handle on where I am. I recognize the faded, white stained wood paneling on the walls. A light glow comes from the lamp I rescued from the dumpster outside the hotel. One of my mother's scarves is draped over the lamp to filter the light and perhaps to keep from blinding me when I wake up. Covers lay over me, and a cold sweat begins to form between my skin and the blankets.

I see the pressed roses in a frame hung on the wall. My rosary beads hang off of one corner of the frame. This is my room. I am home. How did I get here?

"I can't just go in shooting up the place, goddammit. It would ruin years of work and put other people—good people—in jeopardy. This is about the long game, Burke. You've got to be able to see that, or you can't stay."

His response is muffled, but I know it's him. My mind flashes to his hand darting out the car window—reaching for me in the rain. Did I take his hand? Did I lead him here? I move to the floor and peer over the ledge of the loft. I can see down into the living room where books are littering the floor and the cushions of the tattered couch.

A pair of well-dressed legs is pacing around the doorway of the kitchen—it must be Paolo, Burke's driver and friend to Anton. So the one speaking muffled soliloquies from the kitchen is Burke. I press against the railing in an effort to hear what he's saying.

"It's not like that here, Burke. Sure there are laws, but they only apply to certain people in certain situations... No, I haven't assimilated... Yes, I see what happened to her, you don't think I know how awful it is? It happens to hundreds of girls a day down here. It's happening to hundreds of girls at home every day, too. Why is this one special?"

At home? Is Paolo American? They're talking to each other like brothers or co-workers, but how would Burke know Paolo? He just arrived in Cuba yesterday.

Among the muffled responses I can make out the words, 'bullshit,' 'corruption,' and 'truth.' It's Burke, alright.

I'm trying to decide if I should go downstairs and find out

how these men know where I live or if I should keep listening. I begin to move my legs beneath me but they feel weak and lifeless. I raise my arms to steady myself but realize I've lost my balance a moment too late. I fall into the crate that I use as a bedside table, knocking the lamp and causing it to teeter. I squint and wait for the sound of breaking glass. A long, silent pause passes and when I open my eyes, I see a hand placed on top of the lamp to steady it.

"You're up," Burke says. "You should really lie back down."

"Trust me, the last place I want to be right now is on my back." I say it without even thinking. What does he know about what happened to me? Maybe nothing. Maybe I can tell him I just fainted from a long day of work.

Burke moves to me and places his hands in my armpits, lifting me like a mother lifts a child out of the bathtub. I feel my feet hit the ground and he moves to my side and beneath my arm to help me down the stairs. This is more than a faint. Maybe a migraine? Or could it pass for dehydration? He and Paolo are passing meaningful looks between them; Paolo's face is cautionary, a warning, while Burke's face begs Paolo to sympathize.

"How did you know where I live?" I speak to Paolo but the tone of my voice makes it known that anyone who has a good answer should offer it.

"You're in the system. Magdalena Cruz. Felon. Released from Juventud in 1998. On probation. Placed as a laundress at the Hotel Royaliza in Veradero shortly after your release."

"But my address," I remember that I don't legally own this house, and that no one is supposed to know I live here, "Isn't registered."

"You think El Comandante is going to let a felon accused of treason and anti-revolutionary activity live off the grid?"

As soon as he says it, I feel some small form of validation. I had known someone was watching me for months, but people at the hotel said I was being paranoid. Not all of them know my history, but even so, I had let them convince me I was acting crazy. No one would follow me home, catalogue my movements to and from work, check up on me; but that's exactly what they've been doing, and they've been doing so under the command of El Lider himself.

"El Comandante doesn't know who I am. I'm sure he has much bigger—how do you Americans say it?—fish to cook?"

Burke and Paolo chime the correction together, "Fish to fry."

I raise my eyebrows at Paolo who seems to suddenly realize he's left the oven on. He starts to move for the door. "Burke, I've got to go—remember what we talked about. *Please*." The old door creaks open loudly and he fumbles as it leans diagonally from where it's fallen off the top hinge. He's unsurprised, and expertly places the door back in the frame from the outside, and then he's gone. It's as if he's entered and exited that door a thousand times before. His face is one of those you've seen before but you're not sure where—it could've been on a billboard, in a hotel lobby, or he could've taken your sister to a school dance. He's that forgettable.

My breath catches in my throat as I realize I am alone with Burke—as alone as two people can be while being watched.

ELEVEN

1992　1993　1994　1995　1996　1997　1998　1999　2000　**2001**　2002

May 3rd, 2001 – Veradero, Cuba

He's looking at me with the most sorrowful look. "Madge," he whispers, almost inaudibly. I squirm on the lumpy cushions of my tattered loveseat. I remember when I saw it in the alley behind my sister's apartment in Cienfuegos. I had just been released from the camp and had nothing but the clothes on my back. I thought it funny that the first possession I would make mine would be a loveseat when there would be so little love in my life moving forward.

I can't shake the uneasy feeling of being alone with a man after what's just happened. "Who are you Richard Burke, and what do you want with me?" Inadvertently my eyes fill with tears and I can see a glisten start to form in his, too.

"Honestly, I don't know. I feel drawn to you... responsible for you. When I saw you this morning... Wait, let me back up and start at the beginning. I've been trying to get into this country for eight years. Ever since I became a journalism student at Amherst, I've been fighting red tape to get in here.

Any time I see Cuba in the news, any time a new story breaks, I wish it had been me to write it. This... project fell in my lap and I dropped everything to come here. It's been a dream. But when I saw you this morning, half-heartedly filling waters and reluctantly clearing plates with that little wrinkle in your brow..." He pauses, choosing his words carefully. "I was taken off balance."

I want to break in to speak, but something stops me.

He sighs deeply and his eyes take me in, coming to rest on the scars I bare as brazenly as tattoos. "I'm afraid that just by being here I've made your life much worse."

Burke sits on the other side of the love seat, putting as much distance between us as possible. His body is turned to face me while his feet remain firmly planted on the floor. I have my legs tucked up under me, my body facing forward. His look is imploring, but not forceful—curious but not over-zealous.

I look down and examine the old wooden planks that snugly fit together to make up the floor. They're a weathered gray and almost rotted through in some places, but they remain sturdy.

I think back to just this afternoon, at lunch, when he told me the story about making the map. In another time, I would've let him take me right there on the restaurant patio. I would've told him to keep talking—keep saying those beautiful things. But now it feels like a lifetime ago when I was a person who was unafraid. And another lifetime has passed since this afternoon.

"Burke, I—" It's hard to find the words to explain what needs to be said. "I can't explain to you what my life has been like. I can tell you it's been one long ache with bits of joy scattered in. Those joys always have something to do with the idea of a new Cuba, the idea of getting out of here, or of changing things; the idea of a new life. The only thing that's brought joy to my life has been taken away now. I don't believe in escaping anymore, I don't believe in hope anymore.

"But this morning, this sunny, cursed morning when you called me Madge," a catch comes into my throat, "I felt new joy starting to spread and for the first time in many years I recognized myself. It was like a movie going from black and white to full color. What I'm trying to say is that I don't want you to pity me or look at me differently than you did this morning. Yes, something awful happened to me this afternoon... No. It didn't just happen to me—it was done to me, committed upon me. And I'm sure Paolo knows what it was, or if he doesn't, he will soon. Please don't ask me to tell you the details. Don't make me name the men who hurt me so that you can hunt them down. It's much more complicated than that.

"I don't know what this feeling is between us, but I can't let them win. *I can't let them win again.* They're using me as a weapon to make you turn around and run. They're using you as a weapon to make me see what I can never have. It's the dirtiest form of fighting in the world and it's how Castro has been able to trap millions of people in a nightmare for sixty years. And you pitying me or treating me like a victim, or leaving because you're afraid of what might happen if we let ourselves hope, that's letting them win. It's waving the white flag. It's surrendering. We'd be letting their troops advance across the last barricade and into our hearts."

I hear a floorboard creak and realize I'm standing. My arms are outstretched and I feel ten feet tall.

A surprised and impressed smile fills up his whole face. He stands with me, and though I felt tall a moment ago, he is a head taller and much broader than I. He looks down into my face and cups my chin in his hand. His face is less than an inch from mine and he whispers, "On your orders, General."

And I kiss him. It is the kind of kiss that explains why

people fall in love at all. It is infinite and instantaneous, rich and simple, distilled and imperfect. It's the kind of kiss you remember just before death takes you, and you know that it was all worth it.

TWELVE

1992　1993　1994　1995　1996　1997　1998　1999　2000　**2001**　2002

May 3rd, 2001 – Veradero, Cuba

Burke is astute enough to know that a kiss is as far as things will go tonight. When he stands close to me, his smell enters my nose and I can feel the panic filling me. I think he can sense it because he makes a visible, and noble, effort to restrain himself. It angers me that I cannot give myself to a man I want so badly because of men who treated me like trash. I try to force my brain to remember *this* moment—associate the smell with his kiss, his rough hands, his thick forearms—but my senses are not as quick to respond as I want them to be.

 We sit back down on the love seat and I lay my head on his chest. The scent is overwhelming. I try to just be in it without the horrifying images of this afternoon flashing into my head. I force myself upright and bring my knees to my chest. I look at him apologetically, and he concedes with a light smile and a pat on the knee.

 In my house, a book is never out of reach; this is partly because there's nothing in the house but books and a few sticks of furniture. The sheer quantity makes it hard to escape them. Some I have collected from the lost and found at the hotel, others have been passed down to me from friends, acquaintances and even some strangers. Most belonged to the oddly poetic and deep sugar cane farmer who must've abandoned this place.

I like to imagine that he spread tar, thick and sure, across the floorboards of a '57 Chevy. He would've taken out all the heaviest parts—the engine, the hardware, maybe even the steering column—to make it more buoyant. I can just see him, using a few ping-pong paddles to steer the car-boat towards the Florida coast. He would've slipped past the navy patrol boats by floating by silently in the dead of night. He would've picked the night of the island's favorite soap opera finale to drift away.

This is how I would've done it, anyway.

A few days later, dehydrated and starving, he would've washed up on American shores a free man. And the island's loss is my gain, because I don't think anyone's coming back to claim this house, these books, or these sugar crops that have dried up into tall waving brown whips.

"Is this one of your favorites?" he asks, lovingly rubbing his thumb across the cover of a small worn paperback.

"It is," I say. I know the book and I can see him shift as he reads the title. He turns his whole body to face me. His face contains a mixture of equal parts fascination, pride, and shock.

"Surely, this is banned here." He looks back at the cover, the faded blue rainbow bowing over the words *I Know Why The Caged Bird Sings*.

"Yes, most of these are," I say without consequence.

"But you just said they're watching you. Why would they let you have banned books?"

"I suspect it's because they think I'll lead them to the

militia men who are plotting to take down the revolution. It's all just a mind fuck. If I feel free—free enough to have these books, to come and go as I please—then I will begin to act recklessly and lead them straight to who they really want."

He sits up a little straighter and cocks his head in adorable confusion. He wipes his hands on the tops of his legs, I assume an old habit from his youth to dry up sweaty palms.

"And could you?" His eyes, which were staring at the book intensely, flick to me and then quickly to the floor.

My adrenaline begins to rise again, and as usually happens, it brings with it a raging boldness that I sometimes don't recognize or understand. I reach my hand to his face and tilt his chin upwards until he looks me straight in the eyes.

"Yes," I say.

He stutters inaudibly and stands. "I'm going to make us some tea." He doesn't fumble around my kitchen like most visitors would. I hear no calls from him asking where tea bags are, where cream is or how to turn on my antiquated stove. If he has trouble he keeps it to himself. I know he'll be disappointed when he can't find tea. Unlike most countries, tea isn't a popular drink here. It's very expensive and hard to come by.

I notice that something has shifted within me. I'm suddenly aware of the distance between us. I feel like I must've felt the first time I lost a tooth. This thing that was a part of me, connected to me, is now something separate. How strange that is, and I don't like it. I want him next to me, to remain a part of me as he's felt for the last hour. Even being separated from him by a wall is unbearable.

I hear a creak. It's a familiar groan that the house makes when the wind blows out towards the ocean. But this time I wonder if it might be something—or someone—else.

Burke comes back in with an old towel wrapped around

the handle of my teapot and two cups. Steam billows from the spout. In the bottoms of the cups I see a few slivers of cut lemon, but no tea bags.

"I find I can make do with most anything," he says, squeezing the lemon into his cup and pouring the hot water over the rind. I look at him strangely and do the same.

"Isn't this just hot, watery lemon juice?"

"Well, this isn't really about the tea, is it? The tea is just a vehicle for the conversation. So, in this case, let's let the watery-lemon-juice spur us to say the things that need to be said." He takes a sip of the stuff and recoils because of the heat.

"I have a better idea," I say rising to my feet and walking into the kitchen. I open the icebox and remove the last Cola can and pull out the last bit of ice. It's formed into one misshapen block that I smash into pieces on the counter. It feels good to smash something. I pull a handle of rum out of the cabinet, hardly touched since Catalina brought it over to celebrate her getting a job with me at the Royaliza. I grab two new glasses and sweep the ice into them from the counter.

It becomes clear to me how terrible of a waitress I really am when I struggle to carry the can of Cola, the glasses and the rum back into the living room.

"Let me help with that." Burke leans over, grabs the glasses from me and sets them on the table with a thud.

I reach into the scalding hot teacups and pull out the lemons without flinching. I re-squeeze the lemons into the new glasses and give each glass a strong pour of coke and rum.

"This is a Cuba Libre," I tell him, holding one glass close to me and the other glass towards him. "Only now we call it the Mentirita—the little lie. Usually it comes with lime, but I don't want to waste the lemon; it was my last one. My fruit allowance has already been spent this week."

Burke makes a sound—it's not a laugh, but that's the

closest thing to it. "Cuba Libre, my ass. Getting drunk on these is as free as anyone is going to get around here."

I don't smile, though I want to. My body aches from the events of the day, but I don't want to fall asleep, for fear I'll wake up somewhere else. Or even worse, wake up and realize this has all been a dream. I bring my drink to my lips and sip, feeling the alcohol sting a few open cuts. I must wince at the pain because I can see Burke sneaking me a look of frustration and sympathy.

The rum tumbles down into my stomach. I can almost instantly feel my eyes get heavy. I have never been a drinker... rather, I'm someone who likes the idea of drinking but falls asleep as soon as I begin. Burke seems to be the opposite.

As he gulps his drink he refills with more rum and more coke until the coke is gone, then he just keeps pouring rum into the melting ice cubes. He picks up the little blue book and begins to read aloud from the first page. He reads so passionately that it's easy to see why he became a journalist. He is in love with the words, the storyteller, and, perhaps most of all, the sound of his own voice as he relives someone else's experience.

I spar with sleep, if only to hear him read for a while longer. His voice and Maya Angelou's story trickle into my dreams like a leaky faucet drips into a plugged up, stagnant sink. *Drip. Drip. Drip.*

I don't know how late he goes on, or when I fall asleep. I feel myself tossing, hear the sounds of pages flipping, books shuffling, mumbled anger and astonishment. I'm being carried, floating through the creaky floors and stairs and until there's my soft bed, my blankets, the scent of coconuts and lye soap. Now there's nothing but the extinguishing of a light somewhere under a scarf and a warm weight sinking beside me, barely grazing my side.

THIRTEEN

1992　1993　1994　1995　1996　1997　1998　1999　2000　**2001**　2002

May 4th, 2001 – Veradero, Cuba

Sun streams through the slats of the roof. I jump to my feet and search the room for my clock. I realize that today is Thursday, which is my day off from the hotel. I exhale and begin to melt back into bed, but gasp and jump when I see a body lying there.

My bed is an old metal frame bed that reminds me of a nunnery or a mental institution. The black iron frame supports a twin mattress that is thin and flimsy. Burke's bare feet jut out from beneath the white sheet, through the wire foot of the bed and touch the floor. His arms hang down in front of him, knuckles grazing the wood floor. Laying on his side, he must only be taking up a five-inch vertical strip of the bed. His gray, crosshatched trouser legs are peeking out above his feet. I notice his shirt is carefully hung on the back of my wooden chair, and his hat is perched on top of the lamp.

Without thinking, I go to unbutton his pants. I guide the zipper down, trying to remember the last time I removed a man's pants. It feels unfamiliar, and I let myself believe this is the first time I've done this. I'm careful not to wake him. It takes all my strength not to touch him in the firm, muscular place above his hip—and his neck! Oh, his neck could pool water where his collarbone meets his throat. I want to place my finger there and feel it sink in.

Instead, I ball up the pants in my hand and force myself to ignore the blissful smile that's crossed his face. Does he have to smile in his sleep this way—what kind of grown man smiles in his sleep, anyway? At least he's more comfortable now, having rolled over and drawn his legs into himself. Waiting for him to wake will be like waiting for Christmas morning.

I snatch his shirt off the chair on the way out of the room, and begin to wonder how long I can keep him from returning to his hotel room—and what it will look like when he returns. Will there be any evidence of what happened there? Will Anton have had it scrubbed top to bottom in a last-minute bout of remorse? I immediately remove Anton from my mind—he's a point on the map that's too desolate, the elements too harsh for human habitation. I tell myself this again and again each time his cruel face appears to me.

I get the washboard down from the shelf in the pantry, and take down the coconut oil and a bar of my homemade soap. I walk the fifteen minutes to the well and pull water up, splashing it into the basin that I leave next to the well. The well is equidistant between three farms, or what used to be farms. I share the water with the farmer who lives to the west. He raises goats and pigs, and I think he's hiding a few chickens, too. He wants to keep them off the livestock registry. I toss Burke's clothes into the basin so that I can wash them clean of the smells that plague my memory.

I rest the washboard in the basin. I toss more water into it, feeling my muscles burn as I pull the bucket up to meet me again and again. Sweat begins to bead on my temples. I grab the bar of soap and coat the washboard in a thick, creamy lather. Then I coat my hands and forearms in the coconut oil and begin scrubbing the shirt first—feeling the hard, predictable thuds of the washboard as I drag Burke's shirt down and up.

My soap is the best soap in the area. Many people come to trade me for it. I only accept books or food in trade. These are things that aren't so easily tracked. People gladly trade an extra banana or two for handmade soap. Most people on the island can't get any soap at all—there's been a shortage since I can remember. Since I started working at the hotel, I've noticed many of the maids walking around with sagging pockets. Their supervisors let it slide if they set aside an extra bar or two for them. They too can sell soap for almost anything else they want or need. Of course, soap is sold in the tourist gift shops, but there's no way locals can afford it.

My arm travels up and down, and as the bumps on the washboard vibrate to the rest of my body I begin to feel it coming, as I knew it would eventually. I am here, I am alone, and I decide to let it take me. I realize it's no longer my hand shuddering with the washboard, but my body shuddering now. Dry sobs stack in my throat and I let them escape. The wispy grass tickles my legs and the early morning sun bathes me in molten honey. I can't reconcile this world with the people in it, this beauty with the cruelty. I weep for who I was yesterday and who I was ten years ago; those women are dead and buried along with countless bodies lost to starvation, torture, and drowning. They can never come home again. And neither can I.

I can never come home to my body again. I ring the doorbell, I bang on the door, but no one comes to answer. Someone else will always be here, waiting for me. He'll be here whispering to me in my silent moments. He'll watch me when I undress. He'll make sure I know that I'm never alone, that I can never be safe. He'll whisper, "You let this happen, Magdalena. You opened yourself up; you let me in. You wanted me here because you're weak. You belong to me."

In the blurriness of my tears and frustration, I can feel my eyes burning. I don't want to see who it is, I don't want to admit who's whispering, even though I already know. Any Cuban can recognize his voice even at a whisper. Fidel will not be ignored.

I open my mouth to scream and feel the burning trickle into my throat. I recognize the burning sensation as a combination of soap and lack of air. I can't breathe because I've shoved my head under the water. I want to drown out the voices, maybe even shut them up forever.

If I breathe in right now, the water thick with suds, can I be clean again? Could I wash the scents from the insides of my nostrils and lungs? I open my eyes under the water and feel the sharp sting. Real panic rises in my brain now—air, air, you need air! *You want to live.* I don't dignify this with a response, just remain under water, letting the pain and fear envelope me. I may have been out of my senses to put my head under water, but it would be completely insane to take it out now. I don't want to return to this life. I want something else—anything else. Even nothingness is better than this sandy, isolated hell.

Darkness begins to seep in on the sides of my vision and even though I'm forcing myself under, a basic Darwinian call for survival thrusts my head out of the water. Breath, sweet breath—however unwanted—fills my lungs and I fall to the ground. I cough and sputter, the burning in my throat and eyes worse than before.

The shaking is subsiding now, and filling in behind it is an anger; ink soaking a blank page. I grab for the towel I brought with me. It was meant to leech out the water from Burke's clothes, but I need to get this soap out of my eyes before it causes any damage.

    The lye in my soap is strong—it's made by straining water through charred woodchips. I lay on the warm grass, the sterile sting subsiding with my raspy coughs. I can't tell how much time has passed, but start to think Burke might be looking for me. I pull his clothes from the water, drying them by rolling them up in the towel and pressing out the water. I look up and watch the wispy clouds brush past the sun. If I strain my ears, I can hear the waves crashing in the distance.

FOURTEEN

1992 | 1993 | 1994 | 1995 | 1996 | 1997 | 1998 | 1999 | 2000 | **2001** | 2002

May 4th, 2001 – Veradero, Cuba

My thin white nightgown is starting to itch in the baking sun. I've brought Burke's shirt to my nose again and again, trying to make sure I can't detect a hint of his previous smell. I've washed the clothes three more times now, and yet I can still feel the smell in my nose. I think of Lady Macbeth—it's her guilt that propels her to keep washing her hands, to keep seeing blood that isn't there.

I have nothing to feel guilty about, I've done nothing wrong. The realization hits me as I continue wringing Burke's clothes out. Those men are the ones who should be cleansed. They are the ones who robbed me of myself. And I'm the only one who can take it back.

I dump over the basin, stowing the soap and coconut oil under my arm as I run towards the house. My loose leather sandals *thwap, thwap, thwap* the dry ground. I can see the door now, the crooked, fading back door that must've once been painted a bright turquoise. I quickly hang Burke's clothes on the line, my hands moving like little propellers—so fast it's hard to see the details of what I'm doing. I'm about to launch inside when I notice the three rocks—large, medium, small—stacked in front of my cellar door. A message. Los Lobos has the worst timing imaginable.

The message can wait. I barge through the crooked door that leads into my kitchen, careful to reset it and turn the deadbolt—a small, easily broken measure of privacy, but privacy nonetheless. I set the soap on the counter, but keep the coconut oil as I bound up the creaky stairs to the loft.

Burke is awake, sitting at my small desk in his underwear. He is scrawling notes in the tiny black notebook that he flashed to the minder yesterday. He must have heard me coming—no one goes anywhere in this house silently—but he makes no move to turn around, so enthralled is he in his notes. His pen flits like a firefly, his big shoulders hunched trying to accommodate the stepstool he's using for a chair.

As he mumbles to himself I take a small smear of the coconut oil on my pointer finger, and spread it across my opposite palm. Its clumpy white, uneven texture comes to life as I rub my hands together. Fear rises in my ribcage, but I note that it's not the same kind of fear I'm used to. This fear would look more at home on the face of a middle grade girl, the first to walk across the chasm of space to where the boys are shuffling their feet at a school dance. She's decided to be the brave one today; that's when I remember something about myself. I'm brave.

I walk up just behind him, and I know that he feels me here because he stops writing and lifts his head to stare straight at the wall. His breath comes fast, and still he hasn't turned around to acknowledge me. Is this the same brash Burke from yesterday? He seems timid and nervous but also afraid of scaring me away—as if a butterfly has landed on him and he knows that if he moves, it will fly away. He's probably right, so I say nothing.

I rub my oil-soaked hands across his back, and feel the muscles there tense and release. I spread the oil over his arms, his neck and his chest, all from behind. Burke is not tan like most Cuban men; his skin is white and freckled across the shoulders. I slide my fingers up his neck and into his dark blonde hair, massaging his head and temples. He lets out a groan that reminds me of what we're doing and I stop, my hands fused to him. I step back and for the first time he turns to look at me.

The look in his eyes is a warm broth that I want to slurp to the bottom of the bowl. But, he hesitates. His eyes implore me. I can see he wants to ask me, "Are you sure? Is this okay? Do you need more time?" but I press my finger to my lips as I slip the white nightgown over my head.

As he drinks in my body with his eyes, I can feel myself coming more into focus. I resist the urge to cover anything. I'm brave, I remember, some would even say brazen. Others have said reckless. Just as one wipes the fog from a steamed-up mirror, I am seeing myself clearly for the first time since the night of the raid. The night I was taken to Juventud seven years ago.

Burke is bringing me back to life.

I think, *I am Magdalena Cruz.* I take a step toward him. *I am a counter-revolutionary.* Another step. He stands perfectly still, silently insisting that if I need to do this on my own terms, I need to show him what that means.

One downfall of being a man is that even if you want to appear hesitant, your anatomy always gives you away. Burke's erection is pointing at me, stretching the fabric of his underwear. Yet, he does nothing to hide it or tuck it away from me. He lets it stand proudly, doing all the talking that he can't.

I take his face in my hands and press my body up against him. I kiss him powerfully and, although he remains stoic for a moment, I can feel his will break as he moves into the kiss with me. The hardness of him is vertical against me, and he pulls me into him as he begins to grind it into me.

The motion triggers something graphic in my brain, a reminder, a snapshot of yesterday, but I do not react. I push it away, opening my eyes to see the man here with me. He is beautiful and smart and silver-tongued, and I want him.

I remove his underwear in one deft motion, and suddenly here we are, naked and vulnerable to each other by choice—my choice. I move my hands across him, and when he tries to take it further, I stop him. He concedes. I don't want our first time to be riddled with pain. I want him so badly, but I need more time to heal.

He convulses, the breath escaping him beneath my hands. I feel his throbbing heart beating with mine.

Burke is so gentle with me, and yet he finds ways to make me quiver with pleasure. Any time I shrink away in pain, he gives me a look of pure care. He waits patiently until I show him how I can be touched. He never tries to push further than I can withstand.

We explore each other as if our bodies are a course of study. I am a book and he reads me once for the plot, twice for the characters and a third time for the subtleties and nuances he missed previously.

"I'm not sure what I'm doing, but I can't think straight with you," he murmurs. I smile and kiss him gently, hoping to keep him off balance. I keep telling myself he is just a distraction—one that could become useful. I can't afford to lose my senses like he can.

FIFTEEN

1992 1993 1994 1995 1996 1997 1998 1999 2000 **2001** 2002

May 4th, 2001 – Veradero, Cuba

I get up to scrounge some food from the kitchen, which I bring back to bed: a plate of plantains and tamales that my neighbor Maria traded for soap a few days ago. Worries about my ration book tug at my mind—I've shared with Burke almost all my food for the next week, and I won't be able to stock my kitchen again until next Friday, when my ration credits will be accepted again.

I try to let the thoughts flow through me and just enjoy the moments with him. I ease back into my tiny bed and watch his eyes grow big at the sight of food.

"God, I'm famished," he says, taking a big bite of plantain.

"You should be," I smirk, lying on my stomach and breaking a tamale in half. I half-heartedly cross myself at his mention of the almighty.

"Oh, I'm sorry, I didn't realize. I thought this was a communist country." He talks with his mouth full, but somehow remains charming. He isn't condescending in tone, just curious. I have often wondered about this inconsistency myself.

"It's more of a habit than anything. I don't believe in it. My mother was very religious, and any time I would take the Lord's name in vain she would cross herself and say, 'Magdalena! Jesus te oye.'"

He doesn't ask me what it means, but he also never speaks to me in Spanish. I wonder if he speaks it or if he just doesn't want to appear ignorant.

"Where is she now, your mother?" he asks, running his index finger in spirals on my bare shoulder.

"I'm not sure, probably dead." The word "dead" lays in my mouth like a sardine. The spirals stop. He stares at me, trying to detect a note of levity. He doesn't find it.

"You don't know if she's dead or alive?"

"No, when I got released from the camp I went back to Cienfuegos so I could find my way. I had nothing—no one—I'd been there for five years and everyone I knew in Havana was captured with me. I found my sisters through a stroke of luck; one of them worked in a butcher shop. When they took me in, they told me our mother had wandered away one day and never came home.

"They blame me. She was always prone to long bouts of sadness and after I...," I pause, not wanting to be overdramatic, "...went away, they said she couldn't take it anymore. We're all grown and she had no one left to take care of. There was no one to tether her to reality anymore."

"Madge." He says it so sweetly I understand why people started giving each other names at all—to hear them whispered by someone like Richard. "It's no one's fault. Especially not yours." His mouth finds mine, and I let his words work like a salve on an old wound. He fills his hands with my loose black curls and begins to kiss my neck. "So, what did you do to get arrested, anyway, drink too many Cuba Libres?" He chuckles to himself as he takes my breast in his other hand.

I sit up stiffly and spring out of the bed. How easy it is to be seduced by someone who so fundamentally misunderstands my world.

"Madge, come on. I'm sorry. It was only a joke."

"Does this look like a joke to you?" My voice is pinched. I violently gesture to my forearms where the scars around my wrists and up my arms are a constant reminder of my time on Juventud. "Does what happened to me yesterday look like a joke to you? Maybe it is one big joke, and I'm just the punch line." I'm half dressed now, bra, underwear, one leg through my jeans.

"Madge, no, please. I'm sorry, okay. Look at me." He stands from the bed and puts his hands on my shoulders. His nakedness feels strange and out of place now. Then he moves his hands up to my face, and I can't help but look up into his eyes. "I wasn't trying to make light of what's happened to you… what you've fought for." He stops at "fought for," testing me for something—a reaction? A confirmation?

Suddenly I feel even more guarded than I did a few seconds ago. Maybe I've trusted too quickly. Last night I told him I could lead him to the militia—why the fuck did I do that? What if he isn't who he says he is?

I can see the three rocks stacked in front of my cellar door, and suddenly I can put a name to the thing that has been nagging me, forgotten since this morning. The message. I press my lips together and decide to lie to him, at least for now. "I need to get some air," I say, pulling on my white cotton t-shirt.

"Are you sure?" He sits back down on the bed and pulls me into him, breathing hotly onto my stomach. He begins to unbutton my newly buttoned jeans. I almost fall into him. I almost allow myself to giggle, strip for him, let him take me away from this life for the rest of the afternoon. Almost, but something in his earlier pause stops me.

"Yes," I say, firmly re-buttoning my pants and sliding away from him.

"I could go out and get us some real food?"

"I'm not hungry, but sure. Unlike you Americans, Cubans don't eat all the time," I try not to let the note of cruelty slip in, but it lingers there between us.

He smiles his big patented, shameless smile and says, "Why are you the only one who's allowed to make jokes? I'm clearly the funny one in this relationship."

I walk downstairs and out the back door. I slide the rocks out of the way with my foot and unlock the cellar door with the heavy iron key. The cellar is my favorite place in this old house. I store my soap here to cure, and also my cans of fresh jam—guava and strawberry, mostly.

It's also the place where Los Lobos, the counter-revolutionary militia, leaves messages for me. It's usually small things like passing information, but occasionally men and boys stow away down here until they can move to the next stop undetected. I try not to see them—I leave food at the door and knock—and I never get close to them. I don't look them in the eyes. The less I know, the less I can tell the DI if they come looking for information.

I feel the temperature inside the cellar and I suddenly remember what it feels like to be cool. The floor is of black, tamped dirt that emits tepid air. On very hot days, I have to prevent myself from laying down on it, the coolness attracting me like a bee to a flower. I look around warily—Los Lobos never leaves the notes in the same place, and sometimes boys will be asleep on the cot in the corner. Weary runners rest here, or sometimes fugitives escaping something like Juventud.

I see the folded piece of paper tucked under a jam jar on

the third shelf. Just a small corner peeks out into view—something a DI agent surely wouldn't notice if he tried to search the place. I grab the lantern and light it with a match from the box on the surface of my worktable, the sulfur refreshing in my nose.

Pulling the piece of paper from beneath the jar, I begin to unfold it. The thick creamy paper is unusual in Cuba—from the desk of a politician? A rich plantation owner? I'll probably never know. Once unfolded I can see the handwritten note was scrawled hastily:

> *Do not trust Richard Burke. We have not determined his alliances. Stand by for more information. Beware.*

SIXTEEN

1992 1993 1994 1995 1996 1997 1998 1999 2000 **2001** 2002

May 4th, 2001 – Veradero, Cuba

My heart is pounding but I still follow the protocol, feeding the creamy white paper into the lamp and watching it turn to black crust, then crumble away.

How, how could I have been so stupid? His obvious hat, his airs of knowing everything; they reek of a person I've been trained to avoid. He got rid of the handler with no fanfare. Anton has a distinct hate for him; the kind of hate he stokes for people with more authority than he. I can't believe I didn't see it before. And I let him into my bed, into my heart. Through the suspicion, a smile seeps from my scowl. I still flutter at the thought of his touch—even if he's an informant. Even if he's undercover working for the DI, no one—not even Richard Burke himself—can take this day from me.

I palm the spatula I use to stir new batches of soap, sliding it off the tabletop and into my hand. It makes a low rumble as I remove it from the thick wood planked table. I head into the house via the rickety staircase and the door that leads into my kitchen.

I hear his voice speaking to someone and I press my back into the door, trying to shut it as quietly as I can.

"Paolo, would you listen, she's connected. I know what I'm doing."

Pause.

"No, I know that I'm not... yes, I only had one night of training, but I've been doing this for..."

Longer pause.

"Not that good? Listen, I had Kim Jong-il's personal chef's daughter professing her love to me after one night. I can handle a hotel maid..."

My heart has fallen out of my body now, but I remain still, forcing myself to listen.

"She's our in, Paolo. She's in the outlaw sector. She's been beaten down and she wants a way to fight back. She still has contacts. But..." he stops. I can hear him pacing. "You have to promise me we can protect her."

Who is he? A DI agent wouldn't give a fig about protecting me. And he's working with Paolo, who I know is an associate of Anton's. I begin moving toward the door of the kitchen, craning my neck to hear what he says next. There's a note of bravado in Burke's voice that I noticed when he engaged the handler, but it was missing last night as he read to me. Is he just putting on a show?

"No, I won't go on until I have an agreement from Wright. Protect her. Get her out. Let me take her out of here." Long pause. I can't hear Paolo's muffled voice anymore and I wonder if he's considering it.

"I don't care about all that shit. Get on it... just get on it and I'll get you the information you want." He slams the phone shut. I assume it's a paguefono—the kind of phone you buy minutes on at the airport. It's not a number you would give out at a bar.

My head is on fire and my heart has not recovered from the slight about the Korean girl. How could I have thought I was the only one? Was it the way his fingers lingered on my skin as though there was a magnet there?

I glide silently, more silently than I've ever been able to navigate the old warped boards in this borrowed house. The metal spatula grows hot in my hands as I traverse the landing and go still behind the open door of the bathroom. There are no thoughts now, no feelings—there's only action. He's pacing the floor, looking down at the phone. He stubs his toe unexpectedly on the iron bed foot and I take my chance.

He hunches over his blunted toe and curses under his breath. I lunge at him, toppling his already off-balance body hard onto the floor. I scuttle on top of him, punching my legs into the outside of his arms and pinning them there.

"Christ!" Burke yells.

I heave the handle of the spatula down across his throat. Understanding now that he's in danger, he wiggles his arms free and pushes me off of him with relative ease, but I launch at him again. I swing the spatula aimlessly, slicing the air into ribbons.

"Madge, what the fu—" My swinging suddenly makes contact and I see the spatula crack him in the back hard. "Mother fuck!" He screams with such force and surprise that I'm thrown back. He's got the upper hand now, knowing that he's being attacked and that he's got one hundred solid pounds on me.

"Jesus fucking Christ, what's gotten into you?" He takes my arms and pins them to my sides and picks me up forcefully. His fingers dig into my forearms and I can feel my scars begin to itch and whine under the strain. "I'll take this," he says as he plucks the spatula from my hand the way you pull a burr from your skin. I stare at him indignantly, sure that I will never, ever speak to him again.

"You want to tell me what the fuck is going on?" He's bending down into my face, his hands pressing my thighs into the bed. I press my lips together and look away, squinting my eyes all the time.

Don't trust him, don't trust him.

"Look, I guess there's no way around this; I'm going to have to tell you something. You obviously heard me talking to Paolo." His voice is gentle but the grip on my legs is like a clamp. I reach up with my left hand and slap him hard across the face.

"Bastard." The word slips from my mouth, barely a whisper. I can feel tears stinging in my eyes but refuse to acknowledge them.

"Madge, don't. You don't have all the information."

"You wouldn't need to dignify a hotel maid with any important information, would you? Did you need to tell the chef's daughter who you really are, or did you just use her too?"

His eyes fall to the floor and any hint of his previous jocularity is gone. He slowly removes his hands from my legs and sits down beside me on the bed. The room is so quiet and still, I think he must be able to hear my thoughts. "She's dead." His eyes haven't left the floor and his voice is hoarse.

The word dead hangs in the air. I don't move, but stay with my back on the bed and my feet on the floor. If I need to run, I'll be able to do it without much movement. But I don't feel a pressing need to escape.

"She's dead and so is her father." He takes a deep shuddering breath and it seems to empty him completely. "Yuki," I hear him whisper in a faraway voice.

"Yuki was a lot like you. Strong-willed, incensed. Life put

her through the wringer and she was stronger and fiercer for it. What can I say? I have a type." He shrugs his shoulders at his half-hearted attempt at humor. "But you're right. I used her. I didn't love her. I knew she loved me and I exploited her for information, all for a fucking story. Heartless. And now she's dead and I'm still here, and I have to live with that.

"And if you don't do what I say, the same thing might happen to you." He raises his gaze from the floor to look at me—his expression pained and sickly. "And it would be different this time because... I am in love with you. I can feel it down to the very core of my body. And if you were to die because of me—" he turns away again, sniffing and breathing hard, "It won't happen," he says definitively. "I'm going to get you out of here. And we're going to be together."

I let out a puff of air in disbelief. I look into his eyes and feel myself squinting at him. "Who are you, Richard Burke?"

"I'm just your average, run-of-the-mill travel reporter freelancing for the CIA."

I look at him, confused. "That's going to need more texture," I say.

"Well, I am a reporter, that part's true. I'm here working for *Vacation Magazine*. I'm writing on the state of tourism in Cuba. The Cuban government has been fed information that my story will also be filed with an official report to the State Department. In that report will be a recommendation on whether or not it's time to lift the travel embargo."

"That could mean millions in revenue for the island," I say, my eyes wide. Now I understand why it was so easy for him to get rid of his handler.

"Yes, and that's not all. You can imagine that someone writing a story like that would get access to people and places that the average American would never see, right?"

I nod.

"So the CIA took an interest. They've asked me to help them connect the various networks of counter-revolutionaries on the island and funnel them resources to perform a successful coup."

I groan reflexively. "Another Castro assassination plot? Carajo, I'm not getting roped into this. These half-assed plans are a joke on the island. The CIA has been laughed out of Cuba more times than you or I could count."

"I don't know what they're planning, and I don't care. That's got nothing to do with me—with us. We just need to make the connections." He takes both my hands and looks into my eyes intently. "I am going to keep you safe, but I need you to lead me to the people running the counter-revolution. Will you do that?"

"There's a reason the CIA can't break into the Cuban underworld; it's not as easy as finding a smooth talking reporter to sleep with the maids and seduce information out of them," I say with cruelty. He sits back a little, a cloud of hurt forming over his bright, clear eyes. "The reason is because everyone plays both sides when opportunities come up. Anyone who's been slighted by the regime has motive to overthrow them, but the regime is masterful at manipulating people. One day someone is fully committed to the cause; the next, they've been offered a bribe every week for the rest of their life if they turn over all their contacts. When people are hungry and impoverished, it's not hard to convince them to switch sides. Most people work for both sides, and they're the only ones who know it."

I continue, "Once you've been found out, punished, you're in the system forever. They have an entire police force dedicated to surveilling the outlaws—that's what they call us. Castro's terrified of getting called out for more human rights violations, so he hardly ever kills anyone. Which is almost worse. He keeps us alive and makes us work for him. It has driven people mad. So we fight back the only way we know how—in secret, in ways they can't detect."

"So, who are you working with?" He pulls one leg up onto the bed and turns to face me.

I remain with my face forward, not ready to forgive him for his dishonesty. I steal a glance at his eyes, his beautiful eyes that fill me with wonder and dread. He's just confessed to me he's with the CIA. Can I really trust him? I decide silently to myself that I will trade a secret for a secret.

"That's what I'm trying to tell you; I don't know. I'm working with everyone and at the same time, no one. All I know is they call themselves Los Lobos. But I've never been approached directly by anyone who aligns with them. I've never seen a face. I've never heard a name. All the notes are passed into my cellar. I read them and follow instructions. I'm just one link in the chain."

"What kinds of things do the notes say?" His hand is in my hair now, stroking and combing it absentmindedly as he listens. Now, I pull my legs to me and cross them in front of me as I turn to face him. Our eyes meet and it takes everything I have to not consume him with kisses. After what's happened the last half hour, I feel a flush of anger at myself for letting that thought enter my mind.

"Nope, it's my turn. Secret for secret. Who is Paolo and is he working for Anton?"

"Oh, I see how it is. That's technically two questions, but I'll play this game. Paolo is CIA undercover as a DI agent. Paolo's been working this cover for years. It's taken a long time to get in with people like Anton. That's why he wouldn't let me pummel him last night when I saw what had happened to you. It took just about every ounce of strength I had not to kill him. When you came to, Paolo was talking me down." A stricken look comes across his face and I can see he is physically pained by the thought of the night before.

I shift and twitch trying to shake off the thought of Burke's hotel room. "Wait 'til you see your room..." I mutter it before I can stop myself.

His eyes bulge with anger.

"No, no, I shouldn't have said that. The less you know about what happened the better. You're already having a hard time controlling yourself. Please, don't ask me to tell you what happened."

He closes his eyes and takes several deep breaths. He straightens his back and looks as if he's left himself for a moment. He opens his eyes to look at me, a remorseful but understanding wrinkle in his forehead making him look older. "Okay, but I can't promise I won't beat that guy's ass before I leave this god forsaken place."

"Fair enough," I give in. I think about how satisfying it would be to watch that, but don't say it. I don't want to stoke the flames inside Burke any more. It won't do us any good now, especially with the task ahead of us.

"My turn," he says confidently. "What happened," he gestures to my forearms, "to make you an outlaw in the first place?"

"That's like asking what happened to make you a journalist," I say pointedly. "It's what I've always done. It's who I am. I want justice for the people of this island, and Castro almost killed me once for trying to get it. I'm sure I'll eventually die fighting for it."

"Nice speech. But you dodged the question. What did you get arrested for—were there others? What happened to them... to you?" His face is earnest but something still feels strained between us.

I move my face into the space between us, traversing

miles and miles of hostile territory to meet him nose to nose. I gently rub my nose against his and we slide into a kiss—soft and subtle like dewy grass at sunrise. We both know it's a tactic—to forget, to distract, to get lost. We both know, too, that it's working.

SEVENTEEN

1992 1993 1994 1995 1996 1997 1998 1999 2000 **2001** 2002

May 5th, 2001 – Veradero, Cuba

Our second night together passes much differently than the first. We are filled with a rare combination of continuity and dread. I have the feeling that this night encapsulates our entire lives, and it also might be the last time we see each other. This, coupled with being able to tell each other secrets that had previously been off-limits, leaves me giddy and glib and full of the wonder of his face.

We stay up all night talking, telling stories and jokes and discussing our childhoods. He tells me he grew up in Iowa on a dairy farm.

"It was a very iconic American upbringing. Maybe it's why I like to travel—my father was very regimented, strict. He didn't leave Woodburn much at all except to get equipment occasionally. He and my mom drove me to Amherst and it was the first time he'd crossed state lines in his life. There was nothing wrong with my childhood. It just wasn't what I wanted. I wanted to know my way around more than a cow's udder."

"And yet, here you are, shacked up on a farm with a country girl." The dawn light is beginning to seep through the cracks in the ceiling and the sky is indigo now where it once was black and sulky. Through my east-facing window where we counted stars, I can see the sun cresting over the rolling hills. It's a moment I wish I could wrap myself in.

He smiles, voracious and wide. "We have some things that need deciding, but can it wait until tomorrow?"

"It already is tomorrow, love, and I have to be at work in two hours." I knew it was coming, but saying it out loud made it all the more real. I would have to leave the nest of love and comfort Burke had built for me over the last thirty-six hours, and return to the harsh world of Anton and laundry and looking over my shoulder. The thought of it puts a soggy black lump in the pit of my stomach.

"You have to go back," he says, as if realizing it for the first time himself, and understanding what it means for me. I rest my head on his chest and feel his heart pounding like an animal clawing against the bars of a cage. His fists clench and unclench.

"Yes, I have to. And if we're going to make a plan, it has to involve me going back and acting as if nothing has changed. We have to maintain the cover."

He sighs and brings his hand to his forehead, clamping it down over his eyes. I can't tell if he's wiping away tears or frustration. Maybe both.

"Alright. I think I should call Paolo and get him over here. Or meet him somewhere. We can formulate next steps and then... I'll have to let you go."

"I'll wait for you like a lonely house," I say softly, taking his hand from his face and pressing it to my lips.

"'Til you will see me again and live in me. 'Til then, my windows ache." He quotes it back to me without missing a beat.

I'm suddenly filled with fear because I don't know anyone in the world as well as I know this man, whom I've just met. If he goes away there will be no one to say they knew Magdalena Cruz—once a brave counter-revolutionary, now a pathetic, lovesick maid.

Burke calls Paolo on his disposable cell phone and he agrees to meet us in town at the street market. It opens early and is always swarmed with tourists, so we will be able to lose anyone who tries to follow us. It's about a twenty-minute walk from the farmhouse to the city center. I walk slower than usual and Burke has to visibly shorten his stride to keep from getting ahead of me. We don't say much, as both of us are dreading the idea of parting for the first time since Wednesday night.

Today is Friday, so we pass many old women, well-dressed with their heads wrapped in scarves. They scuttle along on their way to morning mass. When they see Burke and I walking together, dressed not for church but for something only sinners would do on a Friday morning, they look at the ground and mutter to each other. One woman winks at us with a knowing grin. Burke smiles and waves at her. She blushes and hurries to catch up with her friends.

"She reminds me of my abuela, my mother's mother," I say.

"She smiled at strangers?" he says with a chuckle.

"No, she was a romantic. Always setting people up, taking such pleasure from seeing two people in love. She once told me that love was the only distraction powerful enough to keep people going."

"Are you saying we're in love? As in, you're in love with me?" He looks so proud he could burst. I feel my face get hot and remember we're not in the loft anymore, but outside where people can see us.

All of a sudden, Paolo is walking beside us, and we're

entering the market through white stone archways. Above us are thatched grass roofs that reflect strange shadows at our feet. The rows and rows of vendors' booths, covered in bits and bobs, each have an accompanying salesman who's hooting and hollering at passersby.

"Pretty lady, need a scarf? Pretty scarves here," one man courts me as we walk through the rows. "Or jewelry, I've got rings, earrings, cheap, eh? Come take a look!" A woman reaches out to touch me, as if desperate for anything I can give. When she looks into my eyes and sees that I'm Cubana, she steps away and moves on to manipulate the next person wandering from booth to booth.

These vendors are some of the richest people in Cuba. They play on the perceptions of the tourists, but the truth is that they get to keep most of the money they make in their booths. There is a waiting list to sell things here, and most people have been on it the majority of their lives. To be face to face with the Canadian and European tourists every day, hawking your wares and splaying your poverty for all to see; it's one of the only legitimate ways to make money in this country.

We walk through two or three rows, dodging around people and tables. Paolo buys a hat and a scarf and places them on us.

"Good morning," he says with staunch cynicism. "Burke caught me up on the phone, but I don't know everything. What's the next step?"

"I say we watch the cellar and see who's dropping the notes. For all we know it could be someone with the DI just waiting for Madge to act on the intel."

"No, it isn't," I say. "The DI knows something is going on, but they don't know what. They want me to act on the intel and lead them to Los Lobos. It's the only reason they've kept me alive. I have never done anything with the information that they give me. Occasionally someone will stay in the cellar overnight—at most, two nights. But they're gone without me knowing where."

"How often do they house someone there?"

"Maybe once a month, but I never know when."

"What do you know about Los Lobos?"

"Nothing, that's the point." I speak curtly as we peruse the shelves and shelves of knick knacks from one vendor to the next. Anyone watching us would think we were talking to ourselves about which tchotchkes to bring home to our loved ones.

"Well, why are they called Los Lobos, for starters?"

"El Comandante—Castro—is called 'El Caballo,' the horse. They wanted to be called something that would hunt a horse. Los Lobos means 'the wolves.'" I pick up a tiny Cuban flag stapled to a sanded wooden rod. I wave it absent-mindedly.

"Sounds like you know more than you say." Paolo is right next to me examining a ceramic bull. Burke is behind us, his back to us talking to another vendor. I see him take money from his wallet and palm something into his pocket.

"They're a local legend. People talk about them but no one knows who they are. I started hearing about them when I got stationed here in Veradero. That was two years ago. Before that I was in Cienfuegos for about a year, and before that…" A catch comes into my throat. "You know where I was."

"How did they recruit you to be a stop on this…" He pauses "Underground railroad?"

Burke comes up behind me and wraps his arms around me. He shamelessly puts his lips on my neck.

"Burke! Are you fucking kidding?" Paolo's face is stern, his whisper sharp. "You know we're being followed. You want them to see you two together?"

"Yes, Paolo, have a little trust. I'll explain later." Burke's nose nuzzles my ear.

I can't help but smile. "One day I was bringing a fresh batch of soap down to the cellar to cure. I mix it out in the field so the lye fumes don't stink up the house. I was carrying my basin inside and there were three rocks stacked in front of the cellar door. Anyone else passing by probably wouldn't have noticed, but I know a signal when I see one."

We're walking towards the archways now, the morning light beginning to flood in hot and strong.

"Hey Paolo, can you drop us at the hotel? Madge's got to work, and I really need to get some sleep," Burke is yelling and falling over me now. I'm not sure what's gotten into him, but I fall into the routine with him, smiling and stroking the base of his neck. "After what this woman's done to me—a man can only take so much, y'know?" He laughs loudly and falls into a table of flowers as he exits the market.

"Sure thing, boss," Paolo says, deadpan. I exchange a brief confused look with him. We walk to the black sedan and Burke clumsily opens the door for me, shooting a look behind him. I see two men who look to be tourists on their phones. They walk together in tandem and are looking straight at us.

The three of us are in the car and it roars away from the curb. "What happened to Red?" Burke asks Paolo with genuine curiosity.

"I drove her back yesterday. I had to pick up the Lincoln. I'm pretty sure that guy thought we'd stolen his car."

I don't ask any questions but rather wait for an explanation. It doesn't come.

"What were you saying about the stones against the cellar door?" Paolo addresses me in the rearview mirror.

"Oh, well I went inside and looked around. There was a note on my worktable. It said:

> Will you help end Cuban oppression? We know you've been imprisoned for your dedication to the cause. We won't put you in harm's way. If yes—one stone in front of the door, if no—two stones.
>
> Burn this note immediately.

I put one stone in front of the cellar door and continued curing the soap."

Paolo and Burke exchange looks in the mirror. I can't tell if they are afraid or empowered.

"Want to let us in on your little show back there?" Paolo asks.

"I have a plan. I don't want to hide my relationship with Madge, and it would be pointless now anyway, since someone likely followed me to and from her house the past two days. If we stopped talking and seeing each other now it would be even more suspicious. So I think we over play it. We act so in love with each other that these government thugs start to underestimate us. We're just two young lovers completely enveloped in each other. Who has time for espionage? It will also help that Madge plies me with rum and keeps me so off balance that I hardly have time to investigate the island for my assignment."

Paolo brings one hand to his chin and rubs the stubble so hard it sounds like sandpaper. "That's good Burke. That's really good. Hedonistic travel journalist falls for local girl. Probably the most recent in a line of many worldly loves. No offense," he says, addressing me. "And he—you—is so busy enjoying the fruits of the land and making a buffoon of himself that he loses all credibility. They may even try to start feeding content to you through Madge. Recruit her, even…" I can see his mental wheels turning as he works through Burke's plan. "Let's go with this approach, Madge—brag about your relationship at work. Talk about it all the time. When people ask you what he's writing, say you never see him writing anything. Tell them you just eat and fuck and spend money on his company credit card. Tell them you could get him to write whatever you want—that he follows you around like a lovesick puppy."

I look at Burke who is already watching me. I think about how little effort this is going to take.

"We're about to pull up. You two—spend all your free time together. Madge, go to his room when you get off work. Look sloppy when you emerge. Make sure Anton sees you—but don't let your performance slip. I don't want to give him any reasons to…"

"He doesn't need a reason," I break in.

The two men go quiet and Burke looks at Paolo expectantly. "How can we protect her from him?"

"Magdalena, can you go to Anton and confide in him that the American is in love with you? Can you collude with him on duping Burke into writing what you want him to write? He'll feel that he's in power again and that you'll be his way in. Make him feel like what he did to you…" he quickly looks at Burke and then continues, "broke you once and for all. That you're his instrument to use as he pleases."

A sick feeling comes over me, and I can't tell if it's the idea that I have to see Anton again in a matter of minutes or that I have to make him feel as if he's won. I concede that it's both. A thin layer of sweat breaks out on my brow and I sit back into the seat, feeling the engine vibrate below me.

"That's not enough. What will keep him from touching her again?"

"Can you play this?" Paolo looks right into my quivering soul. "I need you to be all in, or it won't work. Make Anton think you're playing Burke. Tease him. Tell him that you're giving everything—physically, emotionally—to the con. You can't be distracted. Promise him that after Burke leaves, you'll be all his."

"I... I—" Words are supposed to be coming out, but they aren't. More stammering and noises happen, but what I want to do is scream. How can these men possibly know what they're asking me to do?

"Madge," Burke says softly as we pull up under the parkade next to the front door of the hotel. He nods to Paolo who gets out and makes conversation with the bellhops and taxi drivers. I thank God quietly that the windows are tinted. "This is going to be the hardest thing you'll ever have to do." He takes my face in his hands and moves towards me. "But it will get us closer to the freedom you envision for this country than anything you've ever done. You were of no use to the cause sitting on Juventud and you're of no use doing laundry and making soap. This is where you reclaim who you are." His eyes shine and I think it's a shame he was born in America, a country that was already free, for he would've been a great revolutionary.

"Lovers, eh?" I hear Paolo stalling outside the car. "Not ready to say goodbye." The other drivers chuckle and I see Anton exit the hotel and come to stand at the valet podium. He looks over the sets of keys and checks his watch. He's checking to see if Burke has come back to the hotel yet.

"Take a deep breath."

I do it.

"Take another one. That's good. Let it out."

I look at the clock in the still running car. Four minutes until I have to punch in.

"Magdalena Cruz," Burke says, using my full name for the first time. He guides my face into a soft, slow kiss. All other feelings screech to a halt and all I feel are colorful, flapping butterflies thwacking away inside my chest cavity. Burke pulls out of the kiss and opens his eyes, dreamy and intoxicated. "Are you ready to be in love with me?"

I know he means am I ready to *act* in love with him, but I take it to mean what he's really asking. Am I ready to be in love with this fervent, beautiful, brilliant man?

"Richard Burke. There is no such thing as ready. And I'm already there." He smiles the biggest, most earnest smile I've ever seen and pulls on the door handle, opening the car to bright sun, terra-cotta colored bricks and greedy, staring eyes and eyes and eyes.

EIGHTEEN

1992 1993 1994 1995 1996 1997 1998 1999 2000 **2001** 2002

May 5th, 2001 – Veradero, Cuba

I pull the light blue cotton shirt from my bag with one hand while Burke holds my other. He is leading me up the front steps of the hotel. I can feel Anton seething from the valet stand, his mouth tightly clenched. The flexed muscles in his jaw give his face a bulging appearance and I look away without making eye contact.

We get to the top step and Burke turns to face me. I pull the blue shirt over my head and he reaches up, gently tugging the shirt down past my ears. I thread my arms through the sleeves and pull the uniform shirt over the floral printed dress I put on this morning without thinking. My eyes never leave his, which drink me in. He's partly putting on a show for our viewers, partly enjoying the sight of me.

"I... I had fun." He blushes like a teen saying goodnight after the first date.

"Me, too." I mirror his demeanor. "I get off at four. Meet you in your room?" I run my palm down his chest, across his stomach and rest it on his belt buckle. He shudders imperceptibly. I know that was for me and not the audience.

"Absolutely."

I kiss him again but don't want to feed Anton's imagination any more than we already have. I turn away and walk around to the service entrance of the hotel. Once out of sight I start to run, making it to the punch clock with just one minute to spare. I clock in and exhale with relief.

Catalina waits for me in the basement, holding a handful of fresh picked wildflowers and a faded red paperback. "Sylvia told me what happened. I can't apologize for something like this, M. I only hope you can forgive me. You're my best friend." She starts to cry and I realize that word spreads faster here than a bullet from a gun. Everyone must know, and no doubt each of the men have been bragging to anyone who would listen.

I pity Catalina for saying I'm her best friend, for she is little more to me than a fly on the windowsill. So small and insignificant in my life—she is just another traveler who happens to be waiting at the same bus stop, my bus going north, hers going south; but for a few moments we're together in the same place. I take the flowers and the book that she extends to me.

"What's this?" Looking down at the book I can read the faded, creased title: *The Collected Poems of Langston Hughes*. On the front cover a man stares back at me, not sullen but perhaps a bit apologetic, his head propped up by his own clenched fist. "Do you know what this is?" I ask her.

"It's a book. I traded it for a dress I sewed. A lady in town asked who it was for, and when I said you she pulled out this one. I would've wanted one of the ones with Fabio on the cover, but this guy is handsome, too, I guess. In a different way." She looks dreamily at Mr. Hughes and I laugh, unable to be angry at her.

"You must've talked to Patricia; she can get you anything you want, if you can pay." I come back to the moment at hand. "You didn't have to do this. I'm fine and actually, my life wouldn't have changed if you hadn't missed work Wednesday."

"Ooh, is this the American everyone's buzzing about?"

"Yes." I feel my cheeks go red and my body ache, knowing it's the first time I'll have to be away from him for more than a few minutes since he found his way to my bed. Normally I would say nothing more, but remembering Paolo and Burke's plans, I divulge all the details to Catalina. I know the rest of the hotel staff will know the story word for word by nightfall.

Her face sits in titillated shock. When she realizes the story is over, she takes an exaggerated breath and hugs me like I've won a baseball championship. "I won't lie and say I'm not jealous, because I am. I mean, it could've been me he fell in love with and... he's really handsome, Mona said."

Here's where Catalina shows her age—it's much easier for her to see herself as the object of Burke's affection, but she doesn't give a thought to what I had to pay for it.

"But what are you going to do about..." As if on cue the elevator dings its arrival to the basement.

I look at the floor and busy myself moving the laundry bins to their places in front of each washer. I open the first one in the row and begin throwing towels in. Catalina is not so quick on her feet, so she stands gaping-mouthed as Anton marches into the poorly lit room. She is frozen in fear. I tilt my head toward the elevator, trying to get Catalina to look at me, trying to help her get out before he...

"Catalina, your performance is so poor, it may be time for disciplinary action. You inexplicably miss work Wednesday and now you're down in the basement distracting Señorita Cruz from her work." He circles her like a dog, closely examining her from all angles.

"My shift doesn't start for another hour," she mutters, staring down at her knitted fingers.

"Well since you have so much free time, I can find something for you to do." He's looking right at me as he begins to unbuckle his belt. Catalina's hands begin to shake but she says nothing as she instinctively gets down onto her knees and looks up at him pitifully.

I want to lift my hand and shield my face. I want to climb into one of the giant rolling laundry tubs and go limp, as if I am just another piece of cloth to cleanse and reuse.

I've never seen Anton this drunk on power and I wonder what's driving his aggression. Last week, before Burke, we had a visit from General Ajuapio, Anton's superior officer. They were behind locked doors for many hours. Girls with food and drink went in and out, often leaving more disheveled than when they went in. Is Anton emulating his mentor? Or is he exercising his manhood in the face of Burke, someone whose freedom threatens his very existence? He knows I will go back to Burke and spread word of his intimidation. I can see now that he's using Catalina to spur something in me. No matter what fate she left me to, I can't do the same to her.

He joyfully takes out his pathetic, limp cock and begins to stroke it quickly, unable to get it up for a willing participant. Catalina's eyes flick to me, full of terror and pleading for help.

"I think Burke's magazine would be thrilled to read about how Cubans treat women. Especially the part about entrapment, sexual torture and using rape and coercion to keep us in line. That's just the sort of thing Americans love: the salacious." I let the words escape me casually, looking down to pick up sheets.

I hear the jingle of a belt buckle and reluctantly look up to see him tucking himself away as he storms toward me. Before I can do anything, his hand is around my throat and he's pushing me into a wall. The back of my head slams into the concrete façade but I can't brace against the blow because it means less air coming in against his grip.

I wave behind him to Catalina—*go!* She scurries behind to the hallway where the elevator waits, standing open like the arms of Jesus himself.

"Is this really how you want to play this?" I squeak out the words against the tightening fist. "You could..." I stammer. "You could change the way the world sees Cuba." I pull something up from years ago, a fierce glare that makes my eyes go hollow and dead. I have to get through to him and my mind is starting to go weak.

He puts his face close to mine. The grip loosens enough for me to take a deep breath. "I had no idea you were such a greedy whore. Like a bitch in heat, you ran straight from my cock to his. Filthy, is what you are." He says it like I had some choice in being near his cock at all.

"He loves me," I sputter. "He loves me. We can use that."

The hand still hangs there, fingers relaxing joint by joint. A moment of silence passes, and I think I hear the shuffle of a foot in the hallway. Finally, he steps back from me and begins to rub his chin in thought. "He will write anything I tell him to write," I say, bringing my hand to my throat instinctively. I can see the slow motion of the cogs in his mind as they start to spin. "Imagine the commandante's gratitude for the man who manipulated the American media." I just keep spooning it in, each mouthful exciting him more than the last.

"If you're saying we're in this together, then there's only one problem," he says, burrowing deep into my mind with his black stare, as if he can pick through the piles of thoughts and pull out the truth. I close my eyes and shake my head, as if to jostle him out of there. "How can I possibly trust you? You nearly melted into the floor when he looked at you. Why would I believe *you* aren't in love with *him*?"

"Why wouldn't I run straight to his arms? He has no ration book, no job assignment, no limits. If I want something, why shouldn't I get it? It's about time. Those elitist pigs lording over the world with their almighty dollar. He's here for a quick, spicy fling with a Cubana—and why not me? Why not me if I can change the course of Cuban history?" I find within me what's able to split off. I push down the parts that yearn for Burke's touch, shoving them into trunks at the foot of my consciousness. I take all the hate I have for Anton and the anger and I shove it down there too.

My pelvis glides forward into him and I flick my tongue against my upper lip. The brick wall, once my enemy, now steadies the shaking I'm trying so hard to hide. If I'm going to convince him, I have to make true what Anton has always believed: if exposed to him enough, I will eventually begin to want him. "How can I be in love with him, when I don't believe in love at all?"

His mustache twitches and his eyebrows raise.

"When Burke is gone, only you and I will remain. Why would I bet against that?"

He adjusts his belt again, and I can tell he's changing his mind. "So you've finally been tamed, have you?"

I smile a coquettish grin that even Juan Julio hadn't been able to resist. Anton relents and grabs both my hands, holding them up between us. If someone walked in, they would assume we were two young lovers. The truth is so much stranger and sadder. "I know better than to go into a deal without getting mine. But I don't want him getting wise and starting to suspect our… relationship." He brings the hand back up to my face, but this time, strokes my cheek in an attempt to be tender. I have to steel my muscles to keep from shrinking away. "Bring me his notes—his real notes, not the ones he writes in front of you. Sneak them to me and then I'll give them back to you. I want to know what he's really writing about us—about Cuba. And I want to know where your loyalties lie..." He closes all his fingers but one and jabs it a little too hard beneath my eye. I can feel the brick wall behind me again, reminding me that there's no more space to escape into.

"Okay, I'll do it."

"One more thing." He takes his hands up and down my body, groping and feasting as a starving man who happens upon a banquet. "No more cock for you until you're finished with him. Men can smell whores. He'll know something if we keep giving in to our desires."

"Will you be satisfying yourself," I pause to look disappointed, "elsewhere? Because I've heard the girls whispering about going to the Hotel Workers' Union."

He lets out a puff of air, the closest thing I've seen to a laugh. "The notes. By tomorrow," he reminds me, completely ignoring my veiled threat. He turns to head for the elevator and I hear the scuttling footsteps again. I walk back to my laundry baskets and try to start catching up on the day's work that's already getting behind. I hear the elevator doors shut and breathe a sigh so big it could power a cross-country hot air balloon.

Catalina crawls out from behind two pallets stacked against the wall at the end of the elevator bank. It's hard to ignore how tiny she is; still a little girl, really. But maybe she's cleverer than I thought.

"Heard that whole thing, huh?"

Her face is darker, more cynical looking than I've ever seen it.

"Are you going to do what he asks? Are you going to sell Burke out? After everything you told me. He really does love you…"

"If I don't think of myself, no one else will. You learn that in prison," I tell her with steely eyes and a clenched jaw.

She softens, as if suddenly remembering where we are, and that Cuban girls don't just fall in love and sail away to America. "I hope you like the book. The lady said," she pauses, "it would suit you, she said."

She turns to go, and I notice Mr. Langston Hughes surveying the room with a patient, slow gaze from his place, propped open and standing tall on the corner of a large white dryer.

NINETEEN

1992 1993 1994 1995 1996 1997 1998 1999 2000 **2001** 2002

May 5th, 2001 – Veradero, Cuba

The day moves like an old man walking the beach: ambling, cautious, and slow. Normally, a day like this would make me happy. I get all my work done ahead of schedule and I'm able to sweep and mop the laundry room floor. There are no more disruptions, and so I spend the day in solitude. The maids all show up so I don't have to deliver towels to the rooms. Four days ago, this would have been a perfect day. But today, I'm in anguish.

In college at the University of Havana, my roommate took mushrooms once. They were the wild kind that grow in some of the fields in the Parque Nacional Cienega de Zapata. I did not take them myself but sat with her through her trip. She kept groping at things that weren't there. Feeling things in the room with us that were not real. At the time, I thought she was insane. I'd never seen anyone on drugs before. I was biding my time until morning, thinking that I would take her to the university clinic when day broke. I woke up that morning and found her asleep, curled against me.

Today is the first day I can understand what it was like for her, and why she told me later that it was the most fun she'd ever had. "Madge," I hear Burke whisper, but turn to find no one there. I feel his fingers on me, caressing the skin beneath my clothes, but I know he isn't here. It's turmoil laced with ecstasy to not have him here, yet know that he exists—waiting for me just across the building. It's a feeling I barely remember about being in love—a sweet vanity that comes with knowing you've been chosen.

I remember the last time I was in love and wonder where Juan Julio is. It's a thought I have countless times per day, one constant thread in all my life since the moment he was pulled away from me. Juan Julio did not want to fall in love with me. He fought it to the bitter end. That made the love we shared seem sweeter and more forbidden than it actually was, perhaps.

Maybe it was because he was our leader and I, his follower. He didn't want to show me preference by loving me. But when I crawled into his tent every night and lay against him, whispering poetry and singing lullabies into the mesh window that let the starlight in, he did what any twenty-two-year-old man would do—he loved me. And I felt chosen, lucky and victorious.

I know now why he pushed me away with all his might, and I know how much I wish I would've listened.

Finally, the minute comes when I can clock out on the computer kiosk in the break room. A table of employees sits playing cards and eating. The room smells of roasted chicken and peppers. When I come in, a hush falls over the game and they all turn to watch me. I say nothing, but press the buttons on the computer slowly and deliberately.

I reach up and tug on the elastic keeping my hair up. My

hair falls down to mid-shoulder. On a normal day, it can't decide if it's dark brown or black, but today it seems to reflect a ruddy chestnut tone. The whispering starts when I begin to slide my work shirt up over my shoulders, revealing the top half of the sundress I have on underneath. I crumple the shirt and place it in my purse before turning to head to his room. On the way out, I lock eyes with a familiar face, and I remember him as the young bellhop whose virginity I had no choice in taking. He is looking at me with a mix of pride and shame.

My resolve is shaken, but I keep up the momentum towards his room. Elevator. Hallway. Doors, doors, doors. And then there's his, remarkably indistinguishable from all the rest. I knock and the door opens almost instantly. Burke seems taller than he was this morning, but his face looks to have aged ten years.

"Madge," he says excitedly, "I'm so glad to see you." He lobs his arms around me and envelops me in his crisp white sleeves. He's saying something into the top of my head, but I'm overwhelmed by my stomach churning and have to wrench myself away from him.

I don't make it to the toilet in time but instead grab the small beige trashcan under the sink. I collapse onto my knees and get sick in the trashcan. The heaving in my stomach makes my eyes water, streaming tears down my face. I can't think, everything in my head is white hot. What started as a few tears is now a storm of sobs and chokes.

I hear Burke run to the sink and turn on the water, then he's on his phone. The sound of hangers being pushed around on a metal rod invades my misery. My nose burns like a forest fire with the scent of freshly sliced apples and shaving lather.

The retching from my stomach continues even though there is nothing left to push out. What my body wants to eject has nothing to do with what I've eaten.

Then suddenly everything is quiet. I'm a small child again, fallen asleep on my father's overstuffed armchair. It was the nicest piece of furniture in our tiny house, and my sisters and I would argue over who got to sit in it to read before bedtime. It's my turn, and I've fallen asleep with the book across my lap. I have the transcendent feeling of floating as the book is removed and I am picked up—transported, rearranged, and placed into another soft place where I drift solidly away into a dreamless sleep.

TWENTY

1992 1993 1994 1995 1996 1997 1998 1999 2000 **2001** 2002

May 5th, 2001 – Veradero, Cuba

My eyes fly open and I jump from wherever I am, throwing blankets off as a hand comes to rest on my left forearm. I go still and take a deep breath before looking over to see Burke jotting down notes in his little notebook beside me.

We're in a hotel bed but not the same one in the room where Burke's sleeves were suddenly trapping me. This is a different room.

I look at him and notice for the first time that he's wearing reading glasses with a little chain attached to the ends of each earpiece. He squints at the page and then looks over at me, startling when he sees that my eyes are open.

"Oh, you're up," he says in a whisper. "I thought you were just having another—"

"Where are we?" I interrupt, not sure if he's about to say *nightmare* or *episode*.

"I had us moved to a casita," he says, taking the glasses off and resting them on his smooth chest. I also notice that he isn't wearing a shirt, only his dark green chino pants that feel like canvas between my fingers.

The fabled casitas are just folklore to most of the hotel staff. I've heard there are anywhere from five to fifteen private casitas on the hotel grounds. They're reserved for very high profile guests—kings, dictators, movie stars, drug lords—and each has its own dedicated staff. Casita guests have their own private beach, and each has a patio that frames a perfect view of the sunset. Those are the rumors, anyway. It would appear that the rumors are true.

"Did you clear the move with the driver?"

"He's got some jobs back in Havana today. I couldn't get him on the phone so I made the call. I've left a message for him at the front desk."

I feel unsettled, but his answer is enough for me to lay back into the pillow.

"Madge." The whisper is real now, and it's here next to me. I close my eyes for a moment just so that it can be the only thing. "Are you okay?"

"Much better now," I say, my eyes still closed.

"Was it just, you know, being in there that made you sick?" I feel him roll into me. "Because of what happened?"

"Don't. I know what you're doing," I caution him.

"My imagination is torturing me. I came back to the room this morning and... it was wrecked. There was blood. I asked myself what the average American tourist would do and so I called the cops. The Cuban cops—they came and, well, nothing happened. But I want you to know I can handle it. Just tell me what he did to you. It's making me crazy."

"No. I won't let our life together be about that." I can feel the tears running sideways down my face and across the bridge of my nose. "Instead, it's going to be about how we changed the course of history for Cuba." I crack my eyes open and see him waiting expectantly for more. The green of his eyes is so goddamn beautiful. "But if that's going to work, I need you to let go of this thought of me as some poor, helpless girl. We're in this together." I look at his face for the first time since he opened the hotel room door, and see that he truly is tortured. How can I bring him back to me? "This isn't your fault. It would've happened with or without you here. It was already happening. But the only way you can stop it—stop it for me and for millions of others—is to stop pretending to be Superman. You're human; you didn't come here to save me."

"But I want to save you, doesn't that count for anything?" We're facing each other on the bed now, our hands clasped as if making a pact.

"What you want has nothing to do with what's real. If you act on these stupid, macho, hero feelings, you'll likely get killed, and me too. So save me by not saving me."

A flicker of a grin trembles on his lips and I can see how hard this is for him. He wants to storm the gates, save the damsel, kill the dragon, and saddle up for the sunset ride. I can see it's what he's used to doing, and what he came here for. And not just for me, but for Paolo and anyone else who needs him.

"And what if I'm angry? What if all I can think of is beating Anton until his face looks like the inside of a pomegranate?" His voice is getting louder. He sits up and runs a hand through his hair.

I close my eyes again and hear the *thunk* of the mini-refrigerator opening, the glass-meeting-glass as he empties a small liquor bottle into a tumbler.

"Maybe this isn't going to work," I say, the mattress seeming to drop from beneath me. "What do we really know about each other anyway?" I sit up to gather my things.

"Madge, no, I'm sorry. I just... I can't steel myself like you can. I can't tuck my feelings away. When someone hurts someone I love, I want to fucking kick their teeth in. It's just how us Iowa boys were raised." He takes a long pull from his drink. The alcohol on his breath makes me dizzy.

"And so I wait for you like a lonely house." I say it looking into his eyes, hoping he can hear me. I want to speak to the Burke who let me slather him in coconut oil, the man I thought he was. I don't like this shell of men's maxims and worthless talk.

He seems to understand because he gets on his knees in front of where I sit on the bed, pulling my legs around him. I lean over him and take him in. He wears the clothes I washed for him, even though they've gotten dirty again. He bends his head back and puts his mouth on mine, seeming to become himself as we melt into each other.

The first taps at the door are so light that I barely hear them, especially given that I want to ignore them. The second set of rapping is louder and more ominous.

"Ughhh," he lets out a groan. "My windows ache," he says dryly, standing up to get the door.

"What in the fuck?" Paolo bursts into the room, his voice a harsh whisper trailing behind him.

"We had to move rooms, Paolo," Burke says, the ice tinkling against his glass as he drinks the rest of the whiskey.

Paolo doesn't respond but waves his arms erratically towards the ceiling and walls. *We didn't sweep for bugs,* he mouths as he tries to get behind us and usher us out.

"But I thought you wanted me to stay here with her," Burke whispers. "If you take the bugs out now, they'll know something. They'll know. We haven't blown anything Paolo, just let us play it off." His voice is almost inaudible. Paolo and I have leaned in closely to make sure we understand him. I nod in agreement, remembering a woman in Cienfuegos who found a bug in her lampshade. She wasn't sure what it was, and took it to the town mechanic. His face went pale and he told her to replace it exactly where it was, and never disturb it again. The next day she was taken away in a black car and she never returned to her home. "Go ahead and run the farmhouse op," Burke mouths. "We'll be here. Don't worry, we're good. We can meet for dinner and debrief."

It's amazing how I can still understand every word and gesture when almost no sound is escaping him. "Oh, Burke. Let me show you something," I say at full volume. With three people in a room and no sound, anyone listening would get suspicious. Paolo moves for the door.

"We're good, sir. No need for a driver tonight. I think we'll stay in," Burke says loudly.

Paolo makes a swift exit and I bring my purse up from the floor where Burke must've placed it when he brought me in. I pull out the soft, worn paperback and turn it over to reveal the cover. Burke gasps and gingerly takes the book into his hands. He beholds it as one would a newborn baby. As if caught in the gesture, he turns the book around to face me and wobbles it a bit in his hand. "He's one of the greats," he says, gesturing to Mr. Hughes.

The rest of the night we eat lavish snacks from the minibar and read to each other from the book. When the last page of the book is turned, Burke pulls himself into me smelling of honeyed apricots and salted cashews. I've never seen these two foods on the island before tonight. Burke has to teach me the words. "Cash-*oohs*" he keeps saying, and then rumbling with laughter when I say it back to him in my accent. "*Cah-Shus.*" I try to let the bitterness of inequity pass me by, to maybe be a little more like Catalina and revel in the luxuries this vacation has to offer. I try, but I'm not successful.

One thing I can appreciate about the casita is the soft,

downy white robes that hang heavily on the wooden hangers in a cedar closet by the door. These are different than the robes I wash in the laundry room—much plusher and newer. The ones I wash take on a stiff, scratchy feel that can't be avoided.

Although they are soft to the touch and feel like wearing a cloud, that's not my favorite thing about them. After we make love tonight I wrap Burke in his robe, his eyes languishing with pleasure. Then I place my own over my shoulders and tingle a bit as the luxurious fabric touches my skin. I place my hand between my neck and my hair, pulling it free. I let the robe hang open, feeling him watching me even though he is pretending to fall asleep. I see a smile begin to peek through his mask of slumber. He says nothing—he is the only writer I've ever known who understands the power of silence. He lays on the bed in the closest position to the bathroom, while I stand in the pillar of light coming through the bathroom door. The clock by the bed reads 12:07 a.m. And for a moment, I can see Burke as he will exist in his life; brilliant, confident, smiling, nonchalant. His hulking frame and freckled skin stretched taut to reveal muscles, ribs and, just below the surface, a rapidly pulsing heart. All visible in the space where his robe hasn't come together. And I know this is the moment I will choose to remember when he is gone.

My favorite thing about the robes isn't the softness or the ease, but how Burke's hands slip between the fabric and my skin, like a secret, guiding me into the space where his robe hasn't met. I feel the heat of him inside me and I know it won't last long—but it will be because of me. I am coming at the very thought of him, our bodies, robed and somehow naked all at once.

TWENTY-ONE

1992 1993 1994 1995 1996 1997 1998 1999 2000 **2001** 2002

May 6th, 2001 – Veradero, Cuba

The call from Paolo comes in at 1:26 a.m. on Burke's disposable phone. I rouse from finicky sleep at the sound of Burke's voice.

"What time?" he says huskily. An indecipherable buzzy voice responds. "And you're sure they saw it? ... It's gone? Oh. ... Well, he could've..." Paolo interrupts and Burke looks like a spectator at his first running of the bulls. He pulls himself to the edge of the bed, but I lay still, trying to make out the other end of the line. "So, what now? ... Okay, see you there." He ends the call and turns to me. "I guess we missed dinner."

I can feel the blush in the back of my knees and wonder if he might be the first man ever to make me blush at all, let alone all the way to my knees.

"It's too late now, if we go somewhere to eat there won't be enough people out to cover our conversation."

"Shhh... Paolo's got us covered. Someone from Los Lobos picked up the bait he left at your house." His voice is as quiet as he can make it, but my ears feel like a bomb just went off. I'm taken over by stunned shock. "But—as much as I hate to say this—we have to get dressed. We're meeting him in ten."

I look down to realize I'm still wearing only the robe.

"But if I could have it my way, you would only wear that robe for the rest of our lives."

As happy as it makes me to know he shares my affinity for the white robe, I have to turn my face away to hide the hot, angry tears in my eyes. Paolo set bait for Los Lobos in my cellar without telling me? Without first confirming protocol with me? And Burke knew about it? Was this *Operation Farmhouse*? I stay silent for fear of what might come out—and how loudly—if I start talking. And he just said *'for the rest of our lives'*—can he possibly know that he just shortened that time frame considerably?

"You okay?" He looks at me but can't hide his giddiness.

I turn to the phone and page the front desk. "Please buzz Mr. Burke's driver through to the casita, he needs to run an errand." I hang up before I can hear if the voice on the other end is someone I know. Burke watches me and I simply shake my head at him, signifying that I can't talk about it now.

We walk out the door and down the path, shaded on both sides by lush greenery. Paolo is walking toward us and gestures to an archway cut completely out of shrubbery. I find it remarkable that I've never seen any of this, but then remember that I just go in the side door and go to the basement of the hotel most days. Through the archway is a stone path that leads out to a semi-private beach. Hydrangeas, orchids and hibiscus are lapping at the path in the ocean breeze.

We head down towards the water and I understand why Paolo is leading us down here. We walk by a couple in their bathing suits, making out on a towel. The crashing waves are loud enough to cover any conversation and muffle any recording devices.

Our feet sink into the sand and we take long, purposeful steps to the edge of the beach where huge, carved logs are arranged to delineate the beach from the surrounding greenery. If one was to look about twenty-five meters beyond the logs, the moon could be found glinting off a barbed wire, electric fence. The fence trails up to the edge of the property where it meets with a more cordial-looking black iron fence that trails the front, more visible part of the property. Hotel management would explain that the fence is to keep vagrants out; hungry, desperate townspeople in search of a large suitcase to crawl into, rather than to keep foreigners in. I am starting to wonder.

"Okay, first thing's first, M—can I call you M?" Paolo speaks first and I nod at him, still looking at the fence. "Okay, M; how did the meet with Anton go?"

"I think he bought the story. I told him I would get him Burke's notes on the article by tomorrow. And he said, 'the real notes, not the ones he writes in front of you.' I baited him with the idea of manipulating the American media, that Burke will write anything I want him to write because..." I pause and look at Burke a little shamefully. "He's in love with me." I continue on, looking to the ground when I see his token grin. "I had to play it up, you know, my feelings for him. I made it his idea that we can't be physical while I'm conning Burke. He agreed."

"Okay, so for the time being, that threat is neutralized." Paolo quickly taps his right heel in the sand. "Burke, can you get her some notes?"

Burke removes the little black notebook from his pocket—I didn't see him put it there—and a pen. He flips through the pages, scanning the scrawl as he goes. "These should do," He makes a notation for himself in one of the margins. "I guess I'll need to write about things other than you?" He smiles at me and Paolo looks away, impatient. "I'll have to add some more before you 'swipe' it." He nudges me with an elbow, but I can't look at him.

"And what about you watching my house and leaving something for Los Lobos?" The question explodes over the water crashing against the sand.

"Yes, Operation Farmhouse. Someone came today and picked up the message. I haven't gotten anything back yet, but I anticipate an answer soon."

"What did the note say, and how do you know it was Los Lobos that found it?"

"It said we would offer extradition to the U.S. for anyone who would offer information on how the rebels operate, and asked how the CIA can help with the overall goal of liberating Cuba. It gave directions to a safe house where an agent is waiting by the phone to call me if anyone shows up."

"And how do you know it was them?"

"I watched the house. You said the only ones who know the signal are those rebels who've been communicating with you. I stacked three rocks in front of the door to the cellar and placed the message on a shelf above the worktable."

"Where could you hide that no one could see you? The field that faces the cellar door is bare. No trees, boulders, nothing."

"I hid on the roof and looked down above the door."

I look at him, unwilling to show that I'm a little impressed.

"Two men—boys really—came by about three hours ago. One was a little older, maybe twenty. The other couldn't have been more than fifteen. They came to the door almost silently. The younger one's clothes were filthy, like he'd been lying in dirt for days. When they left—"

"They?" I break in. "They left together?"

"Yes, like they came."

"Usually when two are travelling together, it's a stop on the chain. The older one is dropping off the younger one. He would leave the signal for me that someone was there and I would bring food down, along with a basin for washing. I never talk to them, but they stay a few nights until the next link in the chain picks them up. When someone comes to deliver a message, they always come alone."

The two men look at each other, as if they could read what the other was thinking.

"It's fucking bullshit," I explode. "You did this without bringing me in—at my home. Who has to live there after you get deported? Me. Who is a CIA informer to the largest rebel group in Cuba? Me. They left together because they know better than to deal with CIA. We're burned." I'm so angry that it's hard to see. The roar of the waves sounds like deafening screams.

"Or they went to the safe house." Burke says it looking at Paolo because he won't look at me. "How many days' hike is it from here?"

"It could take anywhere from a few hours to a week to get there, depending on how they're travelling. It's all the way at the southern end of the island."

"Can you catch up with them?" It's like they've forgotten I'm here now, and this infuriates me to the point that I no longer care about Burke, about being a laundress, about anything. I have to pack my things, I have to disappear. If Los Lobos doesn't come to kill me, then the DI will be beating down the door as soon as they pick up those boys off the side of the road. They'll torture them until they give up the safe house, him, me, everything. No one trusts the CIA and this is why.

I wish to God I would've woken Catalina up that morning on my way to work. I could've splashed water on her face, handed her some aspirin, turned on the cold shower spray to rouse her from the hangover that forced me into Burke's life. I never would have met him, and this never would've happened. I could've stayed in my safe, stunted little life. I see myself running, stumbling over rocks, jagged and sprawling beneath my feet. Voices trail behind me but I don't stop—I must get to my purse. It has my ID, my papers, my money that I can use to pay a coyote to smuggle me off this god-forsaken floating rock.

Argentina. That's where I'll go. Fuck America. Fuck Americans. I need to blend in, to speak the language, to look the part. I need to disappear.

The ground comes fast into my eyes like a camera lens zooming in. Every crystal of sand has come into focus, and my cheek is making an impression in the beach. I think they must've already gotten me and look for the closest sharp object. I am not going back to Juventud.

"Madge. Madge! Stop. Stop! It's me. It's me, it's Burke. Stop fighting." He says the string of words several times before I hear them. He is holding my hands and Paolo, my feet. It must've been him that grabbed my feet and caused me to fall. I kick my feet out of his grip but don't run. "Hah. Tag, you're it!" Burke laughs and waves to the couple on the beach a few meters away. The man stands and is approaching us. The woman wears a look of concern paired with the ripeness that comes from kissing for days on end. She holds her bikini top up from where it's been untied. They look Czech. Paolo waves at the man and shoots me a look that says *play along*.

I force a breathy laugh and stand up, dusting the sand from my clothes. "I'm fine. I'm it." I wave to them too, trying to assuage their concern. Their faces melt into unsure smiles and the man goes back to lay with his lady friend. He keeps shooting suspicious glances at us and in response, Burke and Paolo get on either side of me. They walk with me to the path that leads to the casitas. They speak without looking at me, their eyes forward.

"M—we have a few days to figure out if they've burned us or gone to the safe house. I agree you shouldn't go back to your house. You should stay here with Burke for the time being. They won't hurt you in front of him."

"And what happens if they burned us?"

"Then we all get to the safe house and get air lifted back to the states," Burke says, gripping my hand, as if this is what I wanted all along. To leave my home, my cause.

"You knew this, you knew I would be leaving my home for the last time and you didn't tell me? Why didn't you include me? You just assumed I would leave with you—that you could sweep me away from all this? You're an arrogant cochino."

They look at each other again, surprised and yet still calm, biding their time. They must know something that I don't. We're walking slowly up the path and instead of taking the turn that leads to the door of our casita, we turn down the over grown walking trail that leads to six more dimly lit casitas, identical to ours.

"What aren't you telling me?" The air in front of us fills with the question and I can feel Burke and Paolo falter in their steps. We walk slowly and they don't dare look at each other.

"When I went back to Havana, I pulled some strings and got access to your file. I knew the basics—what I told you the other night—but I wanted to see where you stand. Anton says things about you—I didn't know if they were popular opinion, or just him—"

Burke breaks in, "Being an asshole."

"Anyway," Paolo touches his forehead, a surgeon about to deliver bad news. "Your last psych eval. Do you remember it?"

I search my memory. It was only a few months ago. "Yes. Nothing out of the ordinary. I've had one every few months since I was released. The doctor asked me a few questions, marked down a few notes on my chart, and I was told to go."

Burke flicks his eyes at me almost imperceptibly.

"Well, your chart says you failed the evaluation and you've been added to the waiting list for hospitalization. Your diagnosis is manic depressive and delusional. The doctor recommended," Paolo bites his lip nervously, "you be hospitalized indefinitely. They planned to place you at Mazorra. It looks like the decision was made a few weeks ago, and they just haven't communicated it to your parole officer yet."

Finally, he is silent. All I can hear is the cool breeze rustling the leaves of the greenery that surrounds us. My feet walk, my eyes see, but there is nothing else. That wind feels like it's blowing through me, and I remember again that I am nothing—just as I always was. Years and years of secrets, messages, contacts, and notes—of helping people and fighting for what's right—all erased with the flick of a corrupt doctor's pen.

And I'm left with Mazorra. To quote our Commandante, "To say Mazorra is to say Dante's Inferno." Of course, he was saying it to illustrate the ills of a capitalist system in 1953, but nothing has changed since his regime took it over. Mazorra makes the hospital in *One Flew Over the Cuckoo's Nest* look like a daycare. Most of the items on the black market in Havana are said to have come out of Mazorra: food, pills, syringes, blankets, bandages. When Juan Julio and I were traveling the island, we were told to find an orderly named Hugo at Mazorra once we got to Havana. "He can get you anything," our contact said. We never wondered who wasn't getting it if it meant he was bringing it to us.

"Madge," Burke whispers. We're in the casita now and Paolo has gone. I don't remember getting inside and it seems like such a long time since I've spoken that I'm not sure my voice will come out if I try to speak. "I'm sorry," he says to me. I've never heard them said this way before, the two words; so full of helplessness and desolation. This is the moment that I see he is drowning; that the decision to come to Cuba to help the CIA was, for him, a frivolous adventure. Another dot on the map, another way to fill the days, and a chance for him to move chess pieces on a board even though he knew nothing about the opponent. And he has lost.

"Burke," I say to him simply, "if it weren't for you, I would live the rest of my life without knowing love." As I say it I find the familiar pad of white letter paper and pen. I write as I speak.

> If it weren't for you I would be in Mazorra by the end of the week. I might still end up there. That has nothing to do with you. If you want to be sorry for something, be sorry for cutting me out. I could've helped. I could've told Paolo what to do, what to look for. Now those boys are out there, and even if they are going to betray Los Lobos and head to the safe house, they're wanted fugitives. The first police officer to see them will take them in and torture answers out of them. Where do you think that will lead? Why won't you let me help? I have nothing left but this.

The truth pours out of me before I can understand the weight of it. I have nothing left but this. Did I ever have anything more than this? "Please tell me I'm not like the other girls, in all the other places you've been. Tell me I'm yours." I say it to him in earnestness but have to stifle a laugh. I hope somewhere close by a few DI Agents are falling in love as they listen to us.

"There's no one on this earth like you, baby. Can the sky own the stars? Can the ocean own the waves? No. But one would be nothing without the other." He starts kissing his hand and making moaning sounds as he reads my note. He points to me and I start to rustle the covers around, moaning in tandem with him.

He picks up the pen and begins scribbling and now it's my turn to take over the sounds. The sound of his pen scratching the paper truly does have the ability to make my fingertips prickle. Anyone listening would be sure that Burke's hands were doing anything but writing. A few times he is pulled away from his writing by my moaning and gyrations.

He hands me the paper and begins his part of the show. I consume the words as I rub my feet around the sheets and pillows.

> *I wanted to tell you. I want to tell you everything. It's protocol—you're in a need-to-know status and, frankly, the less you know right now, the better. If they manage to separate us, they'll question you. The CIA doesn't give a shit about you or me—they want inroads to Los Lobos. Do you think they care if you get tortured for information? No. They only care if you give up information. It's the same with me—I didn't know about Mazorra until yesterday. Listen, they may not care about what happens to you, but I do. I'm not one of them. I'm just a tool for them to use.*
>
> *P.S. Keep doing that thing with your hips and this will go from a radio show to a live production.*

He sees the effect that word—Mazorra—has on me as I read. A mosquito buzzes down onto my skin, and I slap it, wiping at the crimson smear it leaves behind. "Oh, you like that, huh? You like getting spanked?" I can't hide the school girl shock on my face. He feeds off of it and begins humping the bed with surprising zeal.

I scrawl my response quickly as we come to a climax together.

Then why did you come here? If you knew you were just going to be a victim in all this, why are you here at all?

Tears are running from my eyes, one by one. I hope he doesn't notice me rubbing my face into the sheets a few too many times.

He scribbles on the pad, both of us panting loudly with relief.

I don't know if I can answer that. I'd like to think I came here to find you. But—why did I take the job? Any answer I give will seem flippant now.

Against every instinct I have, I press my face into his chest and cry quietly. Minutes pass and he calls on his powerful silence while I humiliate myself with hushed sobs. When the tears subside, he gently lays me on the bed. "Why don't you get some rest," he says. At the same time he writes:

I've got to work on the notes for Anton.

"Goodnight, my love," he says, loudly and sincerely. The words have meaning but not enough to force a response through my exhaustion. I drift into a fitful sleep. As Burke flicks the lighter to burn our notes, nightmares begin to lap at my mind like the flames that consume our words.

TWENTY-TWO

1992　1993　1994　1995　1996　1997　1998　1999　2000　**2001**　2002

June 14th, 2001 – Veradero, Cuba

I wake to find Burke still working. In the weeks since I left home, I've never woken before he does. Time spreads between me and my old life like butter on toast. We've been holed up in his casita, leaving only to eat and drink. It's been a kind of paradise I've never experienced. What I feel for Burke has grown into something I can no longer manage.

Paolo stops in every day to update us on the progress of the mission, and Burke leaves for a few hours every day around mid-day. We've fallen into a homely routine, the three of us. Anton and his cronies must have fallen for the ruse because he's gone about business as usual.

Burke now leans over his familiar, worn black notebook off to his left. He sways between it and a larger notebook—looking almost identical to the first—in front of him.

I fluctuate between numbness, pounding fear, and fluttering love from moment to moment. It's hard to know which feeling to trust, but I'm able to hide the shaking in my hands as I walk to the bathroom.

"Good morning," I hear him say through his feverish scrawling. I make a sound that's something like "Hi," but I'm overcome with a wave of nausea and dizziness that knocks me into the doorframe. My mind is fuzzy with exhaustion.

Burke comes to find me steadying myself over the sink. He puts his hands over my arms and rubs them up and down. His lips make their way to the soft area behind my ear. I see a smile edging onto my face in the mirror.

"You okay?" he whispers.

"Yes. Just shaky and sore from last night," I say lustily. He crosses his arms across his burly chest and looks proud. We still assume we're being listened to at every moment. I step to move into the bathroom and lose my footing again. The cloud of dizziness will not relent. This time, I crumple to the floor to save myself from falling into something harder. Maybe I do belong in Mazorra. "I'm just so dizzy and tired," I manage to say. Burke helps me up and into the bathroom, but I can hear him looming around the bathroom door.

When I come out, his face is plastered with worry. "I don't think you should work today. I can call in for you? Or would you like to do it?" My head is drawn like a magnet back to the soft downy pillows of the bed. It takes my every effort to wave back at him in a gesture that says, '*You do it.*'

If I'd been able to, I would've thought about the repercussions of calling in after making such a show of sleeping with Burke the last few weeks. A clearer mind would know that Anton wouldn't believe a word about me being sick, despite my inability to stand for longer than a few minutes and exhaustion that could take down a tank.

Only fifteen minutes pass before a violent knocking permeates the room. I just keep hearing the knocking over and over intermixed with male voices—sometimes the same voices, sometimes Burke's. Each time I look up at the clock, hours have passed in what seems like seconds. I think I hear Anton, but when I open my eyes I am alone. The clack, clack, clack of the hotel door shutting again and again startles my eyes open, but they pull themselves shut again like blackout shades.

Day seeps into night without me noticing. Burke helps me to the bathroom when he's in the room, other times I crawl there myself. My stomach is a churning beast that leaps at the thought of food. Nothing will stay down. Burke orders soup from room service that tastes delicious, even as I imagine what it will taste like coming back up. When I'm not throwing up or sleeping, there's a dull ache in my stomach.

I start to feel some relief a few hours later, but Burke's been gone from the room for a few hours. The clock reads 7:14 p.m. and I imagine Burke and Paolo are out hatching plans and scheming without me. It makes me feel like a child left out on the playground.

I sit up in the bed and turn the lamp on, trying to remember what I'd read about the symptoms of trauma patients in the Diagnostic and Statistical Manual that sat on my mother's bookshelf. In secondary school, I'd entertained the idea of becoming a psychotherapist. My mother encouraged me, even though she'd only bought the book to help her diagnose herself. From week to week she landed on a new disease that plagued her mind: bi-polar disorder, manic depression, post-traumatic stress disorder. For all I knew, she was right. Half the island could qualify for any of those before breakfast. I'd gone on to the University of Havana and majored in Psychology. I'd always found people much easier to understand than math. When I left for school my mother pushed that old, worn copy of the DSM into my hands. I know it pained her to say goodbye to it—it was her crystal ball, her soothsayer.

And now here I sit trying to diagnose myself, but instead only able to think of her. The way her smooth hands felt on my face when she held it and kissed me goodbye. "You can be anything you want to be, Magdalena," she said, both of us knowing there wasn't an ounce of truth to her words. I wonder where she is tonight and where she walked off to the night she disappeared. Did she make it to a safe house where a helicopter waited to float her away? No. Maybe if I make it to Mazorra, I will find her there.

Victims of emotional trauma, according to the DSM, can suffer wide-ranging and disparate symptoms including sleeplessness, fatigue, nightmares, and a host of other ailments. Nausea and vomiting don't get mentioned in the list. The state-issued psychologist that performed my evaluation was a bumbling buffoon. He pushed and pushed me to tell him about my experience on Juventud; when I finally told him, he said I had Post-Traumatic Stress Disorder. The diagnosis went into my file about six months ago and he's been giving me pills ever since. But neither he nor I said anything about manic-depressive. I wonder if Anton paid him off to put me away.

The door opens quietly and two sets of feet pad in. Burke peeks around the corner and breathes a loud sigh when he sees I'm awake.

"Darling, are you feeling better? I've got a doctor here, he's going to look you over."

"A doctor? In the room?" I've never heard of a Cuban doctor making house calls—they rarely leave the hospitals where they're holed up like atomic bomb survivors.

"Yes," an old man's voice says. I hear him a few seconds before I see him. He slowly comes into the room, using a cane to steady himself. He has an old leather carrying case that reminds me of army field doctors. His salt and pepper beard hugs a genial, thin face. "Your friend, Mr. Burke, is very persuasive it seems." Burke lifts his arm and puts his hand on the back of his neck, shrugging casually in a way that makes me wish we were alone.

The doctor brings his bag over to the bed and unlatches it, the hinged opening making a small squeak. "What seems to be the trouble?"

"I'm having dizzy spells, nausea, vomiting, and I'm so tired."

"And how long has this been going on?"

"Since this morning at about six." I can't remember the last time I actually trusted a doctor, but something about this man's hands—they make me want to tell him about every hiccup I ever had. He rolls my arms in his cool fingers. He gently pulls my head down and examines my scalp. "Uh huh," he says contemplatively, as Burke studies him from the desk chair in the corner.

He throws the sheets off me and presses at my ankle bones, then flexes both my feet up and down. "I'll need you to lie down, Ms. Cruz." It isn't a request, but it isn't a command either. I lay my head back on the pillow. He prods into my abdomen, his fingers pressed together like forceps. "Okay. I'll take some blood? To do a quick test."

"Is she alright? What are you testing for?" Burke says, at the bedside now.

"Just routine stomach issues, ulcers, that type of thing. I can also give a vitamin shot that should help with the symptoms for the next few days." The doctor is talking into his bag as he pulls some things together. "I think it would be better if we do the shot and the test in private. Would you step out Mr. Burke?"

"I..." he seems shocked that anything should be private from him. "When will you have the results?"

"By the end of the week, I should think. Ms. Cruz, we'll need to be by the faucet. Can you make your way into the bathroom please?" He offers me a hand and I take it reflexively. "Mr. Burke, we'll only be a minute. You can wait out here."

We make our way to the bathroom and the doctor closes the French doors behind us. "I didn't get your name?" I say, wondering if we know any of the same people. Wondering if he's even a real doctor at all.

"Dr. Alvarez. I need you to relax your arm."

I do so as he wraps a rubber band around my arm and ties it.

"Now make a fist."

I do and he cleans the soft crease in my arm with cotton. I feel a sharp sting and then a jolt as he attaches the tube that will catch my blood. A moment later he is pulling the needle out and wrapping my arm in a bandage stuck to a cotton ball. He has a very experienced hand. This is the best medical treatment I've ever received.

He shakes the vial and turns on the faucet full blast behind me. Packing the vial away he pulls out a syringe, and a small, sealed glass jar. Inside is a clear liquid behind letters printed on the glass in a language I don't recognize. He expertly draws the fluid into the syringe, and I notice he is looking at me curiously. It's the look people give you when they're trying to decide something about you—they want to confide something, and they're deciding if you're the one to tell.

"Magdalena," he says softly, "I need you to find a way to call this number." He slides a torn piece of paper to me across the counter. "The boys—the ones who got the note from your friends." He gestures to the door, his voice covered by the rushing water. I take the paper and slip it into a pocket in Burke's baggy pajama pants that hang off my body. "They're safe. They've made it to Camaguey. They're going to need some help getting the rest of the way. Our network in the south is a little sparse. One word from you and it will ensure their safe arrival."

My heart is not beating but running, *thump, thump, thump*. The pounding of feet on pavement. I wish it could run all the way to Camaguey, too.

"This is a B12 shot," he says at normal volume. He turns off the faucet and brings his finger to his lips. I press my lips together in understanding. "I'll give this to you in your hip, so I'll need you to turn around. Please pull your waistband down just a few inches."

I do it and he jabs something into my lower back on the left side. "This will help the symptoms for a week or so." *Get yourself out now*, he mouths. "If you need another shot, have Mr. Burke contact me."

I can feel the confusion on my face, but don't speak about what he said while the water was running. "But what is it? What's the matter with me?"

Burke opens the door to find Dr. Alvarez whispering something else to me, this time close to my ear and without the faucet on. Years of refining and perfecting my poker face were meant for this moment. I set my jaw and nod appreciatively. I pat the doctor's arm and begin to walk back towards the bed. "Thank you for coming to me; I don't know how to thank you."

He nods knowingly with a simple smile creasing his face. Burke follows him out the door of the room and I lay on the bed, enveloped in thought.

I imagine Burke is peeling American bills off of his wad of cash and handing them to the doctor. I imagine him asking Dr. Alvarez what is wrong with me. I wonder what the good doctor is going to tell him.

Burke comes back in a few minutes later, a confused and worried look on his face. He sits down next to me on the bed, his back grazing my leg. He looks away from me.

"What's wrong?" I ask.

"He said you're suffering from shock and trauma. He says you need to rest. I'm just worried about you." His face is telling me there's more he can't say. "Can I get you anything? I've got to go out for a few hours. Can I bring something back?"

"I just want to sleep. I'm not sure I can keep anything down yet." Burke goes to the mini-bar and takes out a bottle of water and a package of long thin crackers. Or are they cookies? He sets them and the water bottle on the bedside table closest to me.

"Thank you," I say wearily, letting my eyes close slowly.

He strokes the side of my face and lets the tips of his fingers linger on my neck, where he brushes my hair away and kisses me ever so slightly. I rub a hand through his hair and consider drawing him back into the bed with me. I can already feel the B12 coursing through my veins. I remember the doctor's words and the errand I must accomplish, so I don't budge.

"I hope you're feeling better when I get back," he says into my ear.

"I think I will be," I say with a hint of a smile.

"Get some rest. I love you." We could be as common as a housewife and a banker; him caring for me before heading off to work, a corner office awaiting him. And me, an entire sink of dishes aren't going to wash themselves. I like thinking of us in this way, instead of the complicated and dangerous mess we find ourselves in the middle of.

I wait for the sound of the bolt to click before sitting up. Then, I wait for Burke's and Paolo's voices to trail off down the path before I spring up out of bed. I turn on the shower and strip off the pajamas that are beginning to feel like a second skin. I palm the scrap of paper with a phone number written on it before it falls to the floor. I lay it on the counter. I shower and brush my teeth quickly, not knowing how much time I have before Burke returns.

Mentally I calculate the time it will take to walk to Patricia's and back. A kilometer to the main roadway and then another third after turning left on *Autopista Sur*. About twenty minutes one way. I can feel fatigue seeping in at the thought of it, but I push it down. I put my worn jeans back on but search Burke's laundry for something that will hide me better than the sundress or the tank top I have with me.

It looks like Burke sent all his clothes through the hotel laundry, because everything is neatly folded with thin sheets of tissue paper between each item. I find a long sleeve t-shirt that's gray with dark blue sleeves. It swallows me but I don't have time to think about my appearance. I pull my wet hair back into a functional bun and carefully place the scrap of paper from the counter into my jeans pocket.

The walk to Patricia's feels like a marathon. I ache to stop and lie down but just keep pushing the idea out of my head. I have to keep reminding myself to behave as I did when I had someone to run from. I peer around trees and up and down the road cautiously, looking for any police, but also looking for Burke and Paolo. The doctor didn't want me to tell them and I'm respecting his wishes. I will tell Burke when I get back, I tell myself. I don't want to be dishonest with him. When I see him again, I will tell him everything.

The sky is the deep purple of a bruise. Hints of blue and gold blend in at the edges, where the earth meets sky. The sun has sunk beneath the horizon, but you can still see it there in the crown of light that dissolves clarity into shadows.

I feel at home in the dark. The dark provides a shield that makes my shoulders and hands relax. I relax my jaw, realizing that it has been clenched shut since I left the room. I can see the soft glow of Patricia's convenience store sign brighten up the road ahead of me. It's programmed to come on just at the point when the darkness surpasses the light.

Walking around like this, looking over my shoulder, I can't help but think of Juan Julio. In the days—weeks, months—after we were caught, the thought of him was so constant that it began to feel like another appendage for them to torture and mutilate. He was so gentle and unassuming and naïve. We all were. I wonder if any of them survived. The ache of not knowing the fates of so many people I love almost brings me to my knees. My mother, Juan Julio, our fellow resisters—are any of them alive? Would the regime have anything to gain from keeping them alive? I start to feel tears rolling down my face.

I still don't know why they kept me alive, and it does give me some hope that there are others out there too, who survived. Juan Julio always called himself a pacifist—no guns, no violence—a pacifist revolutionary. He was never really a threat, and they knew that. If he's not dead I'm sure he's somewhere on Juventud, and he'll be there for the rest of his life. The regime doesn't let people out who have the power to organize with only words.

The stiff, artificial lights are flooding me now and I can just make out her face through squinting eyes.

"Magdalena!" She rushes around the counter to hug me. "Thank God you're alright. I thought you were dead. Where have you been? Last I heard, the girl came and got a book for you, and then nothing. What happened to you?"

I open my mouth to speak, but I know that I won't have to. Patricia knows everyone and everything about everyone. I have to be careful what I say because Patricia's store is wired tighter than the office of El Comandante himself.

"I heard you've been shacking up with a handsome

The Many Names of Magdalena Cruz

American," she goes on. I know I can't let her go on too long.

"Patricia, do you have something for me?" She recognizes the code instantly and keeps right on chattering as she comes around the counter and moseys to the storeroom. It's a store closet, really. I wait here, pawing through the cheap car air fresheners and lip balms. I flick my gaze to the camera, whose eye is watching me from an upper corner of the ceiling behind the register.

Patricia, heavier now than when I first met her, ambles back towards me with a brown paper wrapped package tied with string. "This one's yours, just what you asked for. It may be the only copy on the island." I take the package from her extended hand and purposefully unwrap it in view of the camera. The title of the book peeks out at me as I peel the paper back. *To Kill a Mockingbird*, it reads; and then just below it, *by Harper Lee*. I look at the spine of the paperback and run my fingers down it, an authentic chill going down my spine. I've looked for this book since I started reading books. A grade school teacher told me it was the best book ever written. She'd read it on a trip to America, but tragically forgot it in her hotel room.

I can feel the distinctive lump between the pages. The DI knows that I get black market goods from Patricia's—half the island trades on the black market and although illegal, they do almost nothing to stop it. If you're a wanted fugitive and you're apprehended trading black market goods, it will be used in a case against you. But I've never seen anyone arrested for trading on the black market alone. Most DI agents trade on the market, too. The fact that this kind of activity is largely overlooked—expected—makes it the perfect cover for communication with Los Lobos.

"Thank you, thank you; you don't know what this means to me."

"I don't know what you see in all those books, girl, but everybody's got to have something to get them out of bed in the morning."

"Yes, you're right. I'm going to get this home. I'll be back soon," I say.

"We'll see you later," she calls after me as I slip out the glass doors and into the night. I walk nonchalantly away from the store but then turn and walk down the side and to the back of the store, where the neon lights barely make the black rectangle in my hand visible. I pull it from between the pages of my book. It's more compact than the satellite phones we used six years ago, but the basic functions are the same. The button keys are softer than I expected. I pull the scrap of paper from my pocket and squint at the numbers written there.

I push them in, crossing myself instinctively as the line connects. The ringing sounds more like a cat's purr than a bell.

"*Como?*" A man's faraway voice says. Something in it causes a tingle at the base of my spine.

"This is Magdalena Cruz. I was arrested in 1994 with Juan Julio Vega. I spent five years in Juventud. I have been activated." I hesitate. "I am working with the CIA." The voice on the other end of the line waits. "Two boys are headed south to La Sierra Maestra. They're in Camaguey. Your mission is to get them to the CIA safe house in the mountains undetected."

"*El caballo puede pisotear el suelo a sus pies, pero no puede correr de los lobos que lo cazan.*" The voice, familiar again, repeats the code to tell me he is Los Lobos, and he understands the message. It means 'the horse may trample the ground at his feet, but he cannot run from the wolves that hunt him.' A loud, long beep tells me the line has been severed.

Quickly I walk to the back of wall of Patricia's where the back door has been left slightly ajar. I pull the door open and set the phone inside on a wire shelf that holds boxes of Coca-

The Many Names of Magdalena Cruz

Cola and packaged candy. I step backwards out the door and shut it quietly. I look around; there is no one in sight.

I pad silently back to the road. Headlights travel in both directions, but none of them slow as they approach me. If I can get back to the room, Paolo can drive us to the mountains and we could be there by morning. We can all be out of here by tomorrow. A glowing ring of excitement circles a thick orb of grief inside my chest. I know I must go, but it's the last thing I want. I feel a pang of loss for the farmhouse, for my books. Looking down to see the faded cover I hold in my arm, I wonder if I can go back and grab some of my favorites from the house before we leave.

Those books have been my lifeblood—my sanity—for the last two years. They don't allow books in the prison camp. There is no library, no reward system for good behavior. There is solitude, insanity, and the sense of one day bleeding into the next. When I got out, books were the way I found myself again. As I began to become real again, my collection grew. With every small victory—new ration card, getting a job, learning to make soap—a new book was used to celebrate. I would be set adrift in them, become the people I read about and temporarily lose the ache of who I used to be, what I'd done, and who I'd lost.

The thought of losing all that I've collected, of having to start over, is almost too much to bear. I try to estimate how long I've been gone from the hotel room. Will Burke be coming back soon? I think it's been about half an hour since I left. Even though he said he'd be gone a few hours, I'd rather check back at the room. I don't want to risk him being there alone too long. If he's still gone, I resolve to myself, then I will go gather some books and say goodbye to my little farmhouse once and for all.

I shuffle up to the door of the casita, but my heart lights on fire when I see the door is ajar. The lights are on and someone is inside. No, *people* are inside. I can hear voices yelling as I get closer. I slow my steps, knowing any sound I make now could give me away. I crane my neck to the open door.

"Did you honestly think we wouldn't find anything? That your drunk man act would work?" It's a familiar voice but I can't place it. Behind his words there are papers shuffling, and a protestation.

"I fell in love with her, that's all I can say." It's Burke—my Burke—having his room torn apart in front of him. Something must've tipped them off.

"You just so happened to fall in love with one of Cuba's most notorious rebel leaders?"

It takes me moment to realize he means me, and I realize how far the hopes of my people must've fallen if I am one of their heroes. I hear a thud, and wince as it's followed by another thud. Burke's breathing is jagged now. I peek into the room and all I can see are his feet pointed toes down. His body is writhing on the floor and I realize they—is it two, or three men?—are kicking him.

"Send Señor Bush a message from El Presidente. If the CIA is in Cuba, he knows about it. If they're waiters, reporters, limo drivers," he pauses, "he knows about it. And most of the time you whiney bitches grow fat and drunk and forget your purpose here. This is fine with us. But when you start dredging up old wounds, rekindling the fires of revolution that died long ago—then it's over, Burke."

"I don't even know what she did. I don't even know why she was in Juventud. Honestly." A loud fist lands somewhere on his body. His voice is turned inside out and he's gasping now.

"I've had enough of your mouth," the one in charge says. "You're being deported. If you ever try to contact her again, she's dead. If you ever try to come back to Cuba, she's dead.

Forget everything about this miserable failure of a mission. You're done. Go back to reporting because you're the worst spy I've ever met." He directs his voice to the back of the room, "Collect all the notes, every notebook. Keep every shred of evidence. Get him on the next plane to Miami."

I hear a murmuring voice—someone asking something.

"No, leave him to me. He's no longer an asset to anyone." I know he's talking about Paolo.

I hear the heavy, slow footsteps moving for the door. I move to the side of the casita and quietly slip between the wall and a manicured bush. I am as silent as death. My heart has gone cold. It takes everything I have not to strangle the portly, balding man in a military uniform who walks away from me down the path. I stay hidden.

I can hear the room, and possibly Burke, being torn apart. More than anything I want to go in, to save him—but it's no use. He's outnumbered and I would only make things worse for him later. I try to remember the last things we said to one another, and I can't. I can already feel him slipping away from me, like a dream upon waking.

I do the only thing I can think of. I run, glad I wore my sturdy tennis shoes and jeans; they make it easy to propel myself to full speed. I love to run more than anything, and even now when panic and fear are overwhelming me, I take a little pleasure in the burning inside my throat and lungs.

My senses are so heightened I feel like a spider or a fly who can see everything in my periphery. I run to the service entrance and see a linen delivery truck with an open door. I jump in and feel for the keys that dangle from the wheel.

I speed down the service road and away from the hotel. No one gives the truck a second glance. I take the familiar turns and curves, watching the dust kick up in the rearview mirror. I look back once more at the place I worked for two years, the place that breathed life back into me. I start to feel the twinge of tears and focus on the road in front of me—the only chance I've got.

My foot is all the way to the floor, pressing the gas pedal to its limit. I come upon the turn unexpectedly and swerve, slamming my foot on the brake to keep from passing it.

The little dirt road hasn't changed in the few weeks I've been gone, but it feels like a lifetime ago that I ambled up this path. There is something different now, something my mind won't let me see. It's always doing that, my mind, trying to protect me from what's really happening. Trying to make sense of the chaos swirling just beyond my eyes. I pull the truck up to the side of the farmhouse and slam it into park. I just need to get inside. I need to grab a few books—Pablo Neruda, Huxley, Goethe, where did I leave the Nabokov?—I need what's below the floorboards most of all. My stash of money I've earned from making soap. The fake passport I had made my first week out of Juventud.

I can go back to Patricia's. I can call Los Lobos. They can get me out.

It's now that my brain decides to let down the veil of hope. The blur in my vision, the burning in my eyes, they are not illusions. They are smoke—thick rumbling gray smoke that is tumbling up, up and away, above my head into the sky. I tear around the side of the house, my feet carrying me faster than I can understand what my eyes are seeing.

The billowing smoke is emanating from one central point. A hand reaches out and tosses something onto the fire. It flutters into the air like a baby bird learning to fly. Its pages rustle with the wind and make that beautiful sound I love—the sound of freedom. It lands squarely on the pile of rubble and ash. It stays the same for a moment, and I hope everything is going to be okay. This book is refusing to burn, it's putting up a fight. But then, as everything always does, it crumples into itself as the fire blazes around it. I didn't even get to read the title before it burned away. I realize I am on my knees inches from the fire, staring into the flames. Tears pour down my face.

More tossing, more fluttering pages. Anton's face comes into view through the flames. His mouth is moving but I don't hear him. There is no world in which I care to hear what he's saying.

I put a hand to my belly, pressing into my abdomen gently. It's too early to see the swell, but I wonder if the baby can feel me there. It's just a few cells bonding together now—more out of necessity than fear or loneliness. I was going to tell him tonight—tell him that he'd be a father, that we would be parents together. I could've told him that I wanted to be his wife. That I'm sorry I've been so ill these last few days, that it's because the baby was making a home inside my womb. His baby.

Now, there's an infinite gulf of words that will never be spoken between us.

PART III

LENA

TWENTY-THREE

1992 1993 1994 1995 1996 1997 1998 1999 2000 2001 2002

January 5th, 1992 – University of Havana, Havana, Cuba

My new dorm room smells like old nachos, and I wonder who must've lived here over Christmas break. It's my fourth semester, and I still can't get used to a new room before it's time to move again. Or a new roommate. This one seems to like drugs more than most people and I exhale a sigh of relief because at least we won't have to talk to each other much.

It's rare for me to meet a person that I like—I just assume other people must feel the same way. But then I see the other girls on campus lying in the grass of the courtyards, singing and talking and dancing so freely with anyone who walks by. It's then that I realize I'm the skeptical psychology student who sees everyone as an experiment rather than a friend.

"What's your name again?" My roommate, a pear-shaped girl with dyed blond hair, rolls over on her squeaky cot. She must be coming down from whatever's allowed her to sleep until three in the afternoon.

"Magdalena."

"Never touch my stuff. I'm Rosa." She gets up slowly and gathers her shower accessories and towel, leaving the room without another word. I lay back on my bed, counting the semesters until I graduate—four more here and then eight more at graduate school, which is technically just across the street. Theoretically, there could be many more after that.

Rosa's parents must have money, influence, or both for her to be able to get bleach for her hair. I can tell she's not a natural blonde because her eyebrows are pitch black, like her roots.

I've only seen one box of blonde hair dye in my life and it was being traded for something on the black market. My sister stole it from the back room of the hair salon where our mother went when she could afford it. The front room was for regular customers while the back room was for customers who could pay a little extra or trade something worthwhile. We were front-room-customers in every walk of life. My father was in the army, but he left us when I was five. My mother worked on and off as a cleaning woman but mostly stayed home and took care of my sisters and I, when we weren't taking care of her.

I stand up and part the thin, plastic blinds with my fingers. The one nice thing about my new room is that it looks over the courtyard. The Life Sciences building is just beyond it, where I'll be spending about eighty hours a week starting Monday.

There are clusters of young adults huddled together on the grass. One group has a stereo—the first one I've ever seen—and it's playing an American radio station via a long thin antenna pointing to the sky. Another group is bouncing around something that looks like a ball that's gone a little flat. The third and largest group is sitting on the lawn facing one boy who's kneeling. They all look mesmerized as the boy—who looks to be about twenty-two—speaks calmly to them. Some listeners nod in agreement while others shout affirmations. I try to see if the boy is wearing a cross or some other obvious religious marker. Is he holding church here, right on the lawn of the University of Havana? In a communist state that denounces religion? I look to the armed guards who stand watch at each of the building doorways. None of them seem concerned with the boy or his audience. The group with the radio has started passing a bottle around, and still the guards remain at their posts.

Since it's a Saturday afternoon before the semester has started, I have no legitimate excuse for not pursuing my curiosity. I want to know what this guy could be saying to stir the students—the most apathetic bunch I've come across—from indifference.

I wrap a light sweater around my shoulders and head down the stairs and out the door, passing the armed guard who gives me a once-over and a nod as I pass.

As I get closer, I see the boy's dark hair is shorn unevenly. His clothes are worn and he wears no shoes.

"This very ground," he caresses the blades of grass at the base of his knees, "this is the ground of revolution. In 1959, after seven years of fighting, Che Guevara, Frank País, Raul Castro—and yes, Fidel Castro—with eighty-three others, took over the Cuban government. But many, many years before that, Fidel and my grandfather attended school here, right where we sit. They discussed politics, law, and philosophy. Fidel believed he could change the world with only his words. He went to court. He spoke in defense of himself. And in defense of Cuba. People rallied around him. They trusted him. His words changed the world.

"Somewhere along the way, Fidel took up a gun. He decided that violence was the answer to achieve a better world. The walls of hope were weakened. There was no one to argue with him. People wanted things to get better, and they didn't care how it happened. Fidel's violence was rewarded with more power, and he's kept the cycle going ever since. I believe he could've been a catalyst for change with only his words. In fact, I believe he still can."

A few people at the back of the group stand up and dust themselves off. They walk away shaking their heads. "Sure, words can change the world," I hear one of them whisper. "They can change you from alive to dead." His friend nods. But about fifteen people remain, some asking questions, others writing notes to themselves.

"Who was your grandfather?" a girl asks, sounding a little too chipper for the topic at hand.

"Jaime Vega," he answers. "He fought with Fidel to win Santiago, and most of the southern provinces. He was killed trying to take Santa Ana. My father tells the story all the time, even though he was only seven when it happened." His eyes look stormy at the mention of his father.

"Why would Fidel listen to you? He won't listen to anyone. You could never even get in to see him. Half the island is malnourished, and the other half has starved. He and his cronies are shitting on golden toilets and using kids like us for target practice. You think you can completely change who he's been for the past forty years?" The voice comes from the back row. A russet-skinned boy with hair to match sits picking his teeth with a toothpick.

Lucas.

I am not a girl who chases boys; but if I was, I would be chasing Lucas all over campus. He's every bit of the cool-bad-boy-class-clown that girls like to chase. He always questions authority, even if authority knows better.

Last semester Lucas and I were in *Ideologia y Revolución: Cuba 1959–1962*, which was an elective for me. The first day of class he looked me up and down in a way that made me pull my books closer to my chest. I could tell he was used to being pursued, so I did nothing. It was entertaining to watch him trying to flirt and court me as the class became familiar, but never really finding the right rhythm. Lucas eventually ended up dating another girl in class, one that always ran to catch up with him and asked to compare notes with him after lectures. By midterms, I was so engrossed in the class that I forgot anyone else was in the room with me most of the time.

Now, Lucas's eyes look hollow; from grief or a hangover, I can't tell. I notice he is alone, which means his prosthetic girlfriend must've been removed over Christmas break. He is bitter in his arguments with the Buddha-like boy at the front of the group.

"He would hear me out because I am the grandson of one of his comrades. He would hear me out because I am a citizen of Cuba, and we are brothers in revolution." Determination lines the boy's face. He's not kidding.

"You're a joke. Did you smoke too much on the peace pipe today, Juan Julio? Do you know how many revolutionaries—well, counter-revolutionaries, technically—have been killed by Castro? I've heard he takes pleasure in shooting first at someone who's being executed by firing range. If you walk up to Punto Cedo and knock on the door—assuming you get that far without being shot by a sniper—and by some miracle, El Comandante answers the door, what would you say?" Lucas is standing now, pointing his finger in the direction of Juan Julio. The guards at each building door are looking our direction, but still have not moved.

"It would not be just me, Lucas. It would be the voices of thousands of hungry, unhappy people. We would remind him of the boy he once was—tell him that he was just like us. He didn't like the status quo, and he did something about it. We would tell him that we understand how much he's sacrificed, how much he's given to make Cuba great. And we would also help him see how this vision has gotten lost because of corruption and power struggle, and pride—the very enemies he elected to fight against.

"I do have to say, Lucas, you seem very angry. I want to tell you something you may not understand until much later in life. You cannot approach any goals with fear and anger leading the charge. Fear and anger have only gotten us here. If you want real change, you need to go forward with love. Yes, there is much to fear and much to be angry about. But fear only brings more fear, where love brings more love."

Juan Julio stands up and dusts off his knees. He's wearing a light blue t-shirt and loose jeans. He is barefoot. I honestly wonder where such a cliché could have come from. Are people like this made or born? I have never heard anyone talk the way this boy talks.

Lucas sits, mouth gaping, for a long time as the others gradually get up and approach Juan Julio, patting his shoulders and shaking his hand. Do they actually believe what he's saying, or are they shaking his hand before they go inform on him and have him taken to Mazorra, the mental institution? I've always been able to read people and these onlookers look sincere, earnest even.

I consider approaching, but hold back for fear of blending in with the adoring admirers. I am a skeptical observer, at best. Lucas seems to be in my camp too. He's standing next to me now, his arms crossed. His confidence seems to have been shaken to the core.

"You okay?" I ask, half hoping he'll just nod and walk away.

"I mean who does this guy think he is? He's a freshman, never even taken a class, and he comes in here preaching to us about peace, love and revolution? In Cuba? I don't know if I'm his biggest critic or his biggest supporter. I feel...strange."

"Someone actually made you feel? I'm as shocked as you are."

He looks at me without a trace of jocularity.

I grin and nudge his arm.

He laughs unexpectedly, as if he finally remembers where he's met me before.

"What's funny?" Juan Julio's admirers have moved on now, and he's suddenly standing a few inches from me. I jump. "Juan Julio Vega," he says, jutting his hand towards me with zeal.

"Magdalena Cruz," I say. "Nice to meet you."

"Lena," he says lyrically, pronouncing it just as I say the last part of my first name. *Lay-na*. "Lena," he says again, this time *Lee-na*. He nods lightly as if agreeing this is the best pronunciation of my newly appointed nickname. I don't correct him. I like it. "What was that you said about peace, love, and revolution?" He says it as he turns to Lucas.

"Oh, uh, you heard that. I was just saying that's what it seems like you're talking about... mostly." Lucas plumbs for something meaningful to add. "At least, from my viewpoint." The textbook college qualifier is the hallmark of any liberal arts major.

"I love it. It's what we'll be called, yes?" Juan Julio looks to us expectantly, as if we know why we need to be called anything. "PLR: Peace, Love and Revolution. It's so clear," he says, mostly to himself. "Non-violent. Purposeful. But still cool. It recalls the American hippies..." He trails off.

"Yes, that is what made it interesting. But now that you're picking it apart, it loses its luster. Can you tell me what you're talking about? Who's *we*?" Lucas asks, an edge in his voice.

"We're we. Us. Collectively." He gestures to the courtyard

with a grand sweep of his hand. "We're going to form a non-violent protest movement to request an audience with El Comandante. Didn't you hear what I was saying just now?"

Lucas and I look at each other skeptically. I flick my eyes to the guards on either side of the courtyard. One is scraping something off the bottom of his shoe, but the other—his cold gaze burrows into me. He's been watching us since Juan Julio stopped speaking to the group.

"You're really fucking serious, aren't you?" Lucas is dumbfounded.

I watch the two of them curiously. Something is telling me to walk away—run, maybe—but I can't.

Juan Julio's eyes are a hazel green, a strange combination of brown, green and blue that reminds me of the ocean. They're never quite still, and somehow always calm. Standing next to Lucas, he looks very light skinned. His dark hair falls in waves across his forehead. I see myself running my fingers through his hair. I have to catch my hand and pull it back to me before it reaches for him. I have never had this strong of a physical reaction to a person before—my textbook might call this a pheromone reaction.

I've never been in love—in fact I've never even believed love is a real thing. Just another story we tell each other to survive. I'm still a virgin, despite all the couples pairing off our last year of secondary school, desperate to get rid of their virginities before they went to university. I never let anyone get close and only a few have tried. I've always found more love in books than in people.

"Lena," Juan Julio says. "Lena." He touches my shoulder so gently and leaves his hand there. "Are you alright?"

"Yes, yes, sorry. I've got to go. Maybe we three can talk about this at dinner? My dining hall is over there. They serve dinner at six."

"Oh, I'm glad to know that. I just got here today and wasn't sure where to eat. I would like to talk to you both some more. You seem..." he pauses. "You seem like the kind of people I need on my side," he says definitively.

Lucas draws close to me, putting his arm around me. Three months ago, I would've been swooning, but today I want to disappear. I look at him, confused.

Juan Julio's hand falls to his side.

"I don't want anything to do with this. It's dangerous. Magdalena, you should stay away from this guy," Lucas says. He faces Juan Julio, as if to challenge him.

Juan Julio says nothing. I shrug off Lucas's arm and turn to walk back to my room. "See you at six then," I call back to them.

TWENTY-FOUR

1992　1993　1994　1995　1996　1997　1998　1999　2000　2001　2002

January 5th, 1992 – University of Havana, Havana, Cuba

Dinner in the university cafeteria is very different than dinner at home. I still have to get my ration card punched, but then I go down the line. There's more food here than I've ever seen. They slop beans, rice, tortillas, chicken, and salsa verde on my plate. My mouth is watering. At home, we get our ration card punched at the store and then the clerk hands over the box that's marked with our family's name. Inside there might be some milk or cheese, but mostly beans. Rarely is there any meat or vegetables. A can of tomatoes may appear in the box if my mother can trade something that week. There are always several boxes of Russian condoms. My mother says there are more Russian condoms in Cuba than there are in all of Russia.

    The tables in the dining hall are full of young people my age; they're all shoveling food into their mouths as fast as their forks can carry it. It's nearly silent, except for the sounds of knives, forks and the occasional *whump* of the door to the back kitchen pushing open and closed. Soft shoes pad around on the black and white linoleum floor. A guard stands at the door of the cafeteria, leading out into the courtyard.

Juan Julio sits alone at a table for four. He is the only person in the dining hall who is taking time to chew his food. Then he carefully assembles a bite on his fork and brings it to his mouth. He puts the food in and begins chewing, slowly. He closes his eyes and breathes deeply. A small, serene smile comes across his lips. When I sit down, his eyes are still closed. I watch him. It's as if he's thanking God for each morsel, a silent prayer of thanks each time he takes a bite.

He opens his eyes to look at me, and we just stare at each other for a moment, saying nothing.

"Who are you?" I ask with genuine curiosity.

"I'm Juan Julio Vega, we met earlier…" He's about to retell the story of this afternoon, but I stop him.

"Yes, I remember. I don't have head trauma."

He doesn't laugh but just stares on intently.

"I just mean… where did you come from?"

"I was born in here, in Havana. My parents are Buddhists. They're starting a monastery, the first of its kind in Cuba."

"What's Buddhist?" I have never heard of such a thing.

"It's a way of thinking. A religion, I suppose."

Everyone in my town is Catholic, even though they weren't allowed to say it until three years ago. The state outlawed religion for thirty-two years. Worship was practiced in basements; prayers were said at bedsides. The authorities realized that battling religion was a losing game. The harder times get, the harder people cling to their gods. And times have been hard. So, Cuba recanted its stance on religion and everything stayed the same—except old women are wearing their crosses outside of their houses now.

"Hello, my friend," Juan Julio says, looking up at Lucas, who is approaching our table.

"I didn't think you would come," I say, looking up at him. It's really hard to say who's more attractive. I catch myself staring at them again and shake my head slightly to get my mind back in order. Is it possible I missed the hormones of puberty only to have them sprung on me now? Maybe I'm a late bloomer. How does anyone get anything done thinking about these things all the time?

"I came to warn you," he says. "This kid is dangerous and I don't want you getting pulled down with him."

"Since when do you care to protect me?" I ask Lucas.

Juan Julio begins putting small bites of food in his mouth, staring out the window thoughtfully. Lucas watches him, as if waiting to be acknowledged. He wanted his words to anger Juan Julio, and he seems surprised that they don't. Lucas sits next to me and folds his arms across his barrel chest. We both look at Juan Julio expectantly.

"Didn't you want to talk to us about something?" I finally ask.

He smiles and looks at us both. "This is the beginning of something, my friends. Something that will change Cuba forever."

We both stare on as if he is a crazy prophet shouting on a street corner.

"You, Lucas—you're the brooding, angry, skeptical one. You'll pull us back when we go too far. You'll keep us grounded when we float away, high on idealism. And you, Lena, you'll..." He pauses, his brow crinkling as if he is trying to pick the ripest avocado from the tree. "Your passion will win people over. They may be unsure, or scared, but when they see you believe in me, they will follow us to the ends of the island and back again. Because everything you do, you do with purpose and intention. You never do anything half way."

My chest flutters like a moth at the window. I don't know

how he knows anything about me, but I'm too overwhelmed to ask. I've never had anyone confirm to me the things I have always known about myself. A few teachers took me under their wings in school, writing things on my papers like, 'You'll go far!' and, 'Cuba needs more young women like you!' but no one ever said to my face that I mattered to them. Outside of how I looked or what chores I could do, my mother never encouraged me one way or another. I have always felt that I have a bigger purpose, that I'm important in some way—not in a conceited way, but in a dutiful way. People stop talking when I enter a room. When I ask for things, I get them. Even though I come from an impoverished city and a cruel set of circumstances, I have always been lucky. I've won almost every carnival game I've ever played. I'm meant for something greater. It fills me with something unexplainable to know that Juan Julio can see it, too.

Lucas is leaned forward, his elbow on the table. His hand holds his chin, pointer finger flickering against his stubble. His gaze is completely perplexed.

Juan Julio finishes his food calmly, oblivious that he has just assigned roles to us as if he was a director in a play.

"I think you're too crazy to even know how crazy you sound," Lucas says. "And what exactly is it we're going to do together? Me, the doubting Thomas; she, the Mary Magdalene, and you—our savior himself."

"Let me just stop you there, Lucas, because our story bears little resemblance to the life of Jesus, other than the fact that I'm a male looking to recruit followers. Jesus was a religious leader, trying to persuade the Jews that he was, in fact, the son of God. Those who believed him followed him because they believed in who he was. Mary, the lowly prostitute by some accounts, his lover and mother of his children in others, was merely one of his followers. They fled from the Romans and the Jews and eventually, as I'm sure you know, Jesus was crucified for his beliefs and called a false idol. That bears little resemblance to what we're trying to do."

He speaks so strangely and yet so knowingly about topics that most Cubans have never heard of. Jesus having children with the whore Mary Magdalene? Maybe he is as crazy as Lucas says.

"Our story is much different, better if you ask me," he goes on. "We're going to form a non-violent resistance called PLR—like we talked about earlier. I just love the name. The last few years have seen untold poverty and famine on the Cuban people. Something has to change and I believe that change will start with us. I honestly don't think El Comandante intended this. I believe his words when he took power in 1959. 'Condemn me,' he said. 'It is of no importance. History will absolve me.' He really believed that he was the leader to save the Cuban people from American greed and corruption. He wanted us to become self-sufficient, so that no larger country could bully us ever again. From everything I know, I can't believe that he meant to take us from the mouth of one beast into the mouth of another."

"Then what happened, Juan Julio? There is only one man who refuses democratic elections and insists on holding us hostage by depending on Russia and rejecting American aid. That man is Castro. If he really wanted what was best, he would've stepped down. He would've let people own businesses and take care of themselves." I look around to see if anyone has heard my treasonous comment. Forks and knives scrape plates. Joyful conversation over plantains and rice consume the other students around us.

"He has become clouded. It happens all the time when men get into power. They get blinded and they forget. They forget hunger, they forget dirt, they forget sweat. They forget the sacrifices that were made for them to get where they are so that they could make things better. El Comandante needs a reminder."

This is the first time I see something like anger burn behind Juan Julio's eyes. I wonder what he would do to El Comandante if left alone with him.

Lucas is incredulous. "You're insane. There's an entire army and an entire secret service dedicated to keeping crazies like you from getting within a thousand meters of El Comandante. Why would any of them ever listen to you?"

"The same way El Comandante got all of Cuba to listen to him in 1959. He grew his resistance with strong words and loyalty. Word spread and he charged the capitol. He had the will of the people behind him."

"But, like you said, a lot of sacrifice was made. People had to die. If they weren't shot, they were tortured for information. How will you fight back?" The rest of the room has faded away now, and only the three of us remain.

"Anger is a fire that catches faster than a tinderbox and burns you from the inside out. We cannot march forward in anger. We will be different—it's what will set us apart. We seek understanding. That's why this movement will have no guns, no weapons of any kind. We are pacifists. We go forward in peace, or not at all." He begins to look around as if coming out of a dream. His right hand—which was raised in emphasis—comes back down to the table slowly. I'm swept up in him, even if he isn't convinced of his own powers of persuasion.

Lucas and I stare at Juan Julio in disbelief. He must truly be insane. To gather an uprising with no weapons would make us sitting ducks for the regime to pounce on. We could be annihilated without much effort. Guns are an underground market and these days it's easier to come by an AK-47 than a head of lettuce.

"Do you know what happens to a regime that senselessly slaughters non-violent college students who are peacefully organizing a resistance?" Juan Julio looks down at his plate casually as he speaks, as if wishing there were still food there. Then his eyes rise to meet mine and I see a streak of something familiar. Something I've felt since I can remember. It's a vague curiosity for what it must be like to die, but not only that; to die *for* something. To be martyred. To be a catalyst.

In this moment, an entire lifetime flashes before my eyes. I continue in school, get my doctorate in psychology and begin working for a state hospital. I meet and marry a handsome, bearded man who is a doctor of internal medicine. I get pregnant. I have babies. I begin doing charity work. I watch my children grow up under the thumb of the same regime I did. I watch my husband bed nannies and nurses as I turn further into myself. We are not poor, but we can't become rich. We can't own anything, but the world owns us. Every dollar we make ends up in someone else's pocket. We live in fear. Our lives are not our own. I see a grisly end, death by my own hand. But the worst, most painful part is knowing that my death does nothing but continue the cycle. It spurs no one into action, it inspires no speeches. No battles are won or lost on the foot of my grave. I am born no one, and I die no one. And no one will say the system caused this, no one will connect the dots and see that hopelessness sucked the life from me.

I stand firm in one thing: that is not my life.

"I'm with you to the end." I uncharacteristically take his hand and kiss it gently. The closeness—human closeness—startles and awakens me. I know that this moment will change the course of my life.

PART IV

MAMÁ

TWENTY-FIVE

2002 2003 2004 2005 2006 2007 2008 2009 2010 2011 **2012**

May 14th, 2012 – New York City, New York

Richard Burke awoke from his dreamless sleep to a surging headache. He opened his eyes and became immediately aware of two people in the room. One, a leggy blonde on the floor next to his side of the bed; the other, a brunette, who was stuck to his backside by a film of sweat and what appeared to be drool. Both women were naked. *This would be a dream for most guys,* he thought.

He looked out the window of his Central Park West apartment to see that it was still dark. He didn't have to look at the clock to know that it was four a.m. He'd been waking up at four a.m. on the dot for the past nine years, since he took a job anchoring a morning news show that required him to be on set at five. Though he'd since moved to evening news, the habit remained.

He lumbered out of bed, groaning and stretching. The now-anonymous women in his bedroom began to stir, but he didn't care if he woke them up. Suddenly he yearned for solitude. The kind of solitude he craved could not be achieved around sleeping people, a precarious state that always hung in the balance and could be robbed with a flickering eyelid. He wanted them out, gone, never to be seen again. He didn't care that it was 4 a.m. and they had likely just gone to sleep a few hours before. He didn't even care to re-learn their names or their occupations—details he'd likely heard but not bothered to commit to memory. *Besides, how interesting could they be?* he thought. *Stewardess, waitress, pre-school teacher—it's all the same.*

"What time is it?" the girl on the floor asked in a lusty, phone-sex operator tone.

Do they teach that somewhere? Is there some secret class in school that teaches girls how to give a guy an erection from across the room? To do it after a few beers, sure, but in the middle of the night, when she's half asleep? That's impressive. At this thought he let out a smug, one-syllable chuckle.

"Time for you to gather yourself and your friend and get the hell out." As he said it he tucked his erection into the waistband of his underwear—a trick that had served him well since junior high. With the booze and cocaine nearly out of his system, all he could feel was rage.

"Well, it doesn't look like you want us to leave," she cooed, noticing the lump he'd tried to keep hidden. She crawled seductively toward him. Her friend was awake now, watching the scene but keeping quiet.

He sidestepped her and headed for the bathroom. "The man you met last night is gone. The fun's over. If you're not gone by the time I get out of the shower, I'm calling the cops."

The woman in the bed glared at him. "You don't have to be so mean," she snarled. "We're going."

He turned his back on them. Suddenly the memory of her was so intense that he had to grab the doorframe to keep from collapsing to the floor. What had triggered it? Was it the combative look from that groupie in the bed? Was it just that he could feel her disapproval so strongly?

"Madge," he whispered, and the word rose out of him like steam escaping, hot breath bleeding out into below freezing temperatures. Though it had been 12 years, her face appeared to him as fresh and young as it had on the last day he saw her. He'd heard people—soldiers, children who'd lost their parents—say that they would forget their loved ones' faces after long periods of time. He felt the opposite was happening, that she was stronger now in his memory than she had been a year, or even three years after he'd left her.

Suddenly the predictable feeling of cowardice overtook him as it always did when he thought of her. He'd left Cuba with a black shroud over his head. He was shoved into a helicopter—a government aircraft, he assumed—and flown straight to Miami, where he was ordered to climb down a ladder from the hovering copter onto a US Coast Guard base.

"You're lucky to be alive," a voice screamed in his ear. "If you ever try to find Magdalena Cruz, or contact her in any way, we'll slit her throat. We'll find places inside her..." the voice trailed off as the propeller sped up and the aircraft floated away.

He'd complied. He'd never gone looking for her; he'd never asked anyone about her. He didn't even know if she was still alive. If she even remembered him.

I couldn't have. They would have killed her, he reminded himself. But still, he knew that a brave man wouldn't have settled for that. A brave man couldn't have just walked away.

And so he began his day: sopping up the self-hatred that came on so strongly each morning, when he remembered what he had done, what he'd left behind. His headache seared into his brain. He reached into the cabinet and downed two pills from a small round bottle. In the years since he'd seen her, this bottle of Xanax—and the booze, and occasionally something harder—were the only things that could dull the memory to a blurry ache.

He remembered the story he'd done recently on drug addicts. The focus was on individuals who'd lost everything to drugs and were living homeless in the city. Everyone the reporters interviewed had recognizable hairline wrinkles around their mouths. Their jaws jutted out in unexpected ways. It scared him to see the way drugs so obviously affected their looks. He could see the lines around his mouth beginning to make permanent creases in his face like pillow marks that wouldn't fade away. There was a dullness to his eyes that hadn't been there before—or had it? Being on camera for so many years—all those years re-watching the footage of himself to improve diction, speed, emphasis—he'd grown keenly aware of his appearance, and any little changes that might impact his job security.

He heard his front door slam from down the hall. It was quiet outside the bathroom door. Alone at last. He reached for the coconut oil that he used as shave lotion and moisturizer. It was his way of keeping her with him. After all, if she ever showed up, he wanted to smell as she'd made him smell all those years ago.

He examined himself critically for several minutes, looking for signs that the drugs were showing on his face. The laugh wrinkles around his eyes—they'd been falsely earned wining and dining dignitaries, and partying with bimbos—seemed more pronounced. He used his forefinger to prop up the skin beneath his eyebrow and watched as it sagged when he let go. He took both hands and pulled his forehead skin back, giving himself a temporary facelift. *Maybe I should call that plastic surgeon Jane mentioned.*

You fucking pussy!

His father's voice rang clear, bouncing off the mirror and the shower door, as if he was here instead of back in Iowa, deep in the ground, nestled in the walnut casket that Burke had insisted on. All those years and all that distance had nothing on his father's voice, echoing in the catacombs of his mind.

Do you think Brokaw got plastic surgery? Do you think Grimsby was sitting around worrying about wrinkles? Let me ask my grandma if you can borrow some of her anti-wrinkle cream. Stop pandering to yourself and get it together. There's news to report and you're the man to do it.

Burke wasn't schizophrenic that he knew of. It had always helped him when he was feeling down to get a mental kick in the ass. His father, a remarkably cruel gym teacher, or Walter Cronkite himself could show up at any moment to give Burke the extra motivation he needed. The verbal one-two punch to wake him up, straighten him out and get his ass out of the apartment.

It had to be someone that could motivate him out of his stupor—someone to remind him of where he came from and where he was going. His success came due to his ability to deliver when it mattered—to show up, to shove everything else aside for the job. He'd been successful because he was hard on himself. It was his edge. Edge was everything in the competitive evening news game, and after seven years anchoring the nightly news for NBC, he knew to stick with what worked.

But when she showed up—Madge—it would've taken his father, Walter Cronkite, and Patton all there in the flesh to rouse him from how low he felt. He couldn't count how many times she shoved herself into his head every day. Remembering her had become a chronic pain like a slipped disk or a migraine. Something unexplained and untreatable.

TWENTY-SIX

2002 2003 2004 2005 2006 2007 2008 2009 2010 2011 **2012**

May 14th, 2012 – New York City, New York

These millennial bitches and their cheap drugs, he thought. Where was the class? Where was the pride? Kids today would snort or shoot anything from Theraflu to nail polish remover. As a teen in Iowa, he'd huffed gasoline a few times, but like everyone else, once he'd moved to New York he'd had the good sense to put away childish things. He moved on to pills, like a grown-up.

The night before, these girls had him sniffing out of a little brown bottle labeled *Jungle Juice*. When he first saw it, he'd gotten excited because he thought it was a 5-hour-energy shot. *This must be what getting old is all about,* he thought. *You're way more excited about B Vitamins than drugs.* Golda Meir would definitely not approve of his off-the-clock activities, so he made a mental note to not offer her any poppers when he was interviewing her next week.

Whatever was in poppers was doing a number on him—his eyes burned, his heart pounded and his mouth was a desert. As the water battered down on him in the shower, he wondered what desperate, coal-eyed place he would be reporting on today. Syria. Washington, D.C. Congo. Iraq. Troubled places. No one ever asked him to talk about all the great things happening in the world. He used to love that about the news—no goddamn sugar-coating. He was tasked with showing people how the world really was. It was harsh, cruel and unforgiving. Since losing Madge, he had always enjoyed delivering the blow.

The heat and steam from the shower seemed to have a negative effect on his symptoms—where he thought the steam would draw out the toxins, it seemed to be pushing them down deep inside of him, and sealing them in.

He stepped out and dressed quickly, hoping coffee and a few Adderall would get him through the worst of the hangover.

"Julia," he cooed. "When are you going to leave all this behind and come make coffee for me full time?"

The dark-haired barista with the brooding eyes was used to hiding her frustration under a veil of friendliness. "Richard, you know just what to say to make a girl swoon." Her accent was mostly covered by a life in the city, but he could pick it up. *Puerto Rican*, he pinpointed.

"Or should I call you Dick?" He looked up from his phone at her cold eyes. She laid the word 'dick' before him like an animal she'd slain and dragged back to camp. He had a sudden flash of memory—his hands full of her bouncing Puerto Rican ass as she screamed and moaned. How could he have forgotten that?

"I... I, you know what, I'm switching to green tea—

completely forgot," he said, smacking the side of his head playfully. Julia was not smiling. She crossed her arms and swung her hips to the side incredulously. Burke turned and left the line, nearly sprinting for the door.

When had he taken Julia out? He was racking his brain. This was uncharacteristically forgetful, even for him. To walk into a woman's workplace—his favorite coffee shop—and hit on the barista, completely forgetting that they had already had sex? Had the poppers erased his memory completely? Was he getting Alzheimer's? A brain tumor?

He walked to another coffee shop down the street and was relieved to order from the male barista behind the counter. He tipped generously and then sat at a nearby table to retrace his steps—or dates, rather—from the few weeks before.

He knew he hadn't slept with Julia last weekend because he'd been in Brooklyn at Stacey's apartment. Stacey was a little brunette hipster who hung around the news desk. He thought maybe she was a courier or a girl who worked for the vending machine company. She invited him to a warehouse party. He could tell it was partly as a joke—invite the old, stodgy newsman to a party. There were few things that would make him leave Manhattan, and proving hipsters wrong was one of them. He ended up drinking with Stacey and her friends until dawn, and teaching her transgender roommate Tommy (formerly Tammy) how to shoot a bow and arrow on the roof of their building.

Stacey practically dragged Burke back down to her room where she begged him to fuck her hard from behind without a condom. He would not concede on the condom part, but as a compromise he agreed to choke her. It worked out well for both of them, Stacey coming so hard she refused to let him leave for two days, and Burke actually ejaculating during intercourse for the first time in months.

He knew it was because he couldn't see her face at all. It was either obscured by a pillow or turned completely away from him. She told him she couldn't orgasm if he was looking at her. This made it all the easier for him to imagine Magdalena, as he'd done with every woman since her. The problem was, most women screamed or moaned or talked dirty. It always pulled him away from Magdalena and into reality. As soon as he realized who was there with him, all chance of finishing evaporated.

Stacey made no sound—due to the autoerotic asphyxiation—and didn't want to be looked at. His orgasm was so hard and long, he lay in a heaving pile on her bed for half an hour before he could speak. Madge had been so real in that fraction of time that it was like they were coming together again on her tiny bed in the broken-down farmhouse. But after Stacey left the room to find some coffee and scrambled eggs for the two of them, he broke down sobbing and cried himself to sleep.

He made a note in his phone to call Stacey, then deleted the word call and wrote in 'text'—it was the only way these young girls would respond to him. Now back to the barista.

So that meant Saturday and Sunday were out. What was today? Thursday—that left Monday, Tuesday and... ha! Tuesday, you sneaky devil of the workweek. He'd had to stay late at the office to prepare for a board meeting the next day. His boss, Dobbs, wanted him to present some statistics to the board of directors. He found that when Burke delivered bad news, it somehow softened the blow.

Burke had stepped out for some air and started walking to clear his head. He looked up to find himself in Hell's Kitchen at the twenty-four-hour Starbucks on 47th and 9th. It was two a.m., but he wasn't even close to being ready for the meeting.

This part of town seemed to be alive beneath his feet. He stepped into the familiar atmosphere of the coffee shop and ducked into the bathroom. In the cramped space, he removed a little baggy from inside his wallet and took a deep sniff of cocaine. After a quick mirror check, he went out to place his order.

He was surprised to see Julia behind the counter—his regular shop was on 72nd between Columbus and Amsterdam, a little place called Aroma, over twenty blocks away. And frankly, he was a little disappointed to see Julia working at a Starbuck's. His other shop was bright and spacious; the perfect place to find yourself after a morning jog. It didn't feel like selling out to grab a coffee and an egg white soufflé at Aroma. Inside this sad temple to consumerism, people looked worn and jaded. Burke wanted to turn around and run before she saw him, but then she looked up and her chestnut brown eyes locked with his.

He saw such a look of relief in her face—her shoulders relaxed, her hand shot up and she waved. Julia turned to the other barista and gestured to him, the two women giggled looking at him. He'd been mooning over Julia for months, but only within the window of time when he would see her working at Aroma. She left his head as soon as she had entered it and he went on about his day. It was a casual flirtation. He assumed she flirted back with him to get a good tip, and because she knew he was some famous guy, or whatever.

As he approached the counter, Burke recognized well the look Julia was giving him. It was a look that had gone way past casual flirtation. In the middle of the night in Hell's Kitchen, that look felt fucking good.

He touched a hand to the back of his neck and absentmindedly smoothed his hair. He approached the counter to place his order.

"Hi," he said to her, with that Iowa smile that wouldn't quit.

"Hi," she said back, more shyly than he was expecting.

"I didn't know you worked over here, too." He put his hands on his hips, surveying the place. He projected an air that said he needed to approve of this place if she was going to be spending time there. "Not bad," he said conclusively, nodding.

"A lot of people have to work more than one job, Mr. Burke," she said. He saw the road she was going down, but avoided the trap.

"It must be hard working such long hours. Do you get a break any time soon?" The coke was raging through his head like a tidal wave.

Julia looked at the girl who was standing at the steam wand, making drinks. The girl checked her watch and nodded. "Looks like I can take a break now, if you want…?" She knew she might be assuming too much.

"Can I get a drink, first?" Burke smiled to let her know he was a nice guy.

"Oh, of course!" She blushed and reached over to pick up a cup on the other side of the espresso machine. "The usual, right? I started making it when I saw you come in."

His usual was a small Americano with one heaping tablespoon of whipped cream stirred in. Julia made it perfect every time. His body grew warm with appreciation and longing for her, someone so considerate and earnestly sweet. She lifted the counter at the hinge and stepped out. He reached out his hand for hers, but placed his body so that his groin would graze her as she passed. For most women, this was enough. It was enough to convey his intentions and they could sort out the details together. Julia's pace quickened and she led him by the hand out into the frigid night.

"I know a place…" she breathed—it seemed they were

both desperate to touch each other now in all the places their eyes had explored. He followed her, his hands meeting at her waist. Watching her ass bounce as she practically pulled him behind the coffee shop and into a tight alley. The dumpster for the shop filled most of the space, but there was just enough room to get past it into a square plot that was mostly blocked from the street. They were lit by one stray street lamp that shone down from overhead. To his right was a brick wall covered in ivy.

Cigarette butts littered the ground, and the back door to the coffee shop stood slightly ajar. Burke leaned down and removed the wedge in the door, pushing it shut. "Whoops," he said, but they were already moving towards each other. He reached for his pocket where he kept a few condoms for just such occasions. She stopped his hand and got down on her knees. His pants fell around his ankles and she took all of him into her mouth. Her hands cupped his ass and suddenly he couldn't stop the flood of images rushing into his head. The images were of the only other woman who'd ever been able to do that with her tongue, the thing that Julia was doing. Was she Julia? Or was she Madge? He looked down to see dark hair, beautiful features, and suddenly he couldn't tell anymore.

He reached down and fished out the condom from his pants pocket. He couldn't risk losing Madge in the middle. "Get up," he ordered. "Face the wall." She looked confused but she complied. He jerked her black leggings down as she put her hands on the wall and thrust herself backwards into him. He was still fumbling with the confounded rubber, and Madge was fading.

Finally, it was on, and he pushed into her—into Madge. She was here—the gorgeous line of her back, the dark curls glistening in the streetlights. There was a woman—not Madge—moaning far away. He pumped and pumped, slow and then fast how she liked. He cupped her beautiful hips in his hands and pulled them closer and closer each time.

The faraway voice was getting louder—moaning and saying things but he tried to block it out. He was almost there, Madge. "Just stay with me," he said. He slid his hands in front and felt how surging hot she was.

"Madge, Madge," he uttered, his body shuddering with the beginnings of an orgasm.

"Don't come in me!" A very loud voice—still not Madge's—said. He opened his eyes and Julia was getting off of him and turning around. She was getting back down on her knees again and bringing him into her mouth. He wanted her to stop—no, this wasn't right. He lifted a hand to steady himself on the wall.

"Shit, shit," he said, squinting his eyes shut. He tried to stem the tide. He jerked his pants up and stuffed his shirt into them, pushing her to the ground. He met Julia's eyes only for a moment before squeezing his way past the dumpster and back out into the street, alone.

TWENTY-SEVEN

2002 2003 2004 2005 2006 2007 2008 2009 2010 2011 **2012**

May 14th, 2012 – New York City, New York

Then he'd gotten very, very drunk. That must be why he hadn't remembered the encounter. He'd ended up stumbling back home, completely forgetting about the board meeting. It was good that Dobbs was overly familiar with Burke's habit of botching important dates.

Dobbs McGregor had a great relationship with Burke's doorman and showed up at seven a.m. the morning of the board meeting, armed with coffee and Alka Seltzer.

After replaying the past 48 hours, Burke felt better about his mental condition. He felt relieved that he didn't have Alzheimer's or something worse. It was just a blackout—that he could handle.

He was, however, mourning the coffee shop, Aroma. He clearly could not go back again until Julia stopped working there. A real shame—a good coffee shop is hard to find in New York.

Sure, they're a dime a dozen, but so few have the light

pouring in the windows. So few have just the right mix of hipsters and professionals. Only Aroma had papers from each major news source in the world hanging on the rack—Japanese, Chinese, French, Arabic, and yes, even Cuban. It was part of their whole "global" thing. He doubted anyone besides him even looked at most of the papers. But the employees—including Julia—dutifully hung them out every morning, clamped by large wooden sticks to keep them each together. There were few places he could sit and read newspapers without being bothered.

What a fucking shame it was to lose Aroma.

Burke forced himself to look forward. *Find a new place*, he told himself. *This place is nice. A few too many handlebar mustaches, but tolerable.* It irritated him immensely to have to tweak his morning routine to include a new shop. This meant a new walking route, and a deciding on a new path to work.

Since he'd sworn never to leave New York again, his world had continued shrinking. No airplanes. No subways. No cabs. No bridges. No travel of any kind. This made his transition to head anchor much easier. He didn't have to worry about giving up travel for his job; being anchor required that he stay put.

"No time like the present, I suppose," he said to himself. He looked at his phone clock. It was now six-thirty a.m., time for him to head into the office. Most days, when he wasn't too hung over to function, he got to the office a little before seven a.m. This allowed him to do his own perusing of the world's news before his staff began inundating him with things like today's "social media buzz" and "trending topics."

He emerged onto the street and took a few steps out from the shop to see the name of this coffee shop. Irving Roasters on 79th Street and Columbus. He decided to walk down Broadway towards Rockefeller Center. He estimated it would take about thirty minutes, but he was invigorated by the idea of a crisp morning walk.

Broadway was the most efficient way downtown, which made it a good choice for his morning route; but it was also diagonal, which bothered him in some way. He was so used to the gridded, straight-line streets deciding literally everything for him. He let it go for now and decided to just revel in the walk.

When walking from Aroma, Burke would always take the same route to work. He found comfort in memorizing the streets, the blocks, the people. He knew every flower shop and bar on 72nd all the way to Central Park, which he would cut through. This was a great route—city and nature coming together to form a perfect balance of what man created in harmony with the earth. He savored every second of his morning walk. He walked the two and half blocks to cross back in front of his own building, the Dakota. He loved this part. He passed the Dakota as if he were just another person on the street, marveling at its architecture and pondering over the tourists who sat scattered around the building, waiting for a celebrity to emerge. He pretended he was like them for a moment—and then slowly and purposefully let the idea wash over him that he lived there: the most famous apartment building in New York. This was his home.

The high from this really fueled his jaunt through the park. Most days he turned around two or three times to see The Dakota cresting over the trees, nestled in with the rest of the New York buildings that fringed the edge of the park. He just wanted to ensure it was still there—that it still belonged to him.

About halfway into the park, his building would disappear behind the tree line and he would turn his attention to his immediate surroundings. He would take the trails that leapt through the landscape until he emerged at 7th Avenue and 59th a completely new man. He was ready to take on captains of industry, world leaders, revolutions, wars—whatever the human race had to throw at him today, he was ready for it.

The invincibility usually lasted until he got over to 6th Avenue, which was always thronging with tourists. It was hard to navigate through the sea of people without some folks stopping him to ask for autographs. He thought every day about going one block farther to avoid the crowds, but he just couldn't justify the inefficiency.

The six blocks passed without too much hassle and he found himself at the center of the universe. Rockefeller Center, which housed his news station, NBC, in the top of the Rock.

When he'd returned from Cuba, he'd found himself without a job and without a story. Even Dean couldn't help him, but they had kept in touch a little over the years as unlikely friends. The CIA refused to claim him for fear of an international incident, and had told him "off the record" that if he ever shared any piece of what had happened, he would end up in Guantanamo for treason.

The word treason had frightened Burke, and he complied with their demands. Many times over the years he'd put pen to paper to write the memoir of his time with Madge, just so that he could be closer to her by being in Guantanamo Bay, but his inner coward always won.

Burke had turned to the only woman he could for comfort—Elizabeth Waller. She provided little in the way of ease, at least nothing compared to the bottles of dark rum he kept in every room of their apartment. Even he was surprised when she agreed to marry him and buy him his own apartment in the Dakota for those times when he "needed to be alone." All she asked was that he attend parties with her and occasionally extol her virtues to her socialite friends. In addition to her generosity, she put in a good word for him on a news anchor gig on local New York Channel One. That was the four a.m. gig—he'd always shown up on time, despite whatever ills remained from his binge the night before, because he never wanted Elizabeth to look bad. The small bits of clarity he could achieve through his miserable despair were those of intense gratitude for Elizabeth, as well as compounded shame at failing to be even half a husband to her. He never could've been a real partner to her because he belonged to someone else entirely.

He devoted himself to Madge's absence so completely that his life went on without him. He moved up the ranks quickly from morning show anchor to evening news anchor. He remained at New York One for several years as the evening news anchor—a choice breeding ground for network anchor candidates. It only made sense that he would be chosen by NBC as their evening news anchor when Tom Brokaw retired. Liz always put in a good word for him, even after their amicable divorce.

He passed Tiffany's on 59th and 6th where he'd bought her wedding ring. It was in 2003; the city was still a catastrophe—mentally and physically—from 9/11. "The number of engagements has tripled, Mr. Burke," the saleswoman had told him. "It's as if people have realized that life is temporary after all." He purchased the ring Liz had picked out with a credit card that was paid for through Liz's own checking account.

Back in the now, he pulled out his phone and began the business of composing a text while walking down a crowded street.

To Liz: *Was thinking about you. Walking by Tiffany's. How's tricks?*

They still spoke occasionally. He'd run into her the other night, having oysters with a long-time friend. "Liz is fine, she's always been resilient," he said to himself, trying to negate the gnawing feeling he couldn't shake. Was it guilt?

His phone buzzed as he walked up the steps of the Rockefeller Building.

From Liz: *Oysters were good. It's best to let sleeping dogs lie, Burkie.*

He knew she was right, although his throat suddenly felt dry, like parchment paper. He got in the elevator and checked his watch. It was 7:03. Thirty-three minutes. He cursed the new route to work, blaming all these feelings on getting out of his routine.

Riding up the elevator, he wondered if there was any way to make it up to Julia so that he could go back to Aroma and have his old walking route back. He set himself a reminder to send her something—a heartfelt card and some flowers, possibly.

He could endure a well-intentioned relationship for a few months if it meant he could have the invincibility of his old routine back. Coffee at Irving Roasters coupled with walking down Broadway had turned him into a sour, regretful, neurotic old man. That just would not do.

He took a deep breath as the doors opened on the 33rd floor. The buzzing of computers, phones, and interns put him at ease. Just because he was having a mental breakdown didn't mean the news had stopped.

Work had always been his saving grace. When his entire world fell apart, it was the news that had picked him back up, dusted him off and handed him to the world on a platter. It was the only thing he could trust in this world. No matter how drunk, strung out, depressed or feral he was—he could clean himself up and do the news. It was what made him the best.

"Mr. Burke, today's main stories are on your desk—North Korea's threatening the US with nuclear weapons. The team's briefing in the War Room in fifteen," the news desk manager said.

"But it's only seven—" he broke in, looking at his watch again. Normally the team didn't brief until ten a.m.

"Familiarize yourself with the stories on your desk. Gabby's trying to get a statement from the White House."

He picked up his pace, but not enough for people to notice. This was typical on a big news day. The North Korea thing must've just broken during his walk in. Goddamn social media—it made everything move so fast.

He peeked his head in Dobbs' office. "A briefing at seven-twenty a.m.? Have you people gone totally nuts? From seven to ten is my Zen time. You know that. I can't work like this," Burke said it half joking. They both knew he was as much a diva as Bette Midler, but he still kept his sense of humor about it.

"Burke, North Korea's going ballistic. Then there's Syria and also the Cuban story. This one is so good. We've got a line on a special interview with a member of the tech team that attempted to develop a sort of Cuban Twitter. Turns out they were secretly working for the NSA. Sweeps are next week and I need everyone on their game! Briefing in ten!" Dobbs was calling to him down the hall now as he backed toward the kitchen, empty coffee cup in hand.

Burke continued down the hall to his office. He walked in and shut the door. He faced the closed door and, inhaling deeply, he pushed his head gently into the wood.

"Deep breaths," he chanted. "Feel your feet on the floor. Relax your muscles…"

"Hello, sir," a small voice said from behind him.

TWENTY-EIGHT

2002 2003 2004 2005 2006 2007 2008 2009 2010 2011 **2012**

May 14th, 2012 – New York City, New York

"Uh, hello?" Burke said turning around, surprised.

"Are you a Mister Richard Burke?" A young boy sat in his oversized chair. It made him look much smaller than just a boy—he looked miniature. He was slight with tanned skin and golden brown hair. Something about his eyebrows made Burke's heart start racing.

"I'm sorry, yes, I thought I was alone—I mean, I didn't know anyone was in here." Burke turned around and reached for the doorknob. He thought maybe he'd turned into the wrong office, or that Dobbs was using his office as a waiting room for this unexpected guest. "Does Dobbs know you're in here?"

"Sir, may you please sit down? I having urgent matters to discuss with Mr. Richard Burke."

"Yes, that's me. Okay, I'll sit for a minute, but they said they need me in the briefing…"

The boy unzipped his travel vest. He reached inside,

undid another pocket, and pulled out a Ziploc bag full of papers. Beneath the vest he wore a stained white t-shirt with jeans and tennis shoes. He could've been nine or thirteen. Burke had never been around children and had no idea how to tell their ages.

"Who are you, son?" Burke asked, sounding patronizing even to himself.

"Yes!" The boy's voice rose eight octaves. "Yes! So you already know! Yes, I am your son, Mr. Richard Burke. I am Angelo Cruz. Am very relieved that you are already knowing. I was having very bad nerves to tell you myself. Yes, I am overwhelmed, sir. I am dreaming of this day my whole life." His hands were shaking and a smile pinched his cheeks back to reveal two crooked front teeth standing alone. There were other teeth in his mouth, but they were crowded towards the back, laying in wait for the day when the front ones no longer needed the spotlight.

Burke stared at him blankly. "No, I didn't mean 'son' like you're my son, I meant—did you say your last name was Cruz?"

"Yes, sir—father, I mean dad—I am able to call you dad? Dad, my mother is Magdalena Cruz. This is the letters she has given me to send to you." He pulled the papers from the baggy and Burke lunged across the desk where Angelo's hand met his. Their hands touched for a moment and Burke looked into his eyes. They were her eyes. Dark, kind, mysterious eyes that held all the world.

Burke could feel the tears swelling, the bridge of his nose tingling at the thought of touching his own son—a son with half of Madge's DNA. He was the two of them together. In a way, it was as if they had been together all along.

He tried to push the flood of shame down but it began to rush through him—the shame of everything he'd done in her absence. Tears started pouring from his eyes as he gently took the paper from Angelo's hand. "I'm sorry—it's just... it's been a very long time since I saw your mom and I—I miss her very much."

"I am missing her too, sir—I mean Dad. I have only been gone from her for six days, and I'm missing her very much. Trust me, she has been missing you too." Angelo saw Burke hovering distractedly over the paper. "I need a bathroom. Can you show me how to go there?"

"Um." Burke wiped his eyes with a tissue from the box in his desk drawer. "It's just down the hall, last door on your right."

Burke's fingers caressed the cream-colored paper, still warm from Angelo's breast pocket. She had touched this. This had been in her hands. He lifted the fold and began to read, slowly, savoring every word.

My love,

I hope like hell you haven't forgotten me. By now you've met our son, Angelo. He is a wonder. I know that God sent him to me because I could not bear this world without you. Our last few days together I was suffering through the pains of very early pregnancy. I came back to the room to find you and heard them threaten you. I was coming to tell you we were going to have a child.

He is like you in so many ways, which you'll discover. There's so much to say and yet the blank page is staring at me. I want to tell you how it's been for me these past years, but I don't want to make you feel any guilt. All I want you to feel now is love— overwhelming, unabridged love. I know why you didn't come back, and I know you did it to protect me. I am alive, I am well—though some wounds take longer to heal, and losing you is a chronic illness that I battle every day.

I've done things I'm not proud of, Burke. I have made missing you an occupation, and I have tried to quit it so many times. I have tried to forget you. But every morning I wake to see you in our son.

I devoted my life to Angelo, to raising him, to educating him here in Cienfuegos—he learns Castro's Cuba at school, but I teach him the Cuba of the people at home. I taught him English as we walked in the fields from his school each day. I've told him the great stories of our love, of how we met, of my time as a revolutionary.

There is something you need to know about Angelo. He has a talent with machines. First it started with fixing cars in the neighborhood, and then vacuum cleaners and ceiling fans when he was five and six. At eight he built his first computer. At nine he hacked out of the government's firewall at a computer in the lobby of a hotel. (Remember the Hotel Royaliza? I wonder if this was all just a daydream for you...) He is eleven now—he and two of his friends have gotten into trouble. They've been helping to spread a texting network called ZunZuneo. It is a social thing for fun and it showed up a few years ago. But Angelo has gotten in over his head. I think the CIA is behind it. I can't tell you why, but I feel it in my gut. A lot of Cuban people use ZZ on their phones.

A few weeks ago, a secret police officer and an investigator came to our apartment. We're used to regular security checks, but this was different. He didn't know who he was looking for, just that *someone had been using a computer in our house. I told him I didn't know anything, but they'll be back. They took Angelo's laptop and I'm terrified of what they'll find. I had to send Angelo to you to protect him.*

I gave all my money to a coyote—a smuggler—to get Angelo to New York. That is where I hope you are. Where I hope against hope that he is now, too. He is a smart boy. I pray to God he gets to you.

My love, there is so much unspoken between us, but Angelo needs you now. Please find a way to keep him safe.

My windows ache,
-Madge

Burke lifted the page to reveal more of her perfect, swoopy handwriting.

P.S. My Neruda was burned the night you left, but it's gotten easier to get books. My love for Neruda has almost been eclipsed by Rumi. Almost. This poem is like a balm for my aching heart:

A moment of happiness,
you and I sitting on the verandah,
apparently two, but one in soul, you and I.
We feel the flowing water of life here,
you and I, with the garden's beauty
and the birds singing.
The stars will be watching us,
and we will show them
what it is to be a thin crescent moon.
You and I unselfed, will be together,

> *indifferent to idle speculation, you and I.*
> *The parrots of heaven will be cracking sugar*
> *as we laugh together, you and I.*
> *In one form upon this earth,*
> *and in another form in a timeless sweet land.*
> *-Rumi*

Burke read and re-read the letter until there was a strong knock on his door.

"I see you met our source," Dobbs said. "He's the next Elian Gonzalez, but even better. He's like Elian Gonzalez meets Biz Stone. People love child prodigies, so they'll love a refugee child prodigy even more." He was almost salivating.

Burke had wiped his eyes and blown his nose before Dobbs even looked at his face. "Wait, Angelo is your source? You're going to put him on the show?"

"That's right, Burke, to be interviewed by the best in the business—you."

Burke looked at Dobbs and tried to decide if there were any way he could possibly understand what had transpired over the last fifteen minutes. It was safe to say that Dobbs was Burke's only close friend. He'd picked Burke up off the darkest street corners and nursed more hangovers than Betty Ford. And there was no way Burke was letting Dobbs put Angelo on his show.

"Dobbs, I have to tell you something."

"The briefing's about to start, there's no time," he reached for the door of Burke's office. Burke reached out and gently, but firmly, pushed it shut again.

"No, I have to tell you this now. Sit down." Burke put a hand on Dobbs' shoulder and guided him to the armchair. He moved to face him, sitting on the front of his desk. "You can't use Angelo as a source, Dobbs." The words left him like a puff of smoke.

"What, what have you been taking? This could be the Peabody story, Burkie!"

"No Dobbs, it isn't. It can't be—because he's my son."

"I can't just—" Dobbs continued on as if he hadn't heard Burke, and then he stopped cold. "The Cuban girl? The one that you...?"

Burke hadn't filled Dobbs in on all the classified details, but he had told him that he'd been in love once. With a Cuban girl. "Yes. He's my son. His mother, Magdalena and I—she put a letter in his vest. I know he's mine. He's in trouble, possibly with the CIA or NSA—we can't put him on the show. It could be really dangerous for him. Please, Dobbs. I've got to protect him."

"What are the odds he's yours? Anyone can write a letter," Dobbs's eyebrows were furrowed. He looked up at me, his bloodshot eyes considering all the angles.

I grabbed his shoulders and looked intensely at him. "Trust me. This is real."

"Alright, look. I'm going into this briefing and telling them we're leading with the North Korea story, and to fill in with Syria. They may push to report Angelo's Cuban Twitter story. What do I tell them?"

"Just say he didn't check out—he's a kid, say he was embellishing."

Dobbs nodded, rubbing the stubble on his chin. He looked sad for a second and then opened his mouth to speak. He shut it again and turned to the door.

"Thanks, Dobbs," Burke sighed.

"If you get this mess cleared up I'd still like to interview him. Maybe Diane can do it, or Barbara. Do you think it's a conflict of interest for you to interview your long-lost son?" Dobbs looked hopeful.

"Maybe we can work something out. For now, I've got to make a few phone calls. Can you send the kid back in here?"

Burke's mind was racing and, in a way, he felt like his old self again. Was he really going to do this? The self he had lost somewhere amid the sugar cane and creaking floorboards of Cuba. Twelve years. It had been twelve years, yet it felt like he had never left. A ghost of himself had been roaming Manhattan, focusing on all the wrong things. But being his old self meant that he could fix things, he could do this. He began to form the groundwork of a plan.

Angelo opened the door of his office and Burke immediately wondered what a father would do in this situation. He was on unsure ground. Would a hug be appropriate? Should he offer Angelo a drink? Not booze, of course; he was too young for that. What did eleven-year-old boys like? He thought of himself as an eleven-year-old in Iowa. He remembered root beer and baseball cards and riding his bike around the outskirts of his small hometown. He remembered his father—a figure that loomed so tall in his mind—his presence rooted in fear, respect, and underneath everything, an endless sea of love.

It hit him like a sheet of rain that now he would have to be that for his own son. He, whose moral compass was not only broken but completely smashed.

"Dorothy," Burke said into the speakerphone on his desk. "Run down to the Mexican Market on Columbus and 42nd and grab some Coca Colas in the bottles. Also a few candy bars, some plantain chips and maybe a pack of baseball cards. Thanks." He took his finger off the button and looked hard at Angelo. "I want to help you start to feel at home. I've got a plan for how to get you out of trouble, but I'll need to ask you some questions first. Then we're going to call some of my friends and see what we can do to make things better for you and your mom." Burke tried to sound as reassuring as possible without giving away his ace in the hole.

His mind wouldn't stop buzzing with the possibility that he could get Madge out. He could bring Madge to New York and the three of them could be a family. He could and he would get her out, or he would die trying.

"Okay, Dad." Angelo smiled a big toothy smile. "It is getting easy to remember to call you Dad, Mister Richard Burke."

Burke chuckled as he pulled out a sheet of paper from the clean white stack to his right. He laid it in front of him over the leather inlay and began taking notes. The inlay was ridged and worn from the years of writing notes on top of it.

"Yes, okay. Now Angelo—what can you tell me about this ZunZuneo business?"

"ZunZuneo is like what Americans would call social network. But, since in Cuba we aren't allowed internet, it is based in text messages, like from cell phone to cell phone. All the cell phones are supported by the state company CubaCel. Some men came to our school six months ago and asked my teacher who in class was best with computers and science and these things. She is nice when she tells them me, and Adolfo and Sergio."

"Wait, if Cubans don't have internet, how did you learn to hack?"

"There is internet in the lobbies of the hotels so that tourists don't realize how cut off from the world Cuba is." Burke nodded and motioned for Angelo to continue. "Anyway, my friends Sergio and Adolfo, we are three friends who like computers and coding and things like this. But truly Sergio is more good at coding than me or Adolfo. Anyway, these guys said they're working for ZunZuneo and they need some help. Would any of us like to volunteer to help spread a social network across Cuba. We said yes because they let us code on an open interface which none of us had ever been allowed before.

"Once, I hacked out of government's security in the hotel, but that was the closest I ever seen to the real internet like what's here in America."

Burke was writing furiously. "And who were these guys. Did they recruit anyone else but you three?"

"They were only using of their first names. Like, I think one of them was Angel. I remember because it's like my name without the O. Maybe one of them was something like Paolo?"

"Wait, okay—Paolo? Can you tell me what he looked like?"

"Was tall, thin guy. A little bit older than the others. Seemed like he is leading them, or something strange like that. He would say things like, 'we need to monetize the system,'" Angelo sat up straighter and spoke with a thicker accent, pretending to be someone else, "and weird things like that. They all spoke English to each other when they didn't want us to understand. They do not know I speak it too." He smiled his big grin again, and Burke recognized a particular brand of confidence that must be genetic.

Burke was taking notes, but he was thinking hard at the same time. Paolo. How could he be involved with a project like this? And how could he not know that Angelo was Magdalena's son? Hadn't he kept an eye on her, hadn't he helped them get through tough times? Where had he been hiding, only to pop up in the same town on a completely different assignment twelve years later?

"Okay, so there's Paolo, Angel and one other guy?"

"Yes. Is one other guy. He is the coder—he was like a god to us. He is called only by his hacker name while we were around: C0nd0r. You say it like condor but the O's are zeroes because that is really cool for a hacker to do. It is good because condor is the same word in Español.

"If I was a hacker I would want my name to be Crash Proxy. That is really cool, no?" He looked to Burke for approval, but his father was still looking down at the paper, taking notes. "Crash Proxy," Angelo said again, this time quieter to himself, just to enjoy the sound.

"Okay, Crash—tell me what happened next," Burke said, looking at Angelo from under shaded lids.

"Okay, three guys and us—three kids—we are going with them after school to work on a project for ZunZuneo. ZunZuneo needs money, they tell us, or it will have to shut down. They say the investor will not put any more in. They say all this in English when they think we are not listening. What they say to us is more like, 'Hey kids can you help us code some of this for extra credit, and maybe a bonus project later on?'

"We are learning to code most afternoons, just little things like improvements to the software and the way things worked. Sometimes C0nd0r would call Sergio over to look at some things—he would be inside the CubaCel infrastructure. It was so cool to see how he hacked into there."

"What was he doing inside CubaCel?"

"Well, CubaCel was making all the money from ZunZuneo since it's based in text messages. Every time someone would text, it cost money and CubaCel is where the money goes. My mom says CubaCel is owned by the Castros, but the Castros say it is owned by the people."

Burke felt a strong pain any time Angelo mentioned his mother. He tried to breathe through it and kept taking notes.

"So, I think C0nd0r was trying to reroute the money ZunZuneo was making into their bank account. He could never get it to work though."

"So eventually ZunZuneo would run out of money," Burke

said, "Because they were being funded by the outside but there was no way to make money inside Cuba. Right?"

"Right," Angelo was eyeing the door, no doubt wondering when his sweets would arrive.

"She should be here with those cokes any minute. But tell me the part about why you're in trouble?"

"Well, I am not knowing so much. Last week that guy we talked about before, Paolo, walks me home from ZunZuneo. He is saying that the project is dead, that he won't need our help anymore, but he will make sure I get the extra credit for helping. He says there is no money and the company can't keep giving money to CubaCel because it's against the goal. They want to give Cuban people a free voice, not make the Castros richer. He walks me to our apartment door and my mom comes to the door. She sees Paolo and slams door in his face, very loud. She starts screaming, and Paolo is on the other side saying 'Magdalena, Magdalena, I didn't know!' and she is screaming curse words I never heard in English and Spanish. She is saying 'Fuck you Paolo, CIA Pig, how can I believe you didn't know. This is my fucking son. Get the fuck out of here. Fuck. Fuck." Now Angelo is being gratuitous because he can.

"Okay, pal, enough with the bad language. I mean I don't care or whatever, but not in the office... we have to be professional here." Burke felt strange telling him not to curse—who was he to judge? But he also didn't want Dorothy walking in, arms full of Coca Cola and candy, and witnessing what amounted to a poker game in the army barracks.

"Okay, okay. But really, she said it a lot of times. This is when she starts running the house, gathering things and making calls on a cell phone she hides in the bathroom ceiling. And now I am here. Which I am very glad of because she has told me of you since I was little and I loved you so much in my imagination, and now you are here and I can love you in person."

Burke leaned back in his leather office chair, which squeaked loud as he reclined. He placed his hands behind his head and stretched. Air flowed into his lungs and he closed his eyes.

When he opened them again, Angelo was up examining the pictures on his desk. "Is this mamá?" he asked.

"It's supposed to be," Burke replied, picking up the small, square frame. Inside it was a cocktail napkin on which Burke had drawn what he could remember of Madge's face. He'd been obliterated on whiskey and water at the time, and he'd been overcome with a terror so real—an unreasonable terror—that he would forget what she looked like.

He didn't have any photos of her; there were no mementos of their time together. As time went on in New York, he began to feel she was only a figment of his psyche. The drawing was recognizable, but only just. His shaky hand had not done her justice.

Dorothy barged in unannounced—bearing an armful of Cuban sweets and sodas. Angelo looked ravenous as he walked back around the desk and pulled up the chair opposite Burke.

"This is no breakfast for a kid his age." She was talking to herself. She'd spent so many years giving unheard advice that she rarely directed it at anyone anymore. "He needs protein, fruit, he needs to grow."

"This is just to hold us over until I make some calls. Then I'll take him for a steak or something," Burke mumbled, looking through a small black book on his desk.

"Steak for lunch, are you crazy? He'll get heartburn and have nightmares." She continued towards the door.

"Thank you, Dorothy," Burke said, rolling his eyes at Angelo who reflected the motion back. The boy was halfway through one bottle of coke already.

"Okay, buddy. I've got a friend at the CIA I'm going to call. Can you sit tight for a few minutes with your snacks?"

Angelo gave a thumbs up as he dove headfirst into a crunchy chocolate bar. The number Burke had for Agent Wright was disconnected. He pulled up Google and ran a few searches for the generic switchboard at Langley.

"Office of Public Affairs," a young man's voice said on the other end of the line.

"Yes I'm trying to reach a Dean Wright, he's an old friend and I have... information about a case we worked on together."

A pause. "Sir, do you mean CMO Dean Wright, or Deputy Director Dean Wright?" Burke realized he didn't know, because he hadn't talked to Wright in years.

"Wow, a lot has changed since I last talked to him," Burke muttered to himself. "Uh, the one with the beer paunch and the sad eyes."

"Usually around here, you'll need to be more specific than that. But you're referring to the Deputy Director, I believe. I can put you through to his admin, but you'll need to leave a message with her. He doesn't take unscheduled phone calls."

At this point he normally would've dropped his name and the network he anchored for. Usually this opened a few doors, but he had a feeling the CIA didn't want the press calling them about anything. "Alright, that's totally fine."

The ring was a low whir, not the high-pitched alarm bell ring he pictured.

"Deputy Director Wright's office. Patty speaking,"

"Hi Patty, listen. I know that Dean doesn't take unscheduled calls but I've got a serious situation that has to do with a case we worked many years ago in Cuba. I need to speak with him urgently."

"Who is this?" The young voice seemed nonplussed.

"My name is Richard Burke. Back then I was a reporter

for NPR and he and I worked together for a short time on a classified case."

"Richard Burke. Right. Johnny, can't you think of anyone better to prank call me with? Burke is tired and everyone knows it. What is your weird obsession with anchormen? Even Ron Burgundy would've at least been funny. Besides," her voice lowered to a whisper, "I have a real important, serious"—she hissed the word like a snake—"job now. You can't keep calling me like this."

"Patty." Richard said it in the most anchor-like tone he could manage. Angelo looked up from his baseball cards. "This is Richard Burke. And yes, I am tired. Tired of you not listening. Leave a message on Dean's desk as soon as we hang up. Take out a pen right now and start writing. Tell me when you're ready."

"Uh, I'm ready," she said, quietly humiliated, but seemingly convinced.

"Write this: Dean, Richard Burke called, period. Covered in aphids, that's a-p-h-i-d-s. Urgent. Call him back immediately." Burke gave the number to his office and to his cell phone.

"Deputy Director Wright is in a briefing until eleven. I'll make sure he gets this as soon as he returns."

"Could you have someone run it into the meeting to him?" Burke risked sounding desperate. "Lives are at stake."

"Sir, not to be crass, but every meeting the DD attends is usually the result of lives being at stake."

"I'd say we passed crass about three minutes ago," Burke said angrily and hung up the phone. The girl had sounded young. Pretty, even. He kept hearing her voice again and again, Burke is *tired, tired, tired.* And everyone knows it. He had to shake his head like a dog to stop the echo.

Was he tired? Washed up? Was that what people thought

of him—what people said about him when he wasn't around? Most of the time he walked around in a fog of complacency, convinced that everyone—especially young women—thought he was worldly, accomplished, distinguished, and trustworthy. This was what he'd always known about himself—but what if what he'd always known was fading away, or worse, had never been there in the first place?

"Hey, kid." Burke had meant the word *kid* to come out like a term of endearment, but it sounded like he was calling an orphan on the streets of Calcutta. "Angelo. My friend is going to call me back soon and we'll figure this out. For now, can you tell me more about your mom and what's going on in Cuba these days? Is she still working with revolutionaries? Do we need to..." Burke was going to say *hurry*, as if there were reason to rush to get Madge out. He was trying to ascertain if she was in some kind of trouble, but Angelo broke into tears.

The sobs were so complete that Burke sat shocked for a moment. "Angelo—I'm sorry. I know you must miss your mom." Burke had to fight a sob himself because, although empathy was not his strong suit, on this particular topic, he could feel Angelo's pain like a dark shadow inside himself. He stood up and went to the boy, patting him awkwardly on the shoulder and then crouching down to hug him. Angelo fell into his arms willingly. Tears streamed down both their faces. Angelo took an arm to his eyes and nose, and gave them a long hard wipe.

The streaks left behind made Burke think to take him home where the boy could shower and clean up. Being up close, he remembered how pungent prepubescent boys could be, especially after a long hard journey like Angelo's. But he realized he wasn't sure what his obligation to the station was today, or if Angelo's presence was a free pass for a day off.

"Hold on just a minute, can you, son?" Burke stood up,

ruffling the boy's hair. It felt so soft in his hand, he almost crumbled touching it.

He realized how many years he'd missed out on, all in an instant. "Everything's going to be okay," he managed to say. Burke turned to head for the door of his office, the sounds of Angelo's whimpers behind him.

Burke searched the hallways for Dobbs but realized that everyone was probably still in the briefing. If he walked in now, there would be a lot of questions. Unfortunately, there was no other option. The calendar on his phone said he was scheduled to do a live interview of Adora Green, a southern television chef with a penchant for cooking sherry and young, black male production assistants. The former had gotten her into hot water with the latter. This interview was set to be her public explanation and apology. Not something he could really reschedule or opt out of.

Burke leaned his head in the door of the briefing room—"Dobbs, a word?"—and then back out again before anyone could draw him into the conversation.

Dobbs looked annoyed as he stepped out into the hallway. "What is it now, Burkie?"

"I've got some things I need to sort out here. I'm going to need a few days off," Burke said. "To take care of the kid and all. And to find out what the hell is going on."

"Tonight's the Green interview. She said she'll only talk to you—you know how these older women are. They need someone they can trust. You've got to be on tonight and I don't have time to reschedule. I can find a fill-in for the next few nights."

"What about the rest of today? Can someone work on my questions for Green while I take the kid home and get him cleaned up?"

Dobbs sighed and rubbed a hand up and down his face.

"Be back here at five o'clock sharp—no, four-thirty. Someone can hang with the kid while you get ready and maybe he can watch you on set, if he can keep quiet."

"Dobbs, I won't tell anyone, but you're a seriously decent guy. And a good friend," Burke said, clapping his boss on the shoulder.

"A reputation takes years to build, seconds to destroy." Dobbs snuck a smile in as he headed back into the room where an argument had broken out. "Hey, hey, simmer down," Burke could hear him saying as the door closed behind him.

TWENTY-NINE

2002 2003 2004 2005 2006 2007 2008 2009 2010 2011 **2012**

May 14th, 2012 – New York City, New York

Angelo and Burke zipped down a crowded 5th Avenue towards the park. Barista be damned. Burke was not going to sacrifice his fastest route home.

"We'll get you cleaned up and maybe a nap, how does that sound?" Burke was talking into the wind as he pulled a gaping Angelo down the street. The coyote must've dropped him off in front of the building with nothing but the clothes on his back. The boy craned his neck at every tall building and beautiful woman they passed. Burke was flooded with the memory of the first time he had set foot on a New York street. He'd packed everything into two duffle bags and kissed his mother goodbye on their front porch. His father had driven the plow up to the house to see what the fuss was about. Their house—which used to be on an expanse of farmland—now faced an interstate highway where cars flooded before them day and night. The farm expanded behind the house, but any time his father looked at the highway, he felt the world closing in. Burke had returned home from Amherst just the year before, stripped of his aspirations to write and contribute to the world. He'd gained a new respect for his father and for the earth.

He'd taken up residence again in his parent's home, yearning for a simple life. He was already tired of the rat race, having seen his peers drafted into careers of high finance, consulting, and middle management. He yearned for dirt, for strength in his muscles, for sun on his face.

He'd found that living under his father's thumb made his soul itch. His mother doted and swooned as if he were still a boy. He was a man who'd seen things; he had a degree, and a wealth of knowledge. How could his father not take his ideas seriously? He realized he'd made a mistake coming home to Iowa.

So his two duffel bags and he hitched a ride to New York City. It was a story out of Kerouac's playbook. He realized he'd been longing for a place to call home—but there was no such place anymore.

His ride, a Greek man who smelled of stewed tomatoes and smoked clove cigarettes, had driven him from Cincinnati all the way into the city. He'd dropped Burke off at the edge of the Brooklyn Bridge on the Brooklyn side before going to meet his wife and daughter at Coney Island. The man had been jolly enough, and told Burke to inquire about lodging at a hostel on Amsterdam Street near Columbia University. "Great place for a young guy like you to end up!"

In his four years at Amherst, he'd never made it into the city. As exhausted as he was that first day in New York, he'd stayed out all day. He walked the bridge into Manhattan, sat on park benches, ate hot dogs and soaked in the wonder of it all. How simple and wide-open everything had seemed then.

Now, he watched Angelo as the city washed over him.

Burke hadn't left the city since returning from Cuba, and he had no intention of ever leaving again. Every time he left, someone got hurt—someone he loved.

Angelo's feet slowed almost to a drag as they drew closer to the park and Burke realized how tired his son—still strange to think it—was. Burke raised his hand to hail a cab.

The taxi puttered up to the curb right on cue, and the two of them rode the few remaining blocks to The Dakota in near silence. Burke frantically tried to find a conversation topic that wasn't Madge. He scrolled through the rolodex of appropriate conversation starters and realized he had none that didn't relate to drugs, sex or news. This was a pitiful way to begin his journey as a father.

When he finally landed onto a neutral topic in his mind, he blurted, "How about that A-Rod, huh? Do you guys in Cuba get to hear how well he's doing with the Yankees?"

When no response came, Burke looked over to see Angelo sleeping against the door of the cab, his face smooshed into the window. Just then Burke's cell phone rang and he looked down to see a restricted number. Worrying he wouldn't get Dean on the phone again, he motioned to the driver to take another turn around the block.

"Burke." He answered the phone officially.

"Old Dick Burke, what have you been up to my friend? What's it been, six, seven years?"

"About seven, I'd say, Dean, and it's Richard. Is now and always has been."

"That's right. Richard. So what's this you wanted to talk to me about—I assume this isn't a walk down memory lane?"

"I've got to meet you somewhere, today. It has to do with the case I was on in '01. The one you never let me talk about again—in fact the one that led our friendship astray, if memory serves. How interested would your boss, the Director, be to know about your off-record past?"

"Dick... it's not smart to start with blackmail on a call with a CIA Deputy Director. And that mission—your first and last mission—wasn't off record, it's just better left forgotten since it was such an epic failure."

"You're telling me. I'm sitting in a cab with one of the hackers who worked on a project people are calling 'Cuban Twitter.' I think you may have heard of it—ZunZuneo? There are whispers that the NSA was funding it. My friend here is a Cuban national who just arrived on U.S. soil yesterday. If that hasn't piqued your interest, maybe this will. He's my 11-year-old son."

The other end of the line was dead quiet for the first time since the phone rang. Burke continued.

"I had no idea you've done so well for yourself at the CIA. I've been successful too; you may or may not watch me on NBC?

"Let me tell you—something funny—my producer latched onto this Cuban Twitter story like a wild dog." Burke let out a calculated burst of laughter. "And I happen to know that one of the guys from my operation back in '01, Paolo, is working on this thing. So you can act like the U.S. Government isn't involved but..."

"Alright, Burke. Alright." Dean was not in the mood for details.

"When I found out Angelo was my son, I was able to buy you some time before this whole thing goes public. But not much time. Still want to play games?"

Dean let out a loud and exasperated sigh. "Burke, meet me at Lolita's in the Village. I'll be there by one p.m."

Burke looked at his watch: 9:47a.m. He felt pretty good about getting the CIA Deputy Director to clear his schedule at a moment's notice. "Okay. We'll be there."

Dean sighed and hung up.

The cab driver was looping back around to the front of the Dakota where the doorman moved to open the door for Angelo. "Stop," Burke cried as he burst from his side of the cab. "I got it, I've got him," he said as he scurried to the passenger side of the car. He gingerly opened the door so that Angelo didn't wake up or fall out. This was more of a challenge than he anticipated, and he ended up on his knees easing the snoozing child from the seat ever-so-slowly.

He realized he didn't know how to hold the kid, how to keep his head up or his arms from flailing. Burke nodded to Tony, the doorman, to get his wallet from his back pocket. Tony paid the cabby, keeping his eyes on Burke the whole time. As the cab drove away, Tony whispered, "You've been into some weird shit over the years and I never judged you—but this? I think this is too far." He nodded to the sleeping kid in Burke's arms.

"Tony, please. He's my son; he just got here from Cuba. I didn't even know he existed until two hours ago."

"Oh, now that sounds like the Burke I know," Tony said in his distinct Brooklyn accent, something that he tried over and over to polish away. It always came through on Burke's name, which sounded like *Boy-ke* any time he said it.

THIRTY

2002　2003　2004　2005　2006　2007　2008　2009　2010　2011　**2012**

May 14th, 2012 – New York City, New York

While Angelo slept, Burke tried to pick up his apartment from the morning before. He found a forgotten bra and some pills left on the bathroom counter. He flushed them, and then immediately wished he hadn't. Then he poured himself a drink and sat down to inhale Madge's letter again and again. He imagined the timeless, sweet land that Rumi spoke of, and he realized it was where his mind had been living for the past decade. And it was a comfort to hear that Madge's mind had been living there too, although no one was buying her any condos or rings from Tiffany's. His heart wrenched at that thought more than anything else that day.

Angelo slept in the sun-drenched living room of the apartment until noon, when Burke feared they would miss their appointment and woke him.

"Hey pal, we've got to go meet someone a little ways from here. I wanted to give you time to shower and get cleaned up. I had Tony order you up a few outfits from Saks." Burke drained the last of the whiskey in his glass and uncorked the bottle to pour in a little more. His nerves had been on edge ever since Angelo showed up. Having him here made Burke feel as if Madge were physically in the room with him. His sense that he'd utterly abandoned and disappointed her seemed to grow with every passing second.

Angelo rubbed his sleepy eyes and looked around, confused. "Where are we?" he asked.

"This is my apartment. This is where I live."

"Wow. Is really nice," Angelo stood up slowly and stretched. He ambled through the living room and peeked into the bathroom. "I shower in here?"

"Yes, there's shampoo and everything, and towels hanging outside the shower door."

Angelo went in and Burke heard the sound of the sink running. He flashed to a memory of the bathrooms and plumbing in Cuba and decided to go in and guide him along.

By the time Burke went inside, Angelo had taken the bar soap and lathered it up to put on his hair. He was standing fully clothed. "No, no, it's okay, the water here is clean. That's what this is: a shower. You walk into this area of the bathroom and turn on these knobs. Except, maybe you want to turn on the water first and let it warm up." Burke demonstrated.

Angelo tried to hide his shock and excitement about the shower.

"This is shampoo, and this is body wash—that's soap for, you know, your body. And then that one is conditioner."

"What is conditioner?"

"It goes on your hair after shampoo to keep it from being dry."

"Then why shampoo at all?" He was asking earnestly, and Burke struggled to answer a question he had always wondered himself.

"Because it makes your hair smell better. And gets it clean."

"Okay," Angelo said, stripping off his shirt. "I am showering now. I can have privacy, Dad?"

"Oh yes, sure. I'll put your outfit on the bed in the spare room." As he walked out of the bathroom, he could hear Angelo say, "Dios mio." About the shower, he assumed, which was rather magnificent. He'd had it designed himself to shoot water from all angles. There was no door, just a gap in the tile wall that beckoned one into shower heaven. Burke let the boy enjoy and poured himself another drink.

Lolita's was a quiet place for a late lunch in the West Village. The Mexican food was not that great, but Burke couldn't see Dean wanting to have a meeting at his favorite taco truck. They needed a place off the beaten path with chairs and room to talk.

When they walked in, Dean was already there biting into a corn chip slowly as he looked through a file splayed out on the table. Burke would hardly have recognized him if not for the signature trench coat. He had to admire a government employee who had a sense of humor. Other than that, almost nothing about Dean was the same as Burke remembered. He must've dropped fifty or sixty pounds and his hair had turned from black to heather gray. He sipped a water, not a Corona like Burke had imagined.

Burke put his hand between Angelo's shoulder blades and guided him towards the table where Dean sat.

"Burke, you old son of a—" Burke gestured to him to cut the cursing and wagged his head at the kid. "Well, yes, I mean—It's been a long time," Dean recovered. "You haven't changed a bit."

"Well, you have," Burke exclaimed. "You're wasting away!"

"Yeah, I'm off the sauce and the carbs. I'm a new man," Dean said as he shoved another chip into his mouth.

"You know, chips have carbs…" Burke didn't continue because Dean waved him off.

"Tell me, who's this strapping young buck?" Dean was looking at Angelo with a big smile. Maybe Dean had gotten married and had kids in the years since they'd spoken. He was markedly cheerier and better with children than Burke had imagined he would be.

"This is Angelo, he's my son." Burke said the word with pride for the first time and had to blink away a tingling feeling in his tear duct. He shook his head a bit to clear his mind. "He's the one I told you about on the phone earlier."

Angelo spoke for the first time. "Hello, sir. I am new in America." His white collared polo and khaki pants suited him well. If Burke had seen him on the street, he would've thought he was a student at the Internationale Prep School on 22nd. Just give him a backpack and he would fit right in. Immediately, Burke's mind wandered to tuition costs and admission requirements; he made a mental note to email Dorothy about it.

"Angelo, I need to talk with your dad for a few minutes. But, my friend David has a very cool computer game for you to play. He has it all set up at a table right over there." Burke looked to the other side of the restaurant. A man in the textbook black suit and tie sat across the dining room with a laptop on the table. Burke tried to stop Angelo, but the boy was already typing on the keyboard before Burke could think of what to say.

"Okay, so what the fuck is going on?" Dean's eyes were serious for the first time since they'd arrived. Burke reached into his pocket and pulled out the thick cream paper of Madge's letter. He kept one eye on the boy tinkering with the computer while he slid the paper across the table.

Dean pulled out a swab and passed over the surface of the paper, then repeated it on the other side. "David," he called. "Run this." David walked to the table and took the swab from Dean's hand, then returned to where Angelo was, inserting the strip into a kind of scanner next to the computer. Angelo's fingers were flying on the keyboard.

"Look, I was minding my own business when the kid showed up at the station. My boss had already vetted him and checked him out as a source for this Cuban Twitter thing. I don't know if he used that story to get to me, or if someone tipped off Dobbs—my producer. Angelo might have thought it would look suspicious if he showed up asking for me."

Dean broke in, "Burke, focus."

"Yeah, so he's in my office this morning. I had no idea he even existed. But he handed me the letter and yeah, here we are." Burke put his head in his hands. "Can I get a margarita or something? Or is this just some CIA front—I haven't seen one waitress..."

"David, get Burke a margarita, would you?"

David got up from his table. Angelo continued typing away. Burke looked up to notice that the door was locked, the kitchen was dark.

"We have an arrangement with the owners. Free meeting space. Government jobs do have perks, Burke."

"So let's cut to the chase. Cuban Twitter. What the hell, Dean? Paolo is working on it. He's one of yours. Are we funding third-world-tech-startups with taxpayer dollars?"

"Did Angelo tell you he saw Paolo? How do you know it's

the same Paolo from your mission?"

Burke filled Dean in on the details that Angelo had given him. He continued sipping his water and flipping through the file while Burke talked, stopping him only to ask clarifying questions. David returned a few minutes later with a yellow tinged drink in a martini glass.

"What the hell is this?" Burke asked when he looked at the drink.

"A margarita." David's face was deadpan. Angelo was standing at the computer now, continuing to get more involved in the game he was playing. Burke started to seriously wonder what Angelo was working on.

Burke took a gulp. It was a Lemon Drop, at best. "Is this what you make for your girlfriend when you want her to stay home instead of taking her shift at the strip club?" Burke laughed, continuing to sip the drink.

David reared his hand back as if to smack Burke.

"Simmer down, girls. We're working here. David, if you couldn't make a margarita, you should've said."

"I like the company better over here," said David, who returned to the table with Angelo. He peered at the screen with surprise and gave Dean a head nod as if to say, "The kid is the real deal."

"So what the hell are we going to do, Dean? I took a mulligan for you in '01, but don't think I'm going to do it again. I want her out, she and the boy naturalized as American citizens. Who knows what's happening down there right now? She could be in real danger."

"That's exactly why what you're asking me to do is impossible. Angelo, sure, he's here to stay, but you're asking me to extradite a Cuban national who's been on the watch list for almost twenty years. She's lost to you. You've got to realize that. Taking her out now could cause a major international incident."

"What the actual fuck? She's been dormant for twelve years raising our son. She deserves a life, Dean. A life with her family. We've put her through enough." Burke felt breathless.

"You're asking me to save one person and potentially harm or kill hundreds more. My agents and Cuban citizens could get caught in the crossfire. The Castros are not a priority anymore. We're focused on North Korea, Jordan, Syria—countries with real threat levels. Cuba is the long game—waiting for Fidel and Raul to die. Since Raul took over it's actually been much easier, things have improved. I have a feeling they may re-open the U.S. Embassy in a few years…"

"If that's true, then it shouldn't be hard to get her out." Burke stood firm. "Do you want U.S. citizens to be faced with the reality that the NSA, CIA, and whatever other secret branches you supervise were working on a social media system to try and overthrow the Cuban government? How stupid are you willing to look? Not only that, the program just put millions more dollars in the Castros' pockets through text message fees to CubaCel. Hello, Senate hearings."

Dean sighed heavily and drained the rest of his water while eyeing Burke's Lemon Drop.

Burke continued, "She's more valuable here than there. She has intel that can actually take down the Castros—which must still be a priority since you've resorted to social media…" He smirked.

Dean's face reddened. "Look, it worked in Egypt. The model is currently being piloted in Afghanistan and Kenya with success. Hilary Clinton herself signed off on it. It's the new face of diplomacy. Give people their power back. We want the world to see democracy and this is the best chance we've had in history for that to happen."

Burke instinctively reached for a pen.

"This is off the record!" Dean raised his voice and Angelo looked up from the computer screen. Dean brought his voice back down to a whisper. "Yes, it failed in Cuba. I'm willing to chalk that up to startup costs. But if you put this story out, dictators the world over will squash a great chance their people have at organizing and getting closer to freedom. Who knows how many lives that will amount to? That blood will be on your hands."

It was Burke's turn to drain his drink. "Seems we're at an impasse. This is right about the time a creative solution might come in handy..." he thought for a minute. "Can't we do some kind of covert operation to extract her? You do it all the time."

"Is this what I'm here for, Burke? I get your gal or you go public?"

"I didn't say it like that. But I never can tell what could happen—the media is fierce in this country. I'm mentoring some very good investigative journalists right now... they could find something about this on my desk. Or it could die here."

"You realize how fucking selfish you are, right?"

"Yes. Of course."

Dean exhaled. He put his balled fists on top of each other and closed his eyes. He was thinking. Weighing risks. Developing plans. "All right, I may have an idea. And at least this way I get something out of it, too."

Burke's eyes widened. His excitement was growing at the thought that he might actually have Madge—have her here, in his arms—the two of them finally together again.

"There's a guy, he just surfaced. He's on the most-wanted fugitives list," Dean continued. "He calls himself Rock Solomon. He's a human trafficker of the highest order. This guy delivers tailor-made orders of women and young girls to the world's rich and elite. You want a Brazilian babe with a thirty-eight-inch booty for your sex dungeon? He's your man. A blonde, Swedish twelve-year-old girl for your harem? You call Rock. He's a slippery son of a bitch, and we were just able to identify him before he slipped away again. Our intel says he's here in New York City this weekend for a charity auction." Burke raised a finger to say something and Dean interjected. "Yes, charity auctions in New York City are where he finds some of his best clients. It's sick shit, Burke. And I want him caught. The FBI sent me a memo yesterday that he's earned more money from high dollar sex trafficking than the entire Triad gang. It's in the billions.

"So, here's the plan. We run a sting. A covert CIA-FBI joint task force. You're his next high-dollar client, but this time you need him to up his game. You need not only a Cuban beauty with spirit and an ample—"

"Watch it," Burke snapped.

"Right—you need a specific Cuban person. He delivers to exacting specifications, but he's never had to find an actual, specific person before. He will want a lot of money to do this and it will take some convincing. I'm going to give you a wire, and we've got to act quickly. Once he has the assignment he promises a three-day turnaround. He'll ask for half the fee up front which could be anywhere from $100,000 to $500,000. We can wire you that amount and we'll seize it back when we get him. When he delivers Madge to you, we swoop in and arrest him with all the evidence we need to lock him away forever. Deal?"

"Abso-fucking-lutely." Burke didn't need to consider any other factors. This was what he was going to do. He was getting Madge back—end of story. He looked down at his watch. It was already three o'clock. He'd told Dobbs he'd be in makeup by four-thirty. His heart was pounding. He realized he was going back undercover. Fear coiled in his stomach like a snake. Going undercover had led to the only major failure in his life and had gotten his heart obliterated. And this time, Madge's life was on the line.

"The charity auction is tonight at the Met. It's benefitting St. Jude's Children's Research Hospital. I need you there in a penguin suit at five-thirty to get the tech on."

"Shit—who's going to watch Angelo? And, I'm supposed to—"

"We'll keep him in the surveillance truck with us. He seems pretty at home considering he's just hacked into the Chinese government's mainframe; for five minutes YouTube was accessible to about three billion Chinese people who were very grateful."

Burke whipped his head around and then back to Dean. "How did you...? You were sitting over here with me the whole time."

"I've got a comm in my ear; David's been giving me the play by play while we've been talking. You'll have one of these tonight, too. We've had some pretty awesome advances in tech since '01." Dean reached into his ear and pulled out a little device the shape of his ear canal. "It's got a microphone and a speaker that only you can hear. If you have questions or thoughts, you can speak them quietly and we'll get them loud and clear. We'll also have a camera pinned into your pocket square to get a visual of the crowd and who you're talking to." He picked up another chip, looked it over, then thought better of it and put it back down. "So, you game Burke?"

"I'm supposed to be in makeup at 4:30 so I can interview Adora Green. It's primetime." He sat for a moment, looking to see what kind of reaction Dean would give. "But I can figure something out. Call in a few favors."

"Good, because this may be a once in a lifetime chance to hire Rock, and for the FBI to build a case against him."

"Yeah, I'm getting that. He must be a real pro to have escaped your grasp." Burke meant it as a sideways compliment. Dean laughed his old laugh, the one that sounded like a loud burst. Then his face turned serious.

"But I mean it, Richard." He paused for effect. "Don't screw it up this time."

Burke said nothing as Dean stood and motioned to David to move out. David shut the case, telling Angelo he would see him later. The CIA agent shook the boy's hand in a way that showed he was impressed. Angelo returned to the table with Burke and looked full to the brim with pride.

"Hey, bud," Burke said.

Angelo began to spill all the details of what he had just done on the CIA-man's computer-case. He told Burke of black walls, black nets, government security protocols, and the Chinese government's tracking capabilities when it came to hackers. Burke was half listening. He'd walked to the window to make sure that Dean and David had made a clean getaway. He wanted to leave enough time so that when he left, it wouldn't look as if they'd been together.

Suddenly, a small woman appeared behind the counter and started rolling dough into tortillas. She switched on the heat lamps and turned on all the kitchen lights again. Then she made her way to the front of the restaurant and switched on the neon open sign, which made Burke's face glow red as he stared out the window.

She turned to walk away, then acknowledged him. "Can I get you anything else?" she asked as she went to bus the table he and Dean had been sitting at.

"No," he mumbled. The truth was that the one thing he wanted in his life was finally within his grasp. He remembered the words his Buddhist spiritual advisor—the one he'd gone to for a few weeks a couple of years after leaving Madge—had told him: take life one breath at a time. He could never understand this phrase and he knew now that it was because he hadn't taken a real breath in twelve years. He'd felt so guilty about getting to live this life without Madge, he didn't even feel worthy of breath. Now this part of his life was going to be over—he was going to have her, here—his oxygen. And as he looked back at who he'd become the last twelve years, he wondered if that oxygen might be all it would take to finally set him aflame.

THIRTY-ONE

2002 2003 2004 2005 2006 2007 2008 2009 2010 2011 **2012**

May 14th, 2012 – New York City, New York

Burke's head pounded as he and Angelo got into the cab. He realized that he'd been flying on a jet stream of pure cocaine and poppers until he'd seen Angelo, then switched gears to adrenaline. He was wearing thin.

"Where to now, Dad?" Angelo asked brightly.

"I've got to call in a few favors so that we can do this... thing tonight. The thing where you get to sit in the surveillance truck." Burke wasn't sure what Angelo knew or understood. He tried to keep details to a minimum. He told the cabby to drive around for awhile and tell Angelo about the sights.

"Mister, I'm Armenian. I don't know none of the sights. I just follow the GPS," the cabby shot back.

"Okay, smartass. Take us to the Empire State building. Angelo, I can show you the Statue of Liberty from a hundred and two stories up."

The cabby grudgingly put in the address and they cruised into traffic. Angelo stared upwards out the window, enthralled with the city of his dreams.

Burke drafted a text message to Dobbs:

Just do me this one solid and I'll fucking tackle your sweeps next week. Put a bouquet of 2 dozen long-stemmed red roses in Adora's dressing room. Put on the card: 'TRUST ME. -BURKE'

"This is the Central Park." The cabby gestured halfheartedly to his right. Angelo *ahhhed*.

Burke typed a new message to Barbara Waters:

Want the scoop of your life?

Burke waited while the hook sank into the fish. He looked out at the city with Angelo *oooh*ing and *ahhh*ing at the sights.

He pointed out the statue of General Sherman at the corner of 5th and Park. "When the horse is on its hind legs, it means he died in battle," Burke told Angelo. His head pounded harder and harder. "Hey man, can you make a stop for me? I'll just run in and be right back out. Go to 1900 Park Avenue."

Burke had to find someone who was holding, fast. He knew it was wrong. He'd promised himself no more drugs as soon as Angelo showed up. He needed something to get through this night. To get through what he had to do. After tonight it would be 'Goodbye drugs, Hello Madge.'

"You got it," the cabby replied in his thick accent.

"So this man is the leader here? The man in the statue?" Angelo, oblivious to the cab's new stop, looked confused. Burke had forgotten how different things were in Cuba.

"No, we have a president. President Obama. That man was a general in a war a long time ago."

"And he is important enough to be a statue?" Still more

confusion.

Burke was remembering the statues in the park in Cuba. All of them were of Fidel Castro, with a smattering of Che thrown in.

"In America, we have statues of lots of people, because it takes lots of people to make a country great." Angelo seemed to agree with this and went back to looking out the window.

Burke's phone buzzed with two new messages. *Very eager, eh Barb?* Burke thought to himself.

From: Barb Waters
Burkie, what is it this time?

Burke responded:

I need a favor and last time I checked you owed me. For that little cover up I helped with during the Jeter interview, remember? Anyway, I am supposed to interview Adora Green tonight. She specifically requested me, but I have a huge family conflict. I really need you, Barbie. She won't be expecting you, but use a lot of flattery, talk about how good her food is. Make her see the error of her ways and make it about true sisterhood. You two bond, cry, it will make great TV—and possibly invigorate some opportunities for you?

Burke wrote the last line carefully. They both knew her career needed an infusion of tears and YouTube views. Then he opened the message from Dobbs:

This better be good, asshole.

Burke responded:
TRUST ME.

His phone buzzed again and he could tell he had Barb over a barrel—not like the time in '97 when he literally bent her over a barrel and had his way with her—but in the metaphorical sense.

Barb Waters:
When and where? Is Dobbs expecting me?

Burke:
4:30 p.m., make up room at NBC. I think you know your way around. Dobbs has no idea—let's keep it that way as long as possible.

Barb Waters:
Next time, a little more notice would be nice. I'll be there. Set your DVR, Bitch. ;)

That was just like Barb to throw in a back-handed compliment about the timing of a perfectly amazing opportunity. And the winky-face. Smug. Nonetheless, he breathed a sigh of relief, knowing that his obligation to the station was taken care of. And another sigh came when he felt the cab roll to a stop in front of 1900 Park.

"Hey, bud, I've got to go in and see a friend for just a minute. Will you be okay out here? I promise I'll be right back." He looked at the clock: 3:45. He'd need time to swing back by the apartment for his tux. "Leave the meter running. I'll be right back." The driver nodded and pulled out a flip phone that was ringing.

Burke ran up to the doorman of the building, "Is she in?"

he asked, breathless, his anticipation rising.

"Who would that be, sir?"

"You know who I mean," Burke said. "Don't make me say it."

"I've been instructed not to let anyone into the building who isn't here for a specific resident, sir." His face was stern with a hint of enjoyment in it.

Burke exhaled dramatically. "Trixie Fontanel. May I see Trixie Fontanel, please?"

The doorman buzzed an intercom and whispered into the speaker. "Richard Burke is here, should I let him up?"

"Does he have my money?" a scratchy voice blurted back. The doorman looked at him expectantly.

"Yes, Rebecca—I mean Trixie, I have my checkbook." Burke spoke towards the intercom but was looking towards the taxi to make sure Angelo was alright. The taxi driver was pointing to the tops of more buildings as if he knew their names. Trixie buzzed him up.

"Why do you insist on this ridiculous name? You're a rich girl from Connecticut," Burke said as the gold elevator doors opened on the top floor. The white, faux fur rug trailed into the penthouse apartment with such malaise.

The blonde was lounging, as she always was, in a window seat that was lined with gold trim. She was smoking a cigarette with a cigarette holder, the kind Audrey Hepburn used in *Breakfast at Tiffany's. The cliché is complete,* Burke thought. Her eyes lolled at him.

"It's all about image, Richard. Brand. No one wants a drug dealer named Rebecca Brown. No one wants a drug dealer who's from a nice family in Connecticut. I needed a back-story. Trixie is just more suited to my audience."

"I think the golden elevator and the Park Avenue address earn you the right to be named whatever you want," Burke said, pulling out his checkbook and starting to write.

"Make it to cash, would you?" She started getting up and moved to a pullout drawer in a built-in beneath a flat screen TV. "You're showing your age, Richard. Times have changed. You can't just look the part anymore. You have to be the part, through and through."

He reminded himself not to take professional image advice from his drug dealer. She must be what? Twenty-two? An Ivy League dropout with an ever-soft cushion to land on. His head pounded.

She walked over to him with the rolled-up baggy of powder. "Who's the kid?" she asked, trying to seem interested. She must've seen Angelo from the window.

"He's my—he's my little brother, you know Big Brother, Big Sister thing. I like to give back." He wasn't sure why he'd lied. Did having a son make him seem older? Or was it that he feared her judging him for stopping for drugs with his son in tow? Stopping with his "little brother" wasn't much better.

"Sweet." She said it absentmindedly as she looked out the window. "I should get more involved in the community." She seemed to drift off into a hazy daydream then, and he turned to go, waving the baggy towards her in thanks.

"The check's on the entry table," he called back over his shoulder. She said nothing else and he was relieved. She was a strange and unreliable whisper of a person. But she sold quality goods. Burke was reminded of why she was his favorite dealer when he sniffed the little white mountain out of his palm.

The cocaine shot from his nose straight to his brain. He felt a storm of adrenaline and endorphins being kicked around like a cat in a burlap sack. As the elevator got closer to the ground floor, he felt closer to himself. He took three deep breaths to let the cocaine do its job—he didn't want it to be obvious to Angelo. Just a little kick, that was all he needed. When he had Madge back he wouldn't need the stuff at all.

THIRTY-TWO

2002 2003 2004 2005 2006 2007 2008 2009 2010 2011 **2012**

May 14th, 2012 – New York City, New York

They pulled up to the Metropolitan Museum of Art.

"This is the Met," said the cab driver. "There's some art in there I think, but not sure who it's by. Probably some dead guys." At this he laughed and calculated the meter. Burke, exasperated at the cabby's half-hearted tour, rolled out a few bills from his money clip and paid the man.

"Thank you sincerely, sir," Angelo said to the man. "I much appreciate your information. I am new to this city, too. May we both make it feel like home soon."

Burke was touched at his son's idealism and kindness. The cabby shook Angelo's hand as passing travelers do when they've truly met someone who's worth the journey.

The Met steps sprawled before them. Burke assumed the truck was parked not far away on a side street. The sidewalk was buzzing with tourists and class trips heading back to their busses. The sun was slowly falling below the skyline, giving the sky a periwinkle tinge. The tux Burke had picked up from his apartment stood out, an exclamation point on an odd and beautiful sentence.

"Angelo!" The voice from the sidewalk was David's. "Hey, the guys can't wait to meet you, come get suited up."

"Look man, are you sure it's a good idea to have him in the truck during an operation that involves his mother? I'll have to describe her, maybe say some things he shouldn't hear. I think it's a bad idea for him to be in there with you guys," Burke tried to speak quietly but Angelo was jumping at his feet.

"I can go now, Dad? I can go with David?"

"Hold on, Son."

"We're going to have him watching one of our techs who will be monitoring the cameras and the floor plans. He won't have access to any of the audio. I went over it with Dean." David seemed confident and aware, like anyone who's gone through that level of training. But Madge said Burke needed to protect Angelo, and this didn't feel like protecting.

"Angelo." Burke crouched down, careful not to soil his fresh tuxedo pants. "Listen, some things are going to happen tonight that are going to be very important for our family. If you see anything that upsets you, just don't panic. These guys are professionals and they know what they're doing. Stay calm and I'll see you in a little while, okay?"

"Yes, Dad, yes. I can please go with David now?" The boy was too excited to have heard anything Burke said. Burke had never listened to his father, so why would his son listen to him? He stood and brushed the wrinkles from his suit, watching Angelo sprint to the side street where he jumped in the back of a white van marked *Athena's Catering: The Food of the Gods*. There were three identical vans parked on either side of this one. The one closest to Burke housed a man stacking trays of glasses and flatware.

Dean approached Burke and began to guide him toward

the west side of the museum. "Long time, no see." Dean was always the type of person to use old one-liners like, *'You snooze, you lose'* and, *'Where there's smoke, there's fire.'* It annoyed Burke that Dean couldn't find a shred of personality, or even put forth the effort to pretend.

"What's the deal?" Burke asked nonchalantly, although he was beginning to feel heat rising in his throat.

"I'm going to show you our mission control and get you prepped. You'll need an earpiece and pocket square camera. We want to see what you see. I also want to show you a picture of Rock and few of his crew so you'll know who to look for. Let's talk about your intro."

Burke told Dean his plan for engaging Rock Solomon. "That was always the most disappointing thing about you, Burke; so much promise. But the best laid plans, eh?"

Burke didn't respond. He just stared at the picture of his target. In the surveillance photo, a blonde, middle-aged man was sitting innocently at a café. He had somewhat feminine features. A clean-shaven face. Gelled hair, piercing blue eyes. He was thin, his wrists bony. Was this really the man who was finally going to bring Madge back to him? *He's the best chance I've got*, thought Burke.

"If you're going to ask Solomon to find Magdalena, you'll need to show him a picture of her. I know you don't have any, so I pulled this out of our database. It's a little more recent than what you remember." From his breast pocket, Dean pulled two photos that were paper clipped together. Burke's heartbeat lapped in his ears like a speeding stagecoach tearing towards a fallen bridge. Dean turned the pictures over and Burke tried to move slowly as he took them.

There she was—her head turned, listening for something as she hung a sheet out to dry in a courtyard of apartments. Her dark hair floated in a light breeze. He imagined the smell of papayas and dried tobacco leaves filling the air around her. He couldn't get a good look at her face. She seemed thinner than he remembered but still exquisite; a woman who held her posture like a ballerina and her face like a monk. Expressionless. Unapologetic in her perfection. Burke exhaled in relief.

He flipped to the next photo. Here she was at the market, examining an ear of corn. Things must've been better for her if she could get corn in her ration book. The photo looked as if it were taken from below. A camera planted in the produce, maybe? She was straight on, except for her eyes. Burke's breath left him, seeing her there. The marks that twelve years of life had made were showing on her face, but not in a way that made him cringe. A tear slipped down onto the picture before he could stop it and he tried to wipe it away before Dean noticed.

"Okay. Time to put those in your pocket. Let me have you step over here and my team will put your wire on and install the ear piece." Dean avoided eye contact while Burke composed himself, and Burke felt a surge of appreciation for his old friend. He tucked the photographs into the breast pocket of his jacket, over his heart. A young woman stepped up and began fitting something in his left ear. He felt them running wires up his suddenly un-tucked shirt, heard them asking him to re-tuck it, felt a small pebble of a thing go into his ear; but he was too busy burning her image into his brain to care much about the details of it all.

"Burke," Dean said. Then more forcefully, "Burke—listen. I don't like to get involved in your shit, but here it is. You got too invested in this last time, too tangled in her. You care too much. You lose focus. I need you one hundred percent on the ball tonight, or else I'll get one of my guys to do it. You got it? I need you invested, but competent. You standing here all dewy-eyed is not doing anything for my confidence level."

For a moment Burke considered handing off the mission and going to stand in the truck with Angelo. It sounded more his speed. His own confidence was shot the day he was dropped on the tarmac at that Coast Guard base.

"Are you in or are you out, Burke? You've got to tell me now."

"I'm in," Burke responded, against his better judgment. "I'm going to kill this. I'm the one that asked you to do this, and I'm the one who has to seal the deal." Now *he* was sounding like a stale one-liner.

"Okay. Take a quick break in the bathroom if you need to, and then you're on. Wouldn't hurt to bid on a few things to raise your profile in the crowd. Then hit the target up during intermission. He might need to have a private meeting with you after the auction to firm up the details. He may ask that it be offsite. We're prepared to go mobile if need be, so just follow his lead."

Burke nodded. It was easy. Get in, make the deal, and then sit back and wait. He could do this.

Burke stopped in the bathroom just inside the door of the museum. Men and women in tuxes and glittering gowns were beginning to arrive, dotting the steps like raindrops. He went into the stall. "Don't listen to me take a leak, you perverts," he said into his comm.

"Avert your ears, alpha team," Dean joked. Burke took the small tan envelope out of his pocket and dumped another line of cocaine into his palm. He tried to sniff as quietly as he could, but still felt compelled to whisper, "Allergies," for the benefit of those listening.

Exiting the men's room, he wove himself into the stream of people entering, getting in line at the check-in table and then whirring about into the crowd. He spotted several people he recognized, but not the man in the photo.

"I don't see him yet," Burke said quietly into the comm. He worried that people would stare at him for talking to himself, but no one seemed to notice. Women cooed at each other's gowns and kissed each other on the cheeks. Men headed for the bar. Burke didn't want to look out of place so he followed, standing in the line at the elegant bar placed at the center of the first gallery on the right—Egyptian art. His head was surging with a combination of excitement, terror and exhilaration. Deep down he'd always wanted a second chance to prove himself as a spy. Adrenaline rose and fell inside his veins. "Martini, please; two olives, if you don't mind."

"Richard, it's great to see you out and about." The Italian ambassador jostled Burke's elbow as the bartender skewered the olives for Burke's drink.

"Sergio! Great to see you, too. How are Dina and Marco?" Burke could taste Dina's spaghetti with pork Bolognese on the tip of his tongue as he said her name.

"The family's good. What about you? Any chance of you ever settling down? Kids?" The men were making their way from the bar, drinks in hand.

"Well, actually," Burke weighed the social pros and cons of exposing that he had a long-lost son and decided against it. "I think I'm more of a solo artist than an ensemble."

"Of course, my friend. We need to get together again, there's an Italian soccer player whom I'd love to get on your show. He's setting the Italian team ablaze! They're sure to win the World Cup coming up."

"Tell Dina to whip up some of her Bolognese and I'll be there to talk it over!"

"Burke." Dean's voice in his ear was welcome. "Blending in is good, but don't get distracted. Look for Solomon again. Our guys at the door saw him come in. Auction starting in tminus fifteen."

"Right," he said quietly. Burke had fallen into the social butterfly role, almost forgetting why he'd come. His eyes scanned the crowd for the distinctive blonde hair from the photo. Burke spotted Solomon in line for the check-in table. The thin wrists were picking up an auction paddle and booklet. There were two men flanking him and both were twice the mass of their boss, who was a waif of a man.

Burke's eyes tracked Solomon into the Greek and Roman wing to the left of the entrance. The auction was to be held in the main gallery, which was straight-on from the entrance. He followed with enough distance to appear that he was casually exploring. A few more people waved and tried to talk to him, but he waved and brushed them off with a quick but courteous, "Hey there!"

In the Greek and Roman wing it was less crowded, but there was another bar in the center of the room. The shelves glowed with red light, which illuminated the artifacts from multiple emperors' reigns. Spears, vases and small statues lit with red gave an eerie feeling to the room.

"I love being in the presence of such long-standing, unbridled power." The voice came from behind Burke's left shoulder. "I could be talking about these priceless works of art, or maybe about you. The King of Manhattan."

It had been years since anyone had called him that. The nickname was from a time when he had actually tried to be somebody in the Manhattan social scene. Rock Solomon was already holding a drink—something fizzy in a hurricane glass. It was clear with a lime.

"You're Rock Solomon," Burke said casually.

"You're Richard Burke." Solomon gingerly extended a hand. Burke took it firmly and shook it, not breaking eye contact. "I must say, I'm a fan. You're the only newsman I watch. I have a bit of a crush, I guess you could say."

Burke hadn't wanted to assume but now it was confirmed that Solomon was unmistakably homosexual, and he didn't try to hide it. "I'm flattered. No one's called me The King of Manhattan since—well, a long time. But I play for the other team, actually."

"Oh, I know, Richie. I follow Page Six. A new bedazzled brunette every week, it seems. I like to keep up with what my clientele are into."

His mother had called him Richie as a boy. Burke was always suspicious of people who acted like close friends with him after the first handshake. Friendship took effort; knowing someone was hard work, and to speed it up unnecessarily felt awkward and forced.

"I'm not your clientele," Burke said matter-of-factly, leading Solomon into the next step of their dance together.

"Aren't you?"

Burke looked at Solomon, surprised and sheepish.

"Mr. Burke. I make a very good living knowing what men like you want. You haven't been to a charity auction in three years. You've had your eyes on me since I came in the door. Has it finally gotten lonely for you up in your ivory tower? I know it was devastating for you when Liz left..." He trailed off.

Burke felt the last line stick in him like a knife. Was it a way to show empathy? Maybe.

"Don't get sidetracked, Burke. Make the ask. Finalize the details afterwards." Burke's earpiece hummed with Dean's voice, but he only vaguely registered the advice.

"Okay, you got me. I've admired your work for years, Mr. Solomon. Rock? Can I call you that?"

Solomon looked star-struck for a millisecond and then nodded calmly.

"I mean, the girl you got for Morass—the one with those

big natural tits—never seen tits like that on a Korean. And my god, the Thai chick with a dick for Don Roman? You wouldn't even know she wasn't a woman until she dropped out that huge schlong." Burke shuddered and Solomon beamed. "The best I've seen, though," Burke continued, "is the Columbian girl you got for Senator Harmon. Jesus Christ, the ass on her could cause an earthquake."

Solomon tucked his thumbs into his vest pockets and smiled like a boy who has found his father's nudie magazines. "That's some of my best work, Richie." He was back to Richie now. "The Columbian has a sister, you know. Is that why you're here? I can make a call."

"No, to be honest my request is a little more... specific."

Solomon looked taken aback. "Honey, I've delivered a Japanese hipster with a diamond tattoo on her ass to a sheik in the middle east. He ordered it up, even down to the tattoo. Saw it in a magazine or something. Specific is not a problem, although it does affect the price."

"Price isn't an issue. Twelve years ago I went to Cuba. Tensions were high, I was on assignment for Vacation magazine. I was young, stupid, you know how it is. Anyway, Rock, I..." Burke's eyes got misty and he reached in his breast pocket to feel the photos resting there. He took them out and left them in his hands face down. "I fell in love with a girl. Real love, the kind of love that lasts. I've tried to move on—Liz, the brunettes—but nothing can fill the void. I got deported and they told me if I ever tried to contact her again they would kill her."

"Jesus," Solomon exhaled. "You've got to know something, Burke." The lights flickered, which meant the auction program was about to start. "I don't deal in love. I deal in sex, fetish, kink—it's not pretty or cute, but it's what pays the bills and it's what I'm good at. I can find you a girl that looks just like this, and teach her to speak with a Cuban accent, but *this* girl—that's a lot more complicated than I'm used to." Solomon had taken the photos and turned them over, examining them closely.

Burke willed himself not to look. "So what are we talking then? What would it take for you to bring me my Madge?" Burke's voice was quavering now. He was doing exactly what he told himself he would do—telling the truth when it mattered. He swore he would show Solomon the real love, the real feelings he had for Madge. If this criminal had a heart at all, Burke was about to find out.

Solomon stared at him blankly.

"Do you have anyone in your life that you care about, Rock?"

"Y-yes," Solomon seemed nervous now. Scared.

"Imagine your life separated from that person for twelve years, not knowing if they're safe, not knowing if they still care about you—not knowing if they're getting tortured daily for even having known you. If you had any chance to get them back, you would take it—no matter the cost. And you would trust the goddamn Cunt Connoisseur, the Sex Slave Trader, the Foreign Intimacy Consultant—whatever you want to call it—because he's the best and the only one who can do this for you."

The two men looked around to notice that the room had emptied out. Solomon's bodyguards stood at the door; the bartender was drying glasses, pretending not to eavesdrop on their conversation.

"Let me think about this, Richie. I want to think about it through the auction. We can talk afterwards, okay? There's a lot to consider." Solomon touched Burke's arm in the way a sweet grandmother would; consoling and tender. He led his two men out of the room and into their seats in the main gallery.

"Damn it to hell, Burke, you fucking held out on me. Foreign Intimacy Consultant? You knew all about this guy and you didn't tell me?" Dean's voice was quiet but furious. "I don't like surprises in the middle of a mission."

"I wasn't giving up my ace in the hole, Dean." Burke was walking to his seat, the last to find his place as the auctioneer began rattling bids for the first lot number. "I needed my reaction to be real, unrehearsed. And I didn't want to incriminate my friends unless I had to."

"This better work. We have to get this guy."

Dean went quiet and Burke said nothing else. Burke realized it was suspicious that he'd come alone, gazing to either side of him at the couples filling the audience. Would it seem suspicious now to charm a woman into holding his arm for the rest of the auction?

"I should've brought a date," Burke said into the comm as he sat down.

THIRTY-THREE

2002 | 2003 | 2004 | 2005 | 2006 | 2007 | 2008 | 2009 | 2010 | 2011 | **2012**

May 14th, 2012 – New York City, New York

The auction dragged on. Burke kept eying Solomon to see if he would give any indication that he'd reached a decision. Solomon sat transfixed by the auction items, raising his paddle for a few things and winning a mink stole for $50,000. Burke wondered who would end up wearing that, and pictured Solomon cleaning his modern-post-modern stainless steel kitchen wearing nothing but his prize. Burke shook his head to rid himself of the disturbing image.

Burke raised his paddle for a few paintings and won a charter trip on a yacht embarking from the Hamptons. The trip was for three days at sea on a fully manned yacht, and he'd paid $75,000 for it. A round of applause went up and he mouthed, *It's for the kids!* to the crowd. Some flashbulbs went off. Solomon's eyes stayed on him a few seconds too long, as if he was trying to decide something about Burke's character.

The auction wrapped up with the usual fanfare and a jazz ensemble started playing Duke Ellington's *Satin Doll*. As the chairs were cleared away, people began to dance and wobble to the music. Burke looked around for Solomon, who was chatting up a docent at the edge of the gallery. It looked like he was trying to go upstairs, even though that area of the museum was closed to event guests for the evening.

The docent nodded to a security guard nearby and lifted the velvet rope to allow Solomon and his two men through. Solomon looked back and gave a chin tip to Burke. The docent stood with the rope open, waiting for Burke to come through.

"Looks like we're going upstairs," Burke said into the comm.

"We're tracking you. We won't be visible to you, but not far off."

Dean still sounded put out. But he wasn't halting the mission, which was good. Burke started to tell himself this might actually happen. He wanted to take Madge and Angelo on the yacht, a celebration of their family finally being whole. A tingle at the corner of his eyes made him squeeze them shut before walking beyond the rope.

He followed Solomon up the staircase and into the maze of galleries. The three men weren't slowing down for him, but stayed just far enough ahead that he could see the next turn. One turn after another, he followed them. Burke wondered if Dean's tracking was sophisticated enough to find him in such a complicated floor plan.

"Passing through gallery 823," he whispered into the comm. "Looks like we're going to land in 826."

Gallery 826 housed several van Gogh and Gauguin paintings. The colorful, out-of-focus works of art blurred past him as he kept diving deeper into the bowels of art history.

Solomon's men came to rest outside of Gallery 826, confirming Burke's thought. Their boss stood inside the gallery staring at a colorful painting that Burke had never seen before.

He finally caught up to Solomon and the two stood gazing at the painting for a few moments. Burke read the title to himself. "La Orana Maria," he said. It was by Gauguin. He personally hated Gauguin's paintings for reasons beyond his ability to express.

"Do you know the translation of that title?" Solomon asked in a curious whisper.

"I'm sure you're going to tell me." Burke was less than amused with a symbolic trek across the museum.

"The Hail Mary." He paused to let the weight of that sink in. "Do you know the nature of the relationship Paul Gauguin had with Vincent van Gogh? Some people actually say that Gauguin cut off van Gogh's ear in the middle of a row. He was a fencing expert. They admired each other's work greatly, but when it really came down to it, they couldn't stand each other. Gauguin wanted van Gogh to work on painting from memory, but van Gogh refused to change. Gauguin went back to Paris after a tumultuous time with his former friend and told all the art critics that van Gogh was insane, just copying off of him. Anyway, I digress."

"Yes, it would seem we have. This is my life, Rock. I don't know why we're talking about Gauguin when we should be talking about Madge. What's the plan? How can you bring her home to me?"

"It's been twelve years, Burke. Why are you so intent to bring her home now, right this instant?" Solomon was testing him.

Burke almost fumbled. "My sources say things have relaxed there. I've been monitoring the situation since the day I left. This is the first time I think we could actually get her out. But I'm banned from Cuba and too high profile now to get false credentials. I need someone with know-how to go in and fly her out. It won't be hard."

"And what if she's dead?" Solomon didn't shy away from the word dead, but instead seemed to revel in saying it.

Burke paused, hoping Dean would chime in with some direction about what to do next.

"Don't talk about Angelo, that leads right back to us. Say that you know in your heart she's still alive and still waiting for you. Tell him that you'll pay him full price even if she's dead." Right on cue and exactly what Burke needed.

Burke looked down at his hands meaningfully. "I have to know. I feel it—that she's still alive, that she's waiting for me. And if she isn't," Burke paused, letting the hook sink in. "Well, it will be the easiest $750,000 you've ever made.

"I don't want us to end up like Gauguin and van Gogh, Burke. I want us to be friends. This is a good idea for my business and could put me in a whole new category. Retrieving people from dangerous parts of the world to reunite with their families—that sounds a whole lot better than being the concierge of human trafficking. But $750,000 is a lot of money and this could turn up absolutely nothing for you. That seems bad for business—I'd rather do it for $500,000 and have us both walk away happy. This truly is a Hail Mary, and I want you to know that. I'm not guaranteeing anything. I'm probably the last chance you have at getting Madge back—this dream you've had for so long, you're about to be free of it one way or another."

Burke exhaled, knowing that no matter who was listening, everything Solomon said was true. He reached his hand out to signify that he would take the deal. Solomon offered his hand the way some women do, fingers pointed down with the back of the hand up, as if he wanted his hand to be kissed. Burke pretended not to notice and shook it the best he could.

"Okay, there are several things I'm going to need. Full

name, last known place of residence, these photos to keep, any known aliases, employers, family members' names, hobbies, etc. Just everything you can think of."

Burke handed over the two photos grudgingly and started to tell Solomon about Madge. Everything he could remember, everything he knew. He tried to throw in hints about her current whereabouts, without giving away that he knew she was in Cienfuegos. He told Rock everything, trying to force down the sobs that came with remembering. Rock scratched notes in a small notebook.

After all the crucial details, Burke dribbled out the last of what he could remember. "She made soap and traded it around the village, Veradero, for more ration cards or other goods that were hard to come by then. She used to make it in the basement of her farmhouse after making the lye out in the field. She traded her soap for animal lard with a nearby farmer. Oh, and one last thing..." After Burke had given every last irrelevant detail he could think of, he casually added, "She's a counter-revolutionary—or at least she was. She was under state surveillance from 1998 through when I met her in 2001, and probably still is. She was in a prison camp—I'm not sure how long and I don't know where, prior to '98." He just laid the information there between them, like a fish to be gutted.

Solomon put his hand to his face and shook his head. "There are pros and cons to what you just told me, the biggest con being that you told me after we'd already shaken on it. Because I never would have agreed to do this had I known that little tidbit." Solomon turned away and put his hands on his waistband, pushing his tuxedo jacket into a pucker behind him. "I never go back on a shake, Richie. You should have told me that. You should have told me that before." He was pacing now, upset, his mind whirring.

Burke squirmed.

"Okay, it's okay. I don't like this. It doesn't feel good. But because it's you—you, Richard Burke—I'm going to do this. Consider Magdalena Cruz on her way to being the newest citizen of Manhattan." Solomon turned and started to walk away.

"Wait, what should I do? What are the next steps?" Burke sounded like an eager schoolboy.

"My associates will be in touch during the next twelve hours to receive payment by wire. Have your bank account numbers and the money ready to go in the morning. I'm going to dig through my closet to find some clothes that breathe—God, I hate packing for humidity." His nasal tone echoed behind him as he zigzagged his way back out to the staircase.

Burke remained, staring at *La Orana Maria*. It was garish indeed, much like Rock Solomon himself. Painted in 1891, the painting was of three island women, the foremost one holding a small naked boy on her shoulders. The women were from the Marquesas Islands, but if one didn't know it could've been painted in Veradero. There were bowls of fruit and vegetables in the foreground. The women wore dresses and skirts with floral prints, two of the women topless.

"What was he trying to say? With the painting?"

Dean's voice made Burke jump. Solomon was long gone by then. Burke stayed quiet, staring at the face of the woman holding the boy. She was quite beautiful. "I don't know," he mumbled. "I just remember a girl in my art history class at Amherst railing on Gauguin. She used to say he was propagating and profiting from the Marquesas culture, but all he really did while he was there was drink, objectify women and have sex. God, she hated him. I have to say, I'm not a fan either."

"No, that description doesn't sound like anyone I know at all." Dean was deadpan.

Burke felt things that were once solid, liquefy inside him. The whole time Solomon was talking, he'd imagined himself as van Gogh—the good guy. But he was Gauguin and his masterwork was about to come to life. Burke made a sound that felt inhuman and headed for a nearby trashcan where he puked, twice.

"You okay, there, Burke?" Dean tried to be sympathetic.

"Am I the bad guy, Dean? Am I the Gauguin, running around chopping ears off and fucking up people's lives? What if she doesn't want to be saved? What if she doesn't need me at all? What have I done? She could be killed by this goddamn maniac."

Burke was on his knees taking a sleeve to his mouth. A female agent he recognized from outside appeared and helped him to his feet. The coke was completely worn off and he was left with a sickening dread taking root from his sternum to his groin. He felt powerless and terrified. The agent helped him navigate the maze of galleries back to the elevator bank.

"What's your name?" he asked the auburn-haired girl who was propping him up as they rode down the elevator.

"Jenna, sir. You were great in there. I think you're just coming down off the adrenaline. It happens to a lot of us the first time out."

"Yes, lying for a living can make you feel like shit. Imagine that." Burke was raising a hand to his forehead to wipe away the cold sweat. The elevator settled to the first floor and he lost his balance, catching himself on the wall. The agent was caught between him and the side of the elevator, pinned there for an instant. Her gray eyes looked through him, her soft, pink lips dewy in the fluorescent lights from overhead. Her shiny, straight hair was pulled back into a perfect bun and he could just see her dusty rose bra beneath her white catering uniform shirt.

He went in for the kiss before any of the other neurons could fire off a warning. He felt his pants stiffen as she reciprocated the kiss even to his own surprise. He was pressing against her as she began to lift her skirt. His fingers fumbled to the door close button, but hit the door open button by mistake.

As the door dinged open, Angelo and Dean stood there with pale, stunned faces. Burke felt the air change in the elevator but couldn't quite put his finger on what the difference was. He turned; seeing the open door and who was beyond it for just a millisecond , he flung himself onto the back wall, away from Jenna.

"Really? You were with him for thirty seconds!" Dean's tone was a combination of reverence and disbelief as he trudged off after his agent, who was storming to the catering tent, flushed and humiliated.

Angelo stood speechless, glaring at his father, who continued to lean away from him into the back wall of the elevator. Burke took the other sleeve to his mouth and wiped, as if he could wash away all evidence of what had just happened.

Angelo hung his head but said nothing.

"Hey, pal. How was the surveillance truck? Did you get to see some cool stuff in there?"

"Yes. They keep talking about you. How old you are and how pathetic. They said at least you were doing a good job this time, because boy you really fucked it the last time. I say, 'That's my dad. He is good and he will help bring my mom to me.' So they stop saying these things. But maybe they are right. Maybe you are a pathetic old man." Tears poured down his face but there was no hint of crying in his voice, which cracked sometimes from the early signs of puberty. "I hope my mom has gone to hiding, so neither you or this Rock man will find her!" He ran out the front doors past the staffers breaking down the buffet, past the dining carts, through the open doors and out into the open street.

Burke brought his hand to the back of his neck and rubbed the stubble there. Just as he made a move to leave the elevator, the doors closed again in his face. Exasperated, he pushed the open-door button and walked in the direction of Angelo and the catering tent. Feeling completely suffocated, he took off his tuxedo jacket and removed his cufflinks. He rolled his sleeves up to his elbows as he walked, feeling a hot sweat meet the cool breeze as he stepped outside.

"Nice going, Burke. Is it impossible for you to let one good mission stand on its own? That was great work in there—until—until that last part."

"Where's the kid?" Burke was in no mood for Dean's posturing. He could clearly see in the light of the evening how much of an ass he'd been.

"Went back to the van," Dean said matter-of-factly. He was busy packing up some of the equipment from the tent, now that the high-profile guests had cleared out. "I'm not here to tell you about your personal life, Burke, but you look like shit and it seems like you don't know what you want from a hole in the ground. Get my wire off and return my comm before you pass out on yourself."

Burke unbuttoned his shirt and started to take off the tape that had held the wire to his stomach. He noticed Jenna watching him from across the tent, some of her embarrassment having dissipated.

Dean said nothing more while two agents disconnected and stored Burke's tech. David approached from the van. "Where's Angelo?" he asked.

"I thought he was with you?" Burke's voice shot up three octaves.

"No, he came to find you guys ages ago," David said

innocuously.

    Dean ran to the surveillance van, Burke in tow. They found it empty, full of blinking lights and blank screens.

PART V
LA ALFA LOBA

THIRTY-FOUR

2002 2003 2004 2005 2006 2007 2008 2009 2010 2011 **2012**

May 16th, 2012 – Cienfuegos, Cuba

Having him gone is a knife in my side. Any movements I make, I'm reminded that I have to make them alone, the pain unyielding. The tiny boy who once grew inside me—the only lasting token of love I would ever have—has left me. He's left out of necessity, but I mourn him just as I mourn all the other loves of my life. I have no illusions that I will ever see him again.

Five days. It's been five days since he left. I've heard nothing from the coyote who took my life's savings to get my boy to New York safely. I even gave him an extra fifty for a touchback—that's what they call the courtesy of letting a client's family know when the cargo has arrived safely.

I can only hope he made it to his father—and then I can only keep hoping that Burke has been able to keep himself together these years we've been apart. I scan the radio night and day for any trace of American media, but all I can get are soap operas and Miami news and weather.

In the beige laundry room of my employer's house, I run my fingers across the straight, comforting ridges in the radio dial. I don't know what I'm looking for exactly.

"Magdalena, that static is driving me up the wall. Turn it off and focus on the ironing."

Louisa sweeps in, turning off the radio instead of waiting for me to do it.

"Si, Doña." I say in a whisper, plugging the iron into the outlet near me. I smooth one of her husband's work shirts onto the ironing board, and she watches me quietly.

"Is something wrong, Magdalena?" She has never inquired about me personally before. "How's Angelo?"

I force myself to withhold a cringe at the sound of his name. It makes my womb ache. "He's fine. You know how boys are, they never really let you in, do they?"

Louisa Manchón has three boys, aged five, eight and fourteen. Her daughter Francisca is three. "Yes, especially at that age. Very secretive, as if the world is happening to them and them alone." She looks wistfully at the photo of her family hanging in the hallway outside the laundry quarters.

I have always thought that Louisa and I would be friends if I hadn't been assigned as her housekeeper six years ago. She shows me herself in small, metered glimpses.

Abruptly, she remembers herself. "For today, I want the ironing done. And then I'd like you to look at deep cleaning the carpets upstairs. Don't forget the party next week for the Provincial Election Delegates. I want the veranda to be spotless—as well as inside, of course."

"Si, Doña," I say again and she whips down the hallway. Louisa's husband is some type of political or military man. I'm not sure exactly what he does, but I know it's important. They have parties here for the elected officials of the province. Louisa says that Mr. Manchón could be the next elected official from our province to serve in the National Assembly of People's Power. It's the highest honor in the Cuban political system—that is, if they ever hold elections again. The representatives who serve now were elected in 2008.

I know why I was placed with Louisa. She's the head of the area CDR—Committee for the Defense of the Revolution. Her job is to rat out people like me, people who are involved in counter-revolutionary activity. She and all the other housewives in Cuba make a small wage for reporting suspicious behavior.

Because of her status, and because I wanted to keep Angelo safe, I've been isolated from Los Lobos and the counter-revolution since I started working for her. But I've made up my mind that the only way to get information about Angelo is to re-engage some of my old contacts. They have to know something, to have some connection to the outside.

I ponder my next steps carefully as I scrub the abrasive smelling carpet powder into the thick, shag carpet in the upstairs den. While I wait for the cleansing powder to settle and do its job, I take a pad and pen out onto the veranda and make a list of what needs to be done for the party next week. I walk around the corner and take a deep breath, breathing in the view of the mountains to the south. They're shrouded in clouds that hang low in the sky; they look as if they disappear into another world.

I look down onto the sheet of paper, my pen hovering for a moment as I make a mental list of a different kind. I think:

Rodolpho
Carmen
Sal—

I promptly scratch imaginary lines through all three. They're dead, have been for years. I don't know any other contact I can reach out to. Except one. I can think of only one name:

Paolo

My hands start shaking at the thought of hunting down the man who engaged my son in this mess. The only man who ever knew Burke and me... as Burke and me. What does he know about us? About my son? Has he already reported Angelo's computer to the CIA or to the PNR? I don't know what he's shared. Or with who.

My neighbor said yesterday that a man came to bang on my door when I wasn't home. I believe it might've been Paolo. Now, I need to figure out how to find him.

I feel the walls of my heart closing in as I think about my situation. I don't know how much longer I can cover the fact that Angelo is gone. When they find out, they will likely send me back to prison camp or worse. It could be an international incident like Elian Gonzalez was. God, what a disgrace. I can't have my boy dragged back here like a dog that broke its chain. If I can get some answers out of Paolo, then I can form a plan to get out, or at least settle for knowing that Angelo is safe. I don't know if I'll ever leave this island alive.

THIRTY-FIVE

2002 . 2003 . 2004 . 2005 . 2006 . 2007 . 2008 . 2009 . 2010 . 2011 . **2012**

May 16th, 2012 – Cienfuegos, Cuba

Moving back to Cienfuegos when I was pregnant meant that my sisters would be there to help take care of me, but it also meant leaving my trusted network behind. For the good of everyone, I haven't reached out to any known counter-revolutionaries until tonight.

In my heart, I know the best place to start; the same place I always started ten and twenty years ago. At the gas station and market in the center of town. All illegal business goes through it. So much traffic passes through that the clerk usually knows something by default. After work, I catch the bus up to the Cupet Station at the intersection of Caridad and Central. As always, it's abuzz with shoppers and gossip. I roam the aisles for a few minutes listening in to the conversations.

"They're moving in the next few nights," a man says to another man in passing. The second man makes no indication that he has heard, just goes up to the cashier and pays for his items.

"I heard Fidel died a month ago, but they're not going to tell us. They're just going to let us think he can live forever. Bastardos!" A woman is talking to the clerk, and he shushes her towards the end as she gets emotional.

I wait for five or six more people to pass through. The store is finally empty for a brief second and I head up to the clerk with my ration book in one hand and a few lemons in the other. I can feel the heat on my skin like a furnace every time someone opens the door. The clerk has a small fan placed on a high shelf behind him. The airflow is intoxicating.

"Hola, just the lemons please."

He begins typing in the code then looks at my ration book. He removes two coupons. Just as I'm about to open my mouth to ask about Paolo, he says something quietly under his breath. "Got a message for you." He turns to go into a closet behind him and emerges with a small brown paper bag. He pushes his hand inside it to make space for the lemons. For a second I think I see his hand release something inside the bag.

"Thanks so much," I say nonchalantly. I fold the top of the bag as he hands it to me and walk out of the store. My throat feels dry and clenched as I step out into the simmering night.

I walk back to my apartment drenching the bag with nervous sweat from my hand. The top is soaked and crumpled by the time I set it on my small dining room table—the table where Angelo and I have shared nearly every dinner of his life. I reach my hand in, ignoring the lemons, searching for something else. A piece of paper floats between them, suspended for the moment.

I pull it out. The paper quivers and quakes violently as I unfold it. Deciphering the code comes as easily as riding a bike.

Now that you are free of distractions, it's time
We move in two days

> *Get in the red cab on the SE corner of Defender's Square*
> *-The Alfa*

I don't know anything about who sent this message or what they intend to do to me once I get in that cab. I know that the Alfa is the head of the organization Los Lobos. They are still around kicking up trouble, but nothing consequential. Since Raul took power, things have been better. We can make money now—at least, a little bit. There are rumors that the camps have been eliminated, sending everyone home who was being held there. This has never been proven.

I was so frazzled by the note that I forgot to ask about Paolo, and now I'm not sure if I need to find him. Would the Alfa have better knowledge of Angelo than Paolo would? It seems he knows that Angelo is gone—that must be what he means by 'distractions.'

I decide to go to the cab. If the Alfa knows nothing of Angelo I will simply refuse involvement in whatever they are planning and come home. Then I can hunt down Paolo tomorrow. Defender's Square is just down the street from my apartment. I wonder if any time is best or if the cab will be there no matter the time.

I take the chance and head to the square, checking behind me every few steps for a follower. I see no one, but have a strange feeling. As I cross the street at Valencia and Common Avenue, I walk by a large swath of bushes that line the back of an office complex. The bushes are large and lush and I am swamped with a memory of my sisters and I hiding in bushes like these, waiting for our mother to come home from the market. We rattled the bushes at passersby, who would jump and curse us on their way.

As I push by the end of the bush, an arm leaps out to grab

me. Then another shoots out behind it. I grab at the arm, trying to pull it off me but it holds on tightly. A third hand covers my mouth as I try to scream; it comes out as a garbled growl. I'm thrashing and fighting, my mind struggling to reconcile fond memories with what is happening now.

"Shhh," a voice says. "We're here to help, we're here to help." The hand remains over my mouth in the darkness. I can barely make out the features of a large, muscular white man. He sounds English. The other man is black as night and twice as big. They smell of cheap hotel soaps and Camel lights.

"Stop fighting, we want to take you..." He's cut off when a pipe comes down on his head from behind. The bigger one swipes behind him, seemingly at a fly, but he goes down writhing in pain as well. Behind them is a boy, definitely Cuban, maybe nineteen years old.

"We've got to go, get on." He's riding a bike and is asking me to step onto the axle of the back wheel as he rides.

"Where are we going? What the hell is going on? Who were they?" My mind is a hurricane.

"I don't know. My orders are to get you to the Alfa." The two men on the ground are starting to get up, so I decide to act now and ask questions later. I hop on the back of his bike and he rides like fury to Defender's square, not saying another word.

The adrenaline of the attack is still raging inside me. Even though I don't know what I would've done without the boy, riding so fast on the back of this bike makes me feel like I could do anything. A sudden pang almost overtakes me when I realize that Angelo will be as old as this boy in just a few years.

We get to Defender's Square and the red cab is waiting. The boy rides up so close to the car that the door almost hits us when it opens. I jump from the bicycle to the back seat and the door slams behind me. I look out the back window; there is no evidence of my pursuers—I never saw them leave the bush. Who could they have been? I replay the incident in my mind as the cab pulls away, forcing myself to read the white one's lips as he talked. *We're here to help*, he'd said in English. But help who?

I look out the tinted windows to see where we're going. We leave the city limits, which doesn't take long because Cienfuegos is much smaller than Havana or even the tourist-ridden Veradero where I met Burke.

We drive for twenty minutes down back roads and enter the countryside. I see a road sign that indicates we're driving northwest. The driver is silent; I have nothing to relay to him either, so I use the time to sit and think. They must've been watching me all along. All these years as I was dormant, raising my son alone, struggling—Los Lobos was there, in the shadows. I wonder, *Why me? What do I have to bring to a group like that now?* I ponder this and more questions as the car rumbles on, past hills and miles of tall grass.

Eventually we curve around to the west on Calle 11. We are heading towards the Parque Cienega de Zapata and Playa Larga on the northern edge of the Bay of Pigs. How apt that Los Lobos would be camping here.

We pull into a parking area off the highway, and even in the dark I recognize the crocodile breeding facility where I came with Angelo's class two years ago on a field trip. We followed the guide around as he told us about every stage of crocodile life and at the end of the tour, they took us to the restaurant where they urged us to buy crocodile steaks for lunch.

The driver pulls to the back of the empty parking lot, where a dock floats in a small creek. A speedboat waits for me. The signs read *Villa Guama*. The same man who drove my taxi hops into the boat and starts the engine. It has been a long time since I've heard the burble of a boat's propeller beneath the water. If the sun was up, I imagine I would see clouds of mud rise in the water behind the boat. But, since it's past midnight now, I see nothing but vague outlines of branches, leaves and a deep, cavernous crack leading into the wilderness.

THIRTY-SIX

2002 | 2003 | 2004 | 2005 | 2006 | 2007 | 2008 | 2009 | 2010 | 2011 | **2012**

May 16th, 2012 – Villa Guama, Cuba

There is no such thing as silence, even in the most remote places. Frogs fill the air with their evening singing, in competition of course with the crickets and the roosting birds. When I was a girl, my mother talked about coming to the lagoon to the south of Playa Larga to bird watch—all manner of waterfowl gather here in a kind of bird paradise. People used to flock here from all over the world to watch the birds. Gulls, spoonbills, pelicans, hummingbirds—it was a bird lover's paradise, she would say. As long as I was alive, she never made it here. No matter what chaotic mess I'm heading into, I powerfully wish she was here with me now.

    We putter quietly down a tight stream with lush greenery on either side. A dull headlight stretches in front of us. I hope to God no one decides to leave the lagoon at the same time we're heading in, because there isn't room for two boats to pass each other.

    We putter up to a flimsy-looking dock surrounded by

grass-thatched huts. Each hut is suspended above the water on rafters. On one of the small islands in the lagoon is a larger hut with light emanating from the center. It has no walls and is full of tables. It looks to be a bar, or at least it was at some point. Men gather around the hut talking and drinking. My driver ties up the boat and helps me onto the rickety landing of the dock.

I can feel eyes on me and the few voices I heard as we parked the boat have gone quiet. The driver gestures to the bar in a way that makes it clear that I'm expected. Understanding this, I start to walk towards it and the crowd of men. My driver does not follow.

There are maybe thirty men scattered at tables and around the counter itself. They are dressed in ratty clothes, their knees and arms caked in mud. Some have wiped the mud on their faces like war paint. Their eyes dart from me to one man standing behind the bar. This man does not look up but continues making drinks and filling cups for those around him.

His eyes and cheeks protrude through sunken skin. The wrinkles on his face—or are they scars?—are deep and wandering. His arms look so frail and thin as they pour, serving everyone around him.

Finally, he looks up at me, always aware that I was approaching but waiting for the right moment to look up. It's then that I realize who he is.

"Lena," he mouths. If any sound comes out, I can't hear it over the gasps coming from around us.

"Juan Julio." His name leaves me like smoke escaping a stovepipe. "I… I thought you were dead. Killed I mean, on that night…"

"They did everything but kill me." His green eyes haven't left mine. I am sitting on a barstool now, leaning across the bar. How he has changed. Everyone else watches us, but I've forgotten the world. "Lena, can we talk privately?"

I nod, and he takes my hand as he comes around the bar. My palm and fingers tingle where he touches me. It's been 18 years since I saw Juan Julio dragged away from our camp with forty other boys, bloody and beaten, screaming for their lives.

He walks me into the closest grass hut—also one of the biggest. Inside is a bed, a small desk fashioned of reeds and a glass top. There are some benches carved out of tree trunks. He lights the kerosene lamps, and closes a curtain over the opening we walked through. I look around, bewildered.

"What is this place?" I can't hold back the question.

"It used to be a hotel, Villa Guama. It was an eco-tourism thing. Tourists would come from Veradero to tour the lagoon and stay a few nights. The owner is one of us. When business stopped coming because he refused to paint a pretty picture to the tourists, he closed it. We've converted it into our hub of operations. It feels suitable, no?"

"It's... so strange," I whisper, still looking around the hut, which I think is supposed to be a hotel room. I gather myself, remembering why I've come—to hear about Angelo. I can't forget my way as Juan Julio has always made me do. "Why did you summon me? I've only come to hear if you know anything about my son. I can't get any information on his whereabouts since..."

"Since you sent him to America with a bloodthirsty coyote. I know the whole story, Lena. I got out of prison in 2007—13 years I rotted in that hell-hole a political prisoner. Half of that I spent in prison camp where they tortured me for information. I was so stupid to think we could take Castro with a fistful of ideas." He took a deep breath and looked me up and down. "Do you remember how we were together?" He raises his calloused hand to my chin and holds it.

I remember the first time he touched me like that, in our camp in the mountains. I had never thought myself good enough for him, but I worshipped him nonetheless, just like the other girls did. Until one night he called me into his tent, shivering from a nightmare and the cold mountain air. For all his courage outside the tent, he shook the whole night, even after I climbed into his bedroll and gave him my virginity.

"You were my first, did you ever know that?" He looks at me earnestly, as if eighteen years and another life haven't passed since he disappeared.

"I had some idea." I blush and look away. I look to the bed where an AK-47 lays on top of the bed sheets like a restless child. The mood in the room changes instantly. "What is this? What happened to..." I struggle, expecting him to cling to the ideas that got him tortured and nearly killed, "your principles?" A hint of anger is in my voice now, thinking about all the boys out there—not much older than Angelo—who are following Juan Julio to certain death.

"My principles are the only thing they tortured out of me. The belief that men are anything but bloodthirsty power-mongers, that died long ago, Lena."

"And you, you're one of them?"

"You could say that. I lead these men, and we are going to fight what this regime has done to us and our families. We move in two nights to march against Havana. We have about two hundred remote undercover guerillas who will join us on the way. There are fifty here. Remember when we tried to take Havana with seventy-five well-meaning hippies? I'm not walking into a suicide mission again."

"What do you hope to gain? You're just replacing a dictator with another dictator."

"But this time the dictator will be me. And those who benefit will be my friends, my family... and you Lena. You will be my wife."

"What? What are you talking about? I have to get to

Angelo and Bu…"

"Burke? Richard Burke? The one who left you pregnant and alone with Anton, the animal? The one who sent two young boys—counter-revolutionaries—to death with his careless operation back in 2001? And his bastard son? Who are they compared to being my wife, the future ruler of Cuba? You are the only one."

His hollowed face looks yellow in the lamplight, and I hardly recognize the person he's become. I stand quietly looking at him, considering this future. I could be his wife, or we could both be killed in the coup. "Don't ever call my son a bastard again," I say resolutely.

"How much longer can you hold them off? Soon the head of the household you work for, the leader of the CDR, will learn that Angelo is gone. They'll bring you in, probably put you back at Juventud, because you know as well as I that getting out the first time was luck. Getting out again will never happen. They will break you Lena, and you will never see Angelo again.

"When we win the war, I will send you to New York to bring Angelo back home to us. I can adopt him as my son and he will rule beside us. Isn't that what you want? A free Cuba? We can institute elections, we can bring money back to the island, we can have free press. All brought by a benevolent new leader and his beautiful wife." He smiles at me and, with some effort, gets down on one knee. "Lena, I've been waiting eighteen years to ask you this. Will you marry me?" He slips something on my finger that feels like a real engagement ring.

I forget to breathe for a moment, caught up in a strange mix of hope, love, sadness and nostalgia that I've never quite experienced. I loved Juan Julio once. I was willing to give my life for him. I lost five years in prison and my freedom for him. Could we be together again? Could we make Cuba a better place together? Could we make a family for Angelo? But a voice whispers in my head.

"I wait for you like a lonely house."

It's Burke, my long lost love. The one I can never forget, no matter how hard I try.

"Why me?" I sputter. "Why now? I haven't seen you in over eighteen years. Where were you when I was struggling to raise my boy alone? Where were you while I was scrubbing floors?"

"I wanted to leave you alone. I wanted you to raise Angelo without the threat of me, what knowing me can cost. I am the Alfa. I needed to protect you. But I know now that I cannot do this alone. And Angelo is safe in New York with his father. This is the perfect time for us to be together again. I don't know what's going to happen, Lena, but I want you to be by my side... like we were in the beginning."

I remember the beginning. We hid out in the mountains living off the scraps brought to us by sympathetic local villagers. But we were never hungry. Our militia grew from thirty who left school in Havana to seventy-five seemingly overnight. People were disappearing and starving in the streets, so anything was better than reality. I lived in a dream world with Juan Julio. He was beautiful, but his words were what lulled me into a subconscious haze. I packed lunches, did laundry, gathered groups, strategized, anything and everything we needed, that was what I did. And I felt like someone, someone who was respected and needed by something. We were a movement.

Until we weren't.

"We're lucky we survived the beginning." I turn away toward the bed and I see the gun again. Maybe this time we would actually have a chance.

I can still hear the screams from the night the Policía stormed our camp outside Havana; they still wake me most nights. They burned our camp and trampled us in full riot gear, throwing smoke bombs and raining gunfire. They knew we had no weapons. We were completely defenseless.

Juan Julio and I were entwined against each other, wrapped in his bedroll, sound asleep. I woke to the sound of ripping, our tent being torn by troops sent to take us down. There were hundreds of them all around us. They captured me first and tied my hands behind my back. I kicked one officer in the head and tried to scramble to my feet, frantically searching for Juan Julio. I found him encircled by officers who were closing in slowly. He pleaded, telling them again that we were unarmed, that we just wanted better lives for our people. They covered him in a barrage of arms, batons, guns and legs, moving on him like a mythical beast.

Three officers converged on me and began to drag me away as I craned an ear for the sound of Juan Julio's voice. It shrank to a gargled whisper as I and a few other girls were led away. I called to him as loudly as I could, screaming his name. I still don't know if he heard me. I was sure they killed him right then and there.

Once I awoke on the Isla de Juventud, I followed my mother's instructions. "If you're ever found in the custody of the state—especially in a prison camp—kill yourself as soon as you can find something sharp."

I found a rusty nail along the bottom of the fence line we were forced to walk along every day. I dragged it hard up my forearms once I got back to my cell—heartbroken and alone, deserted by my hope and maimed by my naivety.

"This time will be different," Juan Julio says as he pulls me to him and I feel my shoulders and throat relax, letting out a sob that's been living deep inside me for a long time.

"Guns won't make it different. People will still die," I whisper.

"Yes, but this time, the right people will die." He kisses the top of my head and I look up to meet his eyes. I search for the boy who was so sure in a crowd but so shy when we were alone, and I realize they did kill him that night.

"I'll do it. Yes, I want to marry you. I want to—promise we'll get Angelo back." Big teardrops roll from my eyes.

"I promise you anything you want, my love. You will make me whole again." His hands tighten around me and he pushes his body roughly into mine. I can feel his hip bones through his clothes. I hear the fading whisper again—*I wait for you like a lonely house.* I know that Burke was always a dream for me—one that I was lucky to be awake for—but Juan Julio is my reality now.

I gently kiss his neck, trying to show him the kind of touch I need. He swiftly slides my shirt up over my head and throws me backwards onto the bed. My head bumps into the cold gun and I cry out. "What? Are you hurt? Of course you are." He falls down on top of me and puts his stubbly face on mine. "We all are," he grunts, fumbling with his pants. "We're going to take it back, Lena." He pushes himself inside me hard and I rake my nails up his back in retaliation. He looks skyward and moans.

"Fucking do it, fucking take it, take it all back," I find myself screaming and moving frantically against him. Ferocity shakes loose inside me and I put my hands around his neck, choking him and then releasing. He is harder than ever but still pounding and pounding. The stinging starts between my legs but I use the pain. I clench my legs around him and pull him even harder into me. He puts his hands around my neck now and I feel for a second that it will all end. All the pain and anger melts away into release as waves of pleasure wash over me. I lay back, ready to give in to whatever comes. Juan Julio cannot seem to finish and he curses and sweats as he keeps pumping, but it's no use—his hardness fades to a soft doughy pile between us.

"Shit!" he curses. He pulls a cigarette out of the drawer next to the bed and lights it. He paces naked around the room.

"Is there anything I can do?" I say, half asleep.

"We have our entire lives to fuck. What matters most now is what happens in the next two days." He begins to pull on his pants and starts out the door as I slip into a jet-black sleep.

THIRTY-SEVEN

2002 2003 2004 2005 2006 2007 2008 2009 2010 2011 **2012**

May 17th, 2012 –Los Lobos Camp, Cuba

The sense of movement wakes me, but opening my eyes feels like lifting a thousand pounds. I think they are open, but all I can see is blackness. I try to move my hands to lift them to my face but they're tied. I hear the trickle of water float by me. I'm in a boat.

I start to wriggle out of sheer panic when a hand comes to rest kindly on my back.

"Hello, darling." I don't recognize his pinched voice, or his American southern accent.

The water floats by in rhythmic waves and I realize we're in a canoe. There is someone else in the boat with us, someone rowing. Maybe two people.

"Where am I?" I try to sound calm but my voice shakes.

"You're with us, of course." I can hear a wry smile in his voice. I don't appreciate his callous tone when I'm bound and blindfolded.

"And who are you?"

"There are times for explanations, and there are times for escapes. We're in the middle of the latter, my dear."

"I don't see the big fuss about her," I hear another man's voice, this one with an English accent.

"We're not the ones who decide what the fuss is, Hugo. We're the ones who deliver, even when we get beaten up in a bush by a thirteen-year-old boy," says the man with his hand on my back.

"Can you cut me loose, please?" I say, annoyed.

"Darling, let's wait until we get back to the main road. This goddamn lagoon is miserable, for fuck's sake. Leave it to Cuban counter-revolutionaries to hole themselves up in this mosquito-infested sauna." He lifts his hand for a moment, then places it back, patting me and toying with my hair.

I realize I fell asleep partially naked, but now I have clothes on. My face burns at the idea that one or all of these men helped to dress me.

"This reminds me so much of Bali—remember Bharat? The order was for four Balinese. Tall, with light eyes. He even wanted one of them to be a nursing mother. Shesus, some men never get over being improperly weaned."

The silent man chips in, "Yes, we canoed them away from their village with almost no problem. I hope she's as compliant as the Balinese." This man's accent is Indian. I realize he means me.

"I don't know," the English one again. "She's got a great ass, I guess. I'm starting to see the draw."

I hear a slap and a cry.

"Don't fucking touch her. We're on a timeline, why aren't you rowing?"

The English one grumbles, and the speed of the water passing us increases.

"What's the local time, Bharat?"

"Four a.m., sir."

Four a.m.? That means I slept for a few hours in the camp before they took me. They seem curiously unthreatening, but I do wonder if they've been contracted by the Cuban government to bring me in. It seems unlikely.

"Can you at least tell me who sent you?" I ask, wriggling again to loosen my hands. I am laying in the boat in the fetal position. My hands face the side of the boat. I gently feel around again for something to help cut the ropes. I find a hook where the oars are usually stowed. I try to hook my hand ropes around it and loosen the rope. I feel it working, but try not to move too fast so that the man with his hand on me doesn't notice. It's pitch black in the ravine.

"It may not seem like it right now, Magdalena, but we're here to help you. We were sent by someone who paid a lot of money to get you out of this god forsaken furnace. I also personally believe he loves you, though love is strange."

I stop moving. The sound of my heart is like machine gun fire in my ears. The rope around my hands starts to come loose but I still don't move. "Burke." I breathe it more than say it.

"So you do remember him? I am surprised because that gentleman in the hut had quite a way of making you forget."

I bury my face into the floor of the boat, wishing I could fall through into the lukewarm swamp water. "It's been almost twelve years. I had no idea if he even remembered me. Are you really saying he sent you?"

"Yes, we're taking you to New York to be with your long lost love. That is, if we can get out of here. Do you think any of them will follow us?"

"You do know I still have a blindfold on right? Aren't we all on the same team now?"

"Oh yes, and I think we're just coming up on the parking lot. Sorry we had to tie you up dear, but I wasn't sure how you'd react and the canoe doesn't do well with a whole lot of tossing and turning. There was no way I was ending up in that water."

I feel us come to a stop and bump against a wall.

"Bharat. Pick up Magdalena and carry her up the ladder. Ah—don't think for a moment I trust you with her Hugo. Dear, we'll untie you in the car. We've got to move fast."

I feel myself get picked up and carried upwards, but any sense of fear is gone now and all I feel is excitement and disbelief. I was so close to a life with Juan Julio, which was accepting death in its many forms. The thought of marrying him now makes me cringe beneath the blindfold. Then I remember that my hands are loose. Instinctively, I reach up and pull the blindfold down. I am so weak without Angelo, and now I know how far I would go to get him back.

Carrying me is a large, muscled Indian man—Bharat. Behind us walk two men. One of them must be Hugo, and the other hasn't given a name. A door opens and I am gently placed inside a black shiny car. A man sits in the driver's seat. He cranes his head around to look at me.

"Boss, uh, is she supposed to be able to see us?"

The smaller, blonde man gets in next to me.

"Bharat, did you not notice her blindfold? For fuck's sake men, we've been doing this a long time. Why is Cuba like the kiss of death for you all?" He rubs his face in his hands like bosses do. That must mean Hugo is in back.

"She got loose boss, I'll just tie her up again," says Hugo leaning over the seat to grab my wrists.

"You said I could get untied in the car. What the fuck is going on?" I've had enough bullshit for one night.

"It's just that, Magdalena, darling... a get—that's you—a get has never seen our faces. This business that we do can get very nasty. Your case is kind of special but normally we're not all on the same team, as you so eloquently put it. But, no, Hugo we can't just tie her up again. We're behind schedule and we can't transport her, we need her travelling with us. Also, she's already seen us so that would do no good.

"My God, could this operation go any more wrong?" He continues. He puts his head in his hands and begins to cry. Bharat tries to comfort him but he simply puts his hand up and continues crying. "I should've stayed at the hotel; this is too much for me. I can't handle this kind of stress."

The car is quiet for a while. I place my hand on his back like he did for me in the boat and he lets it stay there. "What is your name?" I ask.

He hesitates. "I really shouldn't say. Please call me boss if you don't mind." He raises his head and dabs his eyes with a handkerchief he fished from the breast pocket of his beige suit. How strange that he would wear a light-colored suit on such an occasion, while the other men all wear black.

"Can I ask you something else?"

He grins and nods, as if he knows what I am about to say.

"Have you seen him? Burke?"

"Yes, dear. I met him and he engaged my services. He's one of our highest profile clients, so I came on the mission myself. That was a mistake, although I do so love your company. Very adept, very sharp."

"Clients?" I say, confused.

"Yes, we're employed by Mr. Burke, and many others, to retrieve women from all over the world."

"Oh," I say, still struggling to understand. "Well, how did he seem to you? Did he have my son with him?"

He pauses for a moment seeming surprised. He crafts his response carefully. "No, he was alone. He's a little worse for the wear, sweetheart. He's definitely not the Burke I used to watch on New York One. I think he may have been on drugs—but who isn't these days? And, of course, he's had some work done around the mouth and forehead. Probably just Botox but, again, who hasn't? None of that would stop me from draggin' him around like a kid does a teddy bear."

This man is one of the strangest people I've ever met.

"I tell you one thing though," he continues. "His whole life's been about finding a way to get you back. Any dings he's taken along the way have been from losing you."

"Are you going to tell him? About how you found me?" I blush, hoping I don't have to remind him.

"Should I?"

I sit quietly for a moment. So much time has passed since Burke and I were together, and even then, it was only for a few weeks. Were our feelings really as intoxicating as I remember? I was sure I would never see him again. He can't have expected me to pause my life, and it doesn't sound like he's paused his. "I'd rather tell him myself. We've been apart a long time with no contact. I don't really know what to expect." I look at the man's face, trying to read his thoughts.

"I didn't think for a moment that either of you hadn't dipped your toes in other pools. But do you still love him?"

I think about my life since the moment Burke was taken from me. Angelo, the best part of my life, is half Burke. I wouldn't know myself without knowing me as a woman who loves Richard Burke.

Right?

I feel an indelible pull back to the hut, with Juan Julio and the counter-revolutionaries. They may take down the Castros, my lifelong dream. And when they do it, I will be a thousand miles away. I will take no credit for their victory. They will build a better Cuba, and I will be a newly-minted American citizen.

It doesn't feel right.

This will be the first time I have ever left Cuba. Burke has sent these men to retrieve me like a lost trinket at the bottom of the sea. What if I didn't want to be retrieved? What if I'm making a terrible mistake?

"My son," I say. "I love my son very much. I need to get to him. The rest I will figure out later."

"That's not the romantic answer I was hoping for," the boss replies.

THIRTY-EIGHT

2007 2008 2009 2010 2011 2012 2013 2014 2015 2016 **2017**

May 17th, 2012 – Whereabouts Unknown

I fall asleep sometime on the drive and wake up on a small plane. At least, I assume it's small—it's the first plane I've ever been on. There are six seats facing forward and one seat behind the pilot that looks more like a bench against the wall. The two men, Bharat and Hugo, sit in the front two seats. Hugo's head hangs back over the top of the headrest, a loud snoring escaping his mouth. Bharat plays on what looks like a cell phone.

    I'm seated in the back; the boss is to my left. He is reading a magazine with a cover that reads *People*. "You know, this is where I find most of my clients. They have everything and yet it isn't enough." He gestures to the very muscular man on the cover, walking down a beach with a rail thin brunette.

    Sleepily, I yawn. I try to open my eyes wider and stare at the picture. Maybe this will help me understand what he's talking about.

    "You're not going to tell me what it is you actually do, are you? Is it easier for you if I just remain cargo?" I feel some kind of angry bile rising in my stomach. "And the four Cuban girls missing out of Camaguey, or the countless children kidnapped all over Mexico and South America every year—you're not going to tell me about them either, are you?"

"Doll, it's more complicated than all that. One time I was on safari with Dorian, my husband. I saw a lion running savagely across the savanna, chasing something too small to be seen. I got out my binoculars, and lo—it was a tiny mouse. The lion held up the mouse and dropped it into his mouth. Gulp. Gone. Dorian was beside himself. Tears streaming down his face, he commanded the driver to stop. Dorian has a way with animals, you see. He searched and searched the savannah for hours, and came back to the jeep with four little mouse babies. 'We're keeping them,' he told me. We go through all the trouble of getting the mice back to New York, buying the cage, getting the bedding. The next morning, our cat, Roseanne, ate all four babies. Dorian was inconsolable."

He sighed the way someone sighs when they're in love with an impossible person. I have sighed that way many times myself.

"So, we're all going to die? That's how you justify kidnapping and human trafficking for the rich and famous?"

"Everybody's got to make a living, Magdalena. Don't you think life will be better for you in America? Food, clean water, the chance to follow a dream?"

"My dream is in Cuba, where I had plenty of food and water and the chance to change things."

"Really? Before you woke, I just heard over the military radio that the Black Wasps—such a cool name for a Special Forces unit, isn't it? Anyway, they gunned down a band of counter-revolutionaries in that hellhole swamp. There was a firefight—twenty Wasps were killed. And not a single counter-revolutionary survived."

I sit staring at his awful face in shock.

"You're welcome," he says pompously.

Juan Julio is dead. Just like he'd been in my mind the past eighteen years. But now it was real, and to hear it from this criminal lunatic makes my blood boil. "You know nothing of dying for something. You only know how to profit off of other people's pain."

"Pain is inevitable. Profit is optional," he quips.

I just want to be alone with my loss. I say nothing else to him or the other men. Tears roll blankly down my cheeks; one thing keeps ringing in my ears: I should've been with them. I should be dead.

I can feel the landing gear go down and wonder where we're landing and if Angelo and Burke will be here waiting. I want to ask but can't stand another half-truth for an answer. The boss whips out his phone and begins typing away. I restrain myself from craning my neck to read his message.

The wheels skid into the asphalt. I look out the window to see trees and ocean. It doesn't look too different from my home so far. Lights ding on inside the plane and Hugo jumps from his sleep wildly.

"Calm down, Hugo. We've landed," the boss says, not looking up from his phone. It buzzes in his hand and I think it's Burke, just on the other side of the message. Just on the other side of the plane wall. I don't know if I want to rip the door to the plane open or crawl into one of the luggage compartments.

The plane begins to slow and gradually it stops. The pilot emerges from the cockpit and opens the door to the outside, pushing a small staircase down and out onto the concrete. He pokes his head back in the door and looks me right in the eye, as if he knows what's at stake for me on the other side of that door. He raises his hand and beckons me out.

I look at the boss, who nods and urges me to stand up and walk towards the opening. I can't stand the suspense so I lean across the aisle and look out the window. On the tarmac is one black car—standing in front of it are Angelo and Burke.

As soon as I see their faces I am running, down the steps onto the concrete and we're holding each other. Angelo's arms are clutched around my waist.

"Mamá, mamá, you're here," he says. His feet bounce up and down a little, jostling me.

Burke gazes at me in disbelief. I meet his eyes. My body hums under his gaze as if no time has passed. I never want this moment to end.

Finally, Burke gathers himself around my shoulders. He nuzzles his head into me. He kisses me on the neck, the shoulder, the face. "Madge, Madge… it's you. You're here," he murmurs in shock. It feels strange to be this close to him after so many years.

I let myself melt into them. I don't ask questions or worry about what's going to happen next. I just feel them—my family—with me together for the first time in our lives. Their limbs are warm around me, the tears from all of our eyes fall in one spot on Angelo's t-shirt.

There is some commotion outside our family huddle. I hear radios and feet stamping all around us. I open my eyes to see men in black suits and body armor storming the plane where I left the boss and his men. The pilot comes out to fight them off. He gets one punch in and then the men take him down, shooting him with a dart. Hugo starts to run down the stairs, his gun drawn. *Thwack.* Another dart hits him in the leg. He falls down the rest of the stairs as two men swarm him, zip tying his limp arms. I hear hollering from the plane—howling like an animal.

Three men in black storm onto the plane and there's a

shuffling sound, accompanied by the boss' cursing. The engine of the plane is so loud it's hard to hear what he's saying. A few seconds later, he's marched down the stairs with his hands above his head and a real gun in his back. Behind him, Bharat is marched out with his hands up. One of the men in black collects Hugo and carries him roughly to a car. He places him in the back seat and remains standing outside.

Another car pulls up next to us, a black SUV. A man in a suit steps out of the back seat on the driver's side. He looks serious but satisfied. He walks up to us, all three speechless while we take in the scene before us.

"Magdalena Cruz?" He asks me as he shoves his hand toward me.

I release my grip on Angelo long enough to shake his hand. "Yes?"

"Dean Wright. Agent Dean Wright, Deputy Director, CIA. Glad the extraction went well. We've gone through hell to get you out. I'd imagine the three of you have a lot of catching up to do." His eyes glisten for a moment before he turns to watch the boss get paraded down the plane stairs and towards the SUV. "You have no idea how long we've been after this guy. Rock Solomon: Human Trafficker to the Stars. You're going down for a long time," he says to anyone who's listening.

"You!" Rock raises his cuffed hands and points in Burke's face. "This is not over. No one crosses me!" The gentle man who had patted my back in the boat this morning is gone, and in his place is a caged rhino. He is red with contempt and coming toward my family.

"You trapped him? You used me to trap him?" I ask Burke.

"Well, it was a sting. It was the only way we knew to get you out."

The plane engine cuts off and he's left yelling too loudly.

Burke gestures at Dean who is putting Solomon in the car.

"But he saved me. He rescued me and brought me to you. Doesn't that mean anything?" I feel lost in this world suddenly. The air smells like gasoline and the sky looks too blue. There are no palm trees or hibiscus lining the bushes. Everything seems dull. "You're supposed to be the hero, but you let him do your dirty work?" I don't know if I'm furious or depressed. My voice shakes.

"Madge, I couldn't go to you. They told me they'd kill you if I tried. I had to find some way to get you out and this—Solomon—was the plan we came up with. Here you are; it doesn't matter how we got here."

"He's a wanted criminal and you trusted him with me? I had to get back to my son, and you trusted a criminal?" I'm feeling hysterical.

Suddenly Dean is beside us, propping me up. "Magdalena. It's been a long night. Go home—er, to Burke's—and get some rest. The man is responsible for trading children, girls and boys, to the highest bidder. You should rid your mind of any guilt about what happens to him. You're the good guy here, you're getting him off the streets."

"It's just—Mr. Wright—there's something good in him. I saw something good."

Burke puts his hand to my face to brush the hair away. I sense his smile—the one he gives when he's been right about something—but I'm too afraid to look at him.

"There's something good in everyone. But I'm sorry, Magdalena; he's wanted for hundreds of crimes and suspected in thousands more. I can't just let him go—you know that. Go home, get some rest and enjoy your family. Burke, I'll call you tomorrow."

From the SUV I hear Solomon call to me, "Magdalena. Find Dorian, tell him where I am. Tell him what happened. I was trying to help you! Magdalena!" The door slams and his cries are muffled. Dean gets in the other side of the car, and they drive away, back down the runway toward the tiny airport, then out onto the street.

Something like guilt begins to creep in and I wonder how I could even find Dorian. I don't have any idea where we are. Overwhelmed, I clutch my boys to me. "I thought I would never see you again." I wipe tears from my face.

"Madge, there is so much to say. I..." Burke starts.

I look at him with a mother's gaze. I gesture to Angelo. "We can talk about it after I've slept." Sleep feels like a fiction that I once believed. I rest my head on Burke's shoulder. "Take me home," I say.

THIRTY-NINE

2002 2003 2004 2005 2006 2007 2008 2009 2010 2011 **2012**

May 17th, 2012 – New York City, New York

Coming back to Burke is one of the strangest, most wondrous things I have ever experienced. Ambivalence overlaid with passion, reality forming from dreams, secrets laid bare beneath a thin façade of time and space.

His face is older than I remember, and he always looks as if he's lost something important. I think, indeed he has, although he isn't sure what it is. His body is still taut, but his hair has gained a manicured sculpt that I can't stand. I almost prefer the white hat to this.

We get to his apartment in what I think is Manhattan. The entire ride there I'm constantly rousing from small naps, assaulted by the lights and sounds of chaos. I'm sure Burke was hoping for a more romantic reunion, but luckily this won't be the first time I disappoint him. I feel the guilt of Juan Julio burn beneath the surface of everything I say to him.

Angelo dotes on me, showing me his new room and around the rest of the apartment. The full weight of the luxury is lost on me in my present state. I see my letter laid out on the side table next to a chair. Burke goes to the liquor cabinet and pours himself a caramel colored drink over ice.

I wake on a couch in my clothes. The sunlight streams in from giant windows. I can see a stretch of green from where I lay. I hear tinkling silverware and glasses behind me; murmuring.

A phone rings loudly, and someone lurches to pick it up. "Hello—yes, Burke here." The sound of his voice in the room with me sends a flutter down my spine. "No, I hadn't heard—"

Angelo comes around to face me with a tray of eggs, bacon, and a round pastry with a hole in it. I've never seen bread like this before. His face is a golden light.

"And what is it you think we can do?" Burke continues.

I put my hands on my son's face and look into his eyes. If there's a word more magical than luck, that's what I feel now.

"Right. Okay. It's something we can talk about. We'll see you at ten then. Thank you, sir." Burke hangs up the phone."Madge. I'm sorry. None of this has gone like I wanted it to." He comes around the couch and kneels before me. Angelo sits down beside me. Burke looks at him with a mix of tenderness and annoyance.

"Hey, bud. Can we have a few minutes to talk, just me and your mom?"

Angelo looks at Burke with a contempt I've never seen. He gets up slowly and turns to at me. "Mamá, estoy tan contenta de que estés a salvo. Tenga cuidado con esta vieja serpiente."

I look at him with shock. This is not the boy who left me.

"Esa serpiente es tu padre. Dale una oportunidad," I say to my son. Angelo walks away silently to his bedroom down the hall. "What happened between you two?" I ask.

"It was a very stressful situation trying to get you back. He helped, in the surveillance truck. He was so useful to them. I was so proud to call him mine. But he heard some things the guys were saying about me, about you. I..." I can see on his face that he is about to lie.

"Don't tell me any lies, my darling. We've been apart too long, haven't we? If the hell we've been through won't make us honest, then nothing will."

"Madge." He is suddenly serious. "I don't want to pretend any more. Losing you destroyed me, and I've spent every day since destroying myself because I never thought we could be together again. Life was meaningless." I watch his face as he talks. Now he is telling the truth. "Now you're here—my ultimate dream come true—and I don't think I can be the man I was when we met."

"And so, I'll wait for you like a lonely house," I say, staring into his green eyes. The very same eyes I swooned over twelve years ago. His face changes to look more like that man—the patient, eloquent, idealistic Burke I love. His cheeks soften, the wrinkles in his forehead relax. He tries to smile but is caught by a sob. He leans in and I lean in, putting my elbows on my knees, coming down to meet him. He pushes up onto his knees, and here I sit, here he kneels.

I take my hand and run it through his hair, through the stiff hair spray and mess it up, pressing it to the side and tousling it until he looks like I remember. "We have to do something about your hair," I say.

He smiles his famous smile, and for the first time since seeing him again, we're right back on the island together. He touches his lips to mine, and I swear I taste seawater. He runs his hands through my hair, "There is some kiss we want with our whole lives," he whispers.

"Rumi," I breathe into his ear, astonished and proud. I want him to take me, like he used to in my old beautiful farmhouse. He picks me up and I wrap my legs around him. He starts to walk back towards his room.

"Wait, Angelo. What if he comes in?"

"We'll have to do what parents do; lock the door and try to keep it down." He burrows into my neck, and I'm ashamed at how much I've missed it.

The morning streams in through thin curtains on the tall windows. Burke tenderly lays me down on the bed, his eyes never leaving my face. The two of us take our own clothes off slowly, still a bit standoffish and shy. Still his eyes travel only between my eyes and my lips, as if he wants to make sure I'm me. He slowly descends on the bed, his hands exploring my body patiently and calmly. I am alive under his fingers. The electricity reminds me why I held onto the idea of Burke for so long after he was gone.

He joins with me, his eyes locked on mine. I dare not look away, even as I shudder and grip the sheets. He sees me, and I see him—our broken landscapes make up something together they never would have been alone. We come together—as the most experienced of lovers do—my soul quaking, awakening, stretching, and yawning. He comes and comes and comes as if an ocean were inside him.

He lays down, a sheen of sweat on his skin, careful not to separate from me. "I'm never letting you out of my sight again," he says, pushing the hair out of my face. I exhale and nod in agreement, too overwhelmed to speak. Tears stream, unexpected, from my eyes. We lay there together for a long time, lounging in each other's gaze.

A soft knock at the door comes—hours or minutes?—

later. "Mami and Burke, Mr. Dean keeps calling. Should I answers?"

"Hold on, son," Burke says. "Just leave it. I'll call him back in a minute."

"What does he want? I thought we were done with him," I say.

"He wants to meet with us this morning. Something happened last night. A plane disappeared from the sky. It didn't crash. Just gone—blinked out of the sky."

I give him a confused look.

"Anyway, there were some high-level people on the flight. He wants to talk to us; you, me, Angelo and—get this—Rock Solomon, about forming a task force. Something where Solomon can work off his time and we can help extract people from dangerous situations, like we did with you. He was really impressed with our work."

I'm sure my face looks worried yet I feel a sense of excitement. I worry about Angelo getting involved in something like this, but I can't deny him what he loves.

"Sounds like the kind of decision a family makes together," I say. And Burke kisses me until our time apart feels like a long, throbbing nightmare from which I have finally awoken.

ACKNOWLEDGMENTS

This book oozed out slowly and intentionally. It took three years of research and writing and it will still never be perfect. But it's pretty damn close. I have so many people to be thankful for. While I was writing I was almost always supposed to be doing something else. So thank you to Rusty, Eva and Cameron for their patience while I stitched this thing together and tore it up again.

To my early readers Teresa Miller, Rusty Rowe, Cristi Drake, Scot Law, John Dixon-Ramsey, Paula Marshall, Jim Stovall and Kelly Morrison - thank you! I know time is dear and reading novels is not always a top priority but you made time for me, gave me comments and made the book better. There will never be enough thank you's.

Finally, to my publisher and editor Daniel Wimberley of Design Vault Press. You have been so understanding and wonderful to work with. Thank you for seeing something in the book and me that was worth investing in. Here's to writing fifty more.

ABOUT THE AUTHOR

Colleen McCarty is a graduate of the University of Tulsa and an entrepreneur. She and her husband own Tulsa restaurant Mod's Coffee and Crepes.

She's been featured on Entrepreneur.com, and in the Wall Street Journal. This is her second novel. Colleen has ghostwritten books for CEOs and New York Times Bestsellers. Colleen lives in Tulsa, Oklahoma with her husband, two kids and two large dogs.

Made in the USA
Lexington, KY
16 July 2017